Karina crept through the jungle, following her quarry by scent as much as by sound.

It was strange to be alone. All her life she'd been used to the strength of the grupo; and now here she was, unprotected, following two True Humans into the secret recesses of the delta.

Why?

Because of her stubbornness. Because she was loyal to her people. Because she wanted to prove to her father that she was capable of looking after herself. Because she was sure there was something in the delta which the felinos ought to know about.

But basically because she was a felina, born to hunt but condemned by her religion to play hunting games—until now.

CAT KARINA

CAT KARINA

MICHAEL CONEY

SF
ace books
A Division of Charter Communications Inc.
A GROSSET & DUNLAP COMPANY
51 Madison Avenue
New York, New York 10010

CAT KARINA
copyright © 1982 by Michael G. Coney

An ACE Book

First Ace printing: August 1982
Published Simultaneously in Canada
2 4 6 8 0 9 7 5 3 1
Manufactured in the United States of America

CAT
KARINA

The Song of Earth

"Step out of your shroud,
Alan-Blue-Cloud,
And sing us a Song of Earth."
　　—Childrens' ditty of the Terminal Millennia.

When everything else had run down, we will still have the legends of Old Earth.

There is a giant computer which straddles the world. It has its roots deep in the Fifty-second Millennium; that so-distant past when Man discovered electricity. It walked through history hand-in-hand with Man; it saw the building of the first Domes, it survived the reversal of the Earth's magnetic field, it watched the Age of Resurgence, it fought Man's wars for him and even, in the Domes, lived his life for him. It became so powerful that it was able to observe practically everything that happened on Earth and, from this, project what was going to happen in the future—or the Ifalong, as it is more correctly called. Now, in these Dying Years, the computer is still there, still observing, thinking and predicting, in countless solar-powered centers all over Earth.

It is called the Rainbow.

I am called Alan-Blue-Cloud. In a way I am the

Rainbow's interpreter. I am one of the few remaining beings who is able to operate a terminal, and I use this ability to draw true stories out of the computer; stories of True Humans and Specialists, of aliens and Bale Wolves and the sad neotenites known cruelly as Blubbers.

But true stories do not give the whole picture. During the later years of Earth people became dissatisfied with bare facts, which are always a little dull when compared with fictions and legends. So, when it seemed that Mankind was doomed forever to listen to the Truth, because that was all he could get out of his terminals and cassettes, an old art-form was rediscovered.

And Romance returned to Earth.

It started with a few bards and minstrels—I will shortly tell you about one named Enriques de Jai'a. They ignored the Rainbow and they used their eyes and ears, listened to rumors and legends and dying old men. And they used their imagination, and their essential humanness. With these ingredients they created a whole new history of Mankind; a tapestry of events which was passed on by word of mouth—and so could never become dull, inflexible, or accurate.

It is called the Song of Earth.

HERE BEGINS THAT PART OF THE SONG OF EARTH KNOWN TO MEN AS "THE GIRL BORN TO GREATNESS"

Where a young felina
meets a wise woman,
hears of her future
and meets a young True Human whose name
will be linked with hers in the Ifalong.

The world of Karina

"The fastest sailcar is the first to the rotted rail"
                            —Old sailway proverb.

Instantly, Karina knew her leg was broken.

Her body swung downwards and she grabbed the log with her right arm, checking her fall. As she hung there, the pain began. The dark night brightened with her pain, so that for a moment she could see nothing except a blinding redness, flaring like a furnace from a core of agony just below her knee.

She made no sound. Felinas don't cry.

So they were tears of pain in her eyes, not weakness. She blinked and her vision cleared, and she wriggled carefully, working her way onto the log until she lay along it, her foot trapped in the supporting crutch, her legs outstretched. She saw the moon reflected from the long, smooth timber rail of the sailway and, far in the distance on top of a hill, the bright glow of a signal tower. As she watched, the signal blinked with moonlight.

That meant there was a sailcar coming.

For a moment she visualized the great car, white sails spread to catch the night breeze, trundling down the track while she lay helpless. She tried to tug her foot free, but the movement sent a screaming current of pain through her body and, for a moment, she blacked out.

She came to with a sense of great loneliness. Her alpaca tunic was wrapped around her waist, the ground was three metres below, and the wind blew coldly over her as she lay exposed to the night's silence. She was lonely for her sisters but they were some distance down the track, far out of earshot, preparing a harmless ambush for the Pegman. A joke which would cost Karina her life. Lying there in pain, she did something which only she could.

She concentrated all her thoughts on her leg and she said, "Please don't hurt so much. Pain, please go away. Little Friends, wherever you are, please make my leg not hurt so much. . . ."

And her Little Friends helped her, whispering through the cells of her body, gathering about the wounded nerve endings and the torn flesh and bone, and soothing. Not mending, because this was beyond their power, but soothing so that the pain faded and Karina could think straight again. . . .

The sailway track consisted of three parallel rows of trimmed logs forming a simple monorail system linking the coastal towns. The middle rail was the thickest and supported the weight of the cars. The other two rails were placed higher, one on either side, and the lateral guidewheels of the sailcars pressed against these. The whole structure marched along the coastal plains on X-shaped gantries; the running rail resting in the crutch of the X and the guiderails pegged to the upper arms.

Karina's foot was jammed between the running rail and the crutch. She pulled at it and twisted it until warning twinges told her that even the Little Friends could not perform miracles. She lay back in despair. Even if she had been able to free her foot, she could still die. She was a felina, and felino bones do not heal readily.

So Karina the cat-girl lay on the sailway track and waited to die. She was eighteen years old and, by human standards, very beautiful. She had the long supple limbs, the oval face and the slanting amber eyes of her people. Only her hair was different, a startling rarity among felinos; red-gold, it fell about her shoulders like fire. Karina, concentrating on her Little Friends to dull the pain, waited.

Then she felt measured footsteps pacing along the rail towards her.

"Karina? You are Karina, daughter of El Tigre?"

Karina sat up, staring at the tall figure which seemed to float towards her dressed all in black so that for one fanciful moment she thought it was Death come to get her. It was a woman's voice, soft yet with a strangely lifeless quality as though the speaker had seen all the sadness of the Universe, and had been unable to help.

"Yes, I'm Karina."

As the woman stepped forward, the moonlight fell upon her face—and Karina flinched with horror. The pallid flesh was seared and puckered with the Mark of Agni, the Fire-God.

"Give me your hand."

But Karina jerked away, her stomach churning at the awful, unnatural evil of that face. The woman was Cursed. Agni only touched those who sinned, and he made sure they stayed touched. So ran the Kikihuahua Examples. . . . "No. . . . Get away from me," she said. The woman was a True Human. She could tell. There was an imperiousness about her manner.

"You're trapped on a sailway track and you'll die unless you can get free—and you won't let me help you." The woman's tone was wondering. "Do I frighten you that much?"

"I'm not afraid of anything!"

"Is it my face? It's only a burn, you know. You see much stranger things in the jungle."

"Go away!"

"So it's because I'm a True Human."

"All right—so it is! I'm a Specialist and you're a True Human. There's nothing we can do for each other. Nothing we can say."

"That's your father speaking."

"True Humans killed my mother!"

Now the woman said an odd thing. "It is beyond our powers to change the facts of the present, and even the possibilities of the Ifalong can seldom be affected. But Karina—on certain happentracks of the Ifalong you will be famous, and the minstrels will sing of you."

The suggestion was ridiculous. "You mean, like the Pegman and his songs?" said Karina sarcastically.

"Don't laugh about the Pegman's songs. They're important too, and in the distant future they'll be a part of the Song of Earth. All of human history will be told in songs like the Pegman's."

"How do you know this? Can you see into the future?"

"No, of course not. No normal human can. But the Dedo—my mistress—can foretell the Ifalong. It's no coincidence I'm here. Your accident was foreseen."

A thread of fear ran down Karina's spine. "You mean you could have prevented it?"

"No doubt I could, and on certain happentracks I did." Cold eyes looked down at the cat-girl. "Just as on certain happentracks you will live, and on others you will die."

"H . . . happentracks? Like sailway tracks?"

"Different possibilities all existing at the same time."

"Oh." The rumbling was closer. Karina had a vision of her crushed body lying in the wake of a speeding sailcar. Her arm would be swinging limply. "I . . . I can hear a sailcar coming. Can't you *do* something?"

"That depends on you, Karina."

"For God's sake, what do you want?"

"Your word."

One leg would be lying on the ground below, severed. "You have it!" cried Karina.

"Karina, we live in a difficult year. It is a year of unpredictable, whirling happentracks. The Dedo foresees this as the year when her great Purpose could come to nothing. You alone can ensure that the Purpose will be fulfilled."

"How? Just tell me, and I'll do it!"

"You must do several things. At intervals before the end of the year you'll be faced with difficult decisions. It is essential to the Purpose that you take the right step every time."

"How will I know?"

"I'll be there to guide you. It won't be easy for you, though."

"I'll do it!" shouted Karina frantically.

"Give me your solemn word, Karina."

Karina composed herself and uttered the most sacred words a Specialist can utter; more sacred even than the Kikihuahua Examples.

"I, Karina, swear by the bones of Mordecai N. Whirst that I will obey the commands of this True Human. . . . Until the end of the year," she added quickly. "Now, get me out of this!"

And suddenly, just for a moment, the woman was transformed and the humanity shone through. "You poor child—I'm so sorry." She placed a hand gently on Karina's leg. "Just keep still, will you." And she reached inside her robe and took out a smooth, dark stone. It was shot with red flecks and totally ordinary in appearance; and she held Karina's leg straight, so that the bones were set.

Karina concentrated on the Little Friends, and felt nothing.

The woman drew the stone down Karina's leg like a cold caress, and said, "You can move it, now."

"That's it?" Karina flexed her leg and was astonished to find the break appeared to be mended. Cautiously she withdrew the Little Friends and they retreated into the recesses of her body, their work done. There was no pain. It was as though the wound had never been. Now, with her new strength and the handmaiden's help, she was able to twist her foot free of the crutch. The skin was broken and it bled slightly. "Can you use the stone again?" she asked.

"No. Your foot must bleed for a while to remind you not to do a stupid thing like this again. You're precious to the world, Karina."

Karina asked, "What's the Purpose you talked about?"

"You can't know the details. If you did, you could destroy it. You are that important, Karina. But as for the overall Purpose, it is directed towards ending the imprisonment of the greatest person the Earth has ever known: Starquin, the Almighty Five-in-One."

"Oh, just another religion." Karina was disappointed.

They swung to the ground. Karina took a deep breath and looked around. Everything looked fresh and new. For a moment something the woman had said touched her mind, and she wondered if she had stepped into a brand-new happentrack, leaving her old self dying on the sailway. . . .

"I feel so *good*," she said happily.

"How do you like your world, Karina?"

"I like it fine. I like the sun and the ocean, and the cars' sails against the trees, and the mountains. . . . And the felino camp, and," her face glowed suddenly with anticipation, "the Tortuga Festival, and all the fun."

"Have you ever thought there was anything else? Haven't you ever wondered what might be *outside* all that?"

"Well, the fishermen tell of queer folk who live on rafts of weed out in the sea. . . . And the mountain people talk about monsters in the jungle. . . ."

"No, I mean *really* outside. Outside this little space and time. Imagine this, Karina. Imagine a million worlds spinning in space, some with people just like us, some with people who don't know what evil means, some with people so evil that folk are scared even to give their planet a name—and all of those people human. And imagine other creatures too, not human, with different customs. . . ."

"Like the kikihuahuas, you mean?"

"Yes, and more besides."

"It's all in the Examples." Karina was suddenly impatient. A whole world was waiting for her. Maybe a narrow world by this queer woman's standards, but a world full of fun and excitement all the same.

"All right, I won't keep you. Just remember, Karina. Every so often, I want you to look up at the stars and to think of the Greataway, which is all the dimensions of Time and Space—which Mankind used to travel through, thirty thousand years ago before he lost the will and the ability. The Greataway will be rediscovered, and you may play your part. Always remember Starquin, and your promise."

And the warmth faded from the woman's voice, and her expression faded too; her face became hard and the Mark of Agni showed again in mottled, livid scars.

"What's your name?" asked Karina. "You didn't tell me."

The handmaiden didn't reply.

"Who is the Dedo?"

"She is the flesh of Starquin—a part of his body in human form."

"Wait! You haven't—"

But the Dedo's handmaiden was gone, gliding away into the night. For a moment Karina stood there, shaken by the transformation; it was as though she'd been talking to two different women. Her mood of exaltation faded and she shivered, and suddenly the night was cold and the stars hard and threatening, bright terrible little eyes. The Greataway. . . .

So Karina summoned the Little Friends without quite realizing it; and this time they entered her mind and soothed her. She began to walk north towards the distant black mound of Camelback, the wooded hill where the ambush was to take place. Above her, the sailway track was silent. The approaching car had stopped.

The man who wanted to change the past.

The Pegman—Enriques de Jaia'a, called Enri—was indulging in a curious private ritual. Balanced precariously on the guiderail some six meters from the ground, he was flapping his single arm like a bird and uttering screeches. There was no logical reason for him to do this. The idea had occured to him a few moments ago, so he had stopped the sailcar, climbed onto the rail, and surrendered himself to irrationality.

"Har! Har! Har!" he shouted, and the cry was borne by the winds across the coastal plain and into the foothills and the forest where the howler monkeys, hearing a faint strange sound, paused and looked up.

But the world didn't change.

Enri climbed down, kicked his toe against the side of

the sailcar fourteen times, took off the brake, picked up the ropes and pulled in the boom. The *Estrella del Oeste* began to move, jerkily. Enri grimaced, squeezing up his eyes and sucking his teeth, and began to think of the Tigre grupo—the name which people gave the head-strong sisterhood consisting of Karina, Runa, Teressa and, what was the name of the quiet one? Saba.

Charming, vicious, lovely young inhuman girls who, he suspected, would ambush him tonight. Pity they didn't have a mother to keep them in check, or a brother to lend a little finesse to their outlandish behavior.

But life would be dull without them. . . .

"I am the captain of the sailcar *Estrella del Oeste!*" Enri shouted suddenly to a group of rheas feeding harm-lessly below the track. "I sail for distant cantons with a cargo of ripe tortuga which I will sell for enough money to buy the moon. Or at least, the Sister of the Moon," he conceded, his mind wandering to a strange, gigantic dome-thing he'd once seen down the coast; a thing almost as big as a mountain, its top lost in the clouds. "One day I will be rich!" he shouted. "I'll buy my own sailcar! I'll have a fleet of sailcars!"

But the *Estrella del Oeste* didn't even belong to him. It was an ancient Canton car, its days of fast passenger work long over, a broken-down hulk with patched sails and frayed ropes eking out its last years as a track main-tenance vehicle. In its time it had held twenty passengers in its cylindrical hull, but now the seats were gone, and the drapes and the luxuries, leaving only a bare cavern some ten metres long filled with the tools of Enri's trade: wooden pegs, mallets, rope, bone needles and thread, a shovel, a flint spokeshave, and several barrels of stink-ing tumpfat for greasing the rails and bearings. Enri's living quarters were there too; a tiny cabin with a bed, a table and a few possessions.

Enri rode on deck, behind the car's single mast, gripping the mainsheet—the rope which controlled the angle of the sail to the wind—like any crewman on one of the prestigious Company craft, controlling the sailcar's speed by the tension of the rope and by occasional judicious application of the brake. The wind was light tonight, and he didn't have to use the brake much.

The *Estrella del Oeste* lumbered on while the Pegman dreamed of changing the course of history, and a small part of his mind—the professional part—gauged the state of the track by the feel of the deck's motion through the seat of his pants. Soon the car slowed. He had reached the long climb past Camelback.

The wind chose that moment to slacken.

"Huff! Huff!" He shouted the traditional crewman's cry and blew pointlessly into the limp sail. The wind dropped altogether.

The car was rolling to a halt.

He stood, a tall, thin figure in the moonlight, and shook the boom, inviting the wind. His mood of elation had evaporated. Now he saw himself as a broken-down True Human in a broken-down car. "God damn everything to hell!" he yelled. It would be morning before he reached Rangua at this rate.

The car stopped. He swung one-handed to the running rail and jammed a chock under the rear wheel to prevent the car rolling back down the grade and losing him what little ground he'd gained. Walking back to a crutch, he swung his mallet to check the security of the fastenings.

The mallet struck the crutch with a solid thunk. In the distance, the moon reflected pale silver on the sea.

"Sabotage!" he suddenly shouted, driving his fist at the sky. "I'm a saboteur and I'm going to remove a couple of pegs from this crutch, so that it will collapse when

14

the dawn car from Torres hits it. Ten important people will die in the splintered wreckage. The southbound track will be damaged too, and the next car from Rangua will pile into the mess. More people will die!"

Obsessed by his vision of destruction he sat down, his imagination racing. The Canton Lord would be on the Torres car. Enri would be waiting near and would pull the Lord free, the instant before Agni struck the wreck into flames. The Lord would give him land and Specialists, whom he would set to building cars. Monkey-Specialists, with deft fingers and tiny minds.

And then. . . . And then he would search the whole world for Corriente, his love. And he would find her, and she would cling to him, and they would live happily ever—

The wind was blowing.

He walked slowly back to the *Estrella del Oeste*. There was no hurry, and he was lingering over the dream.

The rail trembled. A dry bearing squeaked like a rat.

Corriente, so warm, so loving. . . .

The *Estrella del Oeste* was moving!

It was impossible—yet the dark bulk of the old car was receding from him, wheels rumbling on the running rail, rigging straining to the fresh breeze. He began to run, awkwardly, one-armed and unbalanced on the narrow rail slippery with tumpfat.

"Yaah!" he shouted, like a felino trying to halt a shruglegger.

A burst of clear, feminine laughter answered him. Now he shouted at himself, calling himself a fool. The Tigre grupo had outwitted him again. He could see them now—four girls, leaning on the after-rail, waving. They had sheeted the sail in tight and now, for all he knew, were going to take the *Estrella* all the way to Rangua South Stage. "Stop!" he yelled.

15

"Not for a man who dreams of sabotage!" came the cry. "You ought to be ashamed of yourself—and you a pegman, too!"

Damned felinas! He ran on, muttering. Teressa was at the bottom of this. She'd put them up to it, the little bitch. Saba was too timid and Runa would see the consequences, and Karina . . . Karina was too nice. But Teressa could sway them all. She would grow up to be a *bandida*, that girl.

Somebody must have touched the brake—Karina probably—because he heard a scraping sound and the sailcar slowed. He reached the door and swung himself inside, blundered through the tools and stink and climbed the short ladder to the deck.

"Hello, Pegman!"

The four girls lay about the deck in attitudes of innocence, and Teressa was even mending a frayed rope. Helplessly he regarded them: cat-girls, descendants of some ancient genetic experiment, come back to haunt Man in the person of him, Enriques de Jai'a, pegman for the Rangua Canton. "I am human!" he suddenly shouted. "I am Mankind!"

"Of course you are, Enri," said Karina. "So are we." There was a slight reproach in her tone.

He'd meant no harm; he'd hardly been aware of his own outburst. "You're goddamned jaguar girls," he muttered.

"But you love us," said Teressa, not even looking up from her work.

"Aah, what the hell!" To his intense embarrassment he found tears in his eyes and he turned away, facing north. The wind was strengthening with every moment and he must pull himself together. There was some difficult sailing between here and Rangua; the sailway turned inland for a short distance and cars had been

16

known to jib in the sudden shift of wind. Last year, the *Reine de la Plata* had had her mast carried away and a crewman killed. Felinos and shrugleggers had towed the disgraced craft into Rangua, laughing derisively.

No, the Camelback Funnel, as it was called, was a difficult stretch for a man with one arm.

"And you couldn't do without us," said Runa seriously. "Not in this wind." She handled the sheets, slackening them off while Saba eased the halliard and Karina, climbing to the lookout post, jerked the sail downwards. Teressa threaded a line through the cringles and in no time the sail was neatly reefed—a manoeuver he was totally unable to carry out himself. The car rode more steadily as the pressure on the lee guiderail eased.

"They shouldn't expect you to do it all yourself," said Karina.

"It's this or no job at all."

"Then don't work. Plenty of people in South Stage don't work. Other people look after them."

"Listen!" he was suddenly bellowing, placing his hands at the side of his head like mules' ears. "You're talking about a felino camp! You people are different! You go around in grupos! True humans aren't like that. We're more. . . . solitary. The weak ones die. It's good for the species."

Karina said quietly, "Tonight a True Human helped me."

"Huh?"

"I broke my leg. I was lying trapped on the rail. She came and mended my leg, and set me free."

"If you broke your leg you wouldn't be able to stand on it now."

"She healed it right away, with a stone."

"Ah, what the hell." He wasn't going to argue.

But her sisters had already descended on Karina and

17

the four girls had become a struggling, fighting mass on the deck; half-play, half-serious. "Broken leg, eh?" Teressa was shouting, twisting viciously at Karina's ankle. Meanwhile Runa was dragging Karina's alpaca tunic over her head and Saba, safe now Karina was effectively trussed and blinded, was pounding away at her body with her fists. The *Estrella del Oeste* rolled on through the night. Enriques de Jai'a turned away, checking the set of the sail. Felinas had no sense of decency, and Karina wore no pants, and how much was a man supposed to take?

"Har! Har! Haaaar!" he roared into the wind, acutely embarrassed by his own emotions.

The struggling mass rolled across the deck and brought up with a crash against the after rail. He stole a glance and saw that Karina, freed from the tunic and naked, was fighting back. She'd thrown an arm around Teressa's neck from behind and was throttling her, meanwhile getting a devastating kick into Runa's stomach. Saba, smaller than her sisters and weaker, left the battle and joined him on the foredeck. She was panting and her colour was not good. Enri put an arm around her.

"Too rough for you, sweetheart?"

"I just get tired so quickly, that's all. I wish I was like Teressa, I really do."

It had been a multiple birth, a normal occurence among felinos. More unusually, the babies had all been girls. Although male felino children generally leave the grupos at puberty, either to squire an unrelated grupo or to join the bachelors at the other end of the camp, their presence in the childhood grupo provides a steadying influence in the formative years. The death of the mother had not helped and, with the formidable El Tigre too involved with his revolutionary plotting to guide the four wild daughters of one of his five wives, the girls had gone their own way.

Now Runa was vomiting over the side, Teressa was leaning against the mast, mauve-faced and gagging, and Karina was getting dressed.

"Teressa doesn't look very happy," said the Pegman.

Saba looked round, smiled and said, "I'd change places with her even now. She's strong."

Karina joined them. The wind had freshened and her hair streamed like flames. "Aren't you glad we're here, Pegman? What would you do without us? That last gust would have taken the mast right out of this old tub, if we hadn't reefed for you." She made no mention of the fight. It was an everyday occurrence in the grupo, a part of growing up.

But Enri asked, curious, "Why do you always win, Karina?"

"Because nothing hurts her," said Saba.

"No, I'm just better than them, that's all," said Karina. She had never told anyone about the Little Friends. That was her secret, and instinctively she knew she'd better keep it. Felinos with real peculiarities—as distinct from Saba who was simply not strong—had a habit of being found dead.

The sailcar reached the downgrade and roared through Camelback Funnel with the speed of a galloping horse, and the girls shouted and laughed with excitement as the craft bucked from side to side and the guiderails screamed a warning. Teressa stood guard over the brake lever, daring Enri to approach, knowing that this strange True Human friend of theirs would never get involved in a physical struggle with them.

"Karina—just go and put that brake on, will you?" Enri pleaded, hanging onto a stanchion with his one hand.

But Karina was yelling with the fun of it, standing on the prow of the *Estrella del Oeste* like a beautiful figurehead, braced against the handrails. "No way!" she shouted back against the bedlam screeching of tortured wood. Enri sniffed, smelling hot bearings.

Then he thought: *what the hell.* Just for a few moments he'd forgotten his need to rearrange the world's history.

Too soon they reached Rangua South Stage, the shanty-town of vampiro tents at the foot of the hill on which stood Rangua Town. Teressa surrendered the brake, laughing at him with slanting eyes as he hauled on the handle and managed to bring the runaway car to a halt. The girls climbed down, calling to the felinos and showing their legs. The felinos, mostly bachelors but with a few fathers among them, muttered disapprovingly at the association between the girls and a True Human.

"He'll kiss you while he stabs you in the back, Teressa!" one of them shouted, repeating the traditional saying about True Humans, although in expurgated form out of deference to her age.

Then they hitched up the shrugleggers for the two-kilometer climb to the town. The running rail descended to ground level for this purpose; the gradient was too steep for any sailcar to climb unassisted in anything but gale-force winds. Ten shrugleggers sufficed for the job, and with oaths and yells from the felinos the *Estrella del Oeste* was soon moving again.

Enri slackened off the halliard and furled the sail. Now that the girls were gone and the exhilarating ride over, he felt let down. A surly felino sat on deck, another led the shrugleggers. The wheels creaked, the car felt heavy and dead. The felino on deck had his back to him, sitting on the prow where the lovely Karina had stood, his legs dangling and his head bowed, half asleep, his neck vulnerable to an ax blow. . . .

Now *that* would change history.

That would be just the kind of open clash between True Human and felino which was needed to spark off the present tinder-box of relations.

There was an ax hanging from the shrouds for use in an emergency. Enri took it down and hefted it in his hand. It was heavy but well-balanced, and the blade was the keenest flaked stone. Enri often did illogical, crazy things. . . .

But the felino would bleed, and maybe *hurt*.

Enri put the ax back and stared at the eastern sky which was brightening with dawn.

"Haaaar!" he cried. "Har! Har! Har!" And he slapped his hand against the mast, again and again.

The felino looked round; a quick askance look.

Then Enri heard a noise below, a clatter and thump against the squeaking and rumbling of *Estrella*. Somebody was down there. An intruder, in his private domain. Somebody fooling with his things, robbing him, most likely—maybe even a *bandido*.

He took up the ax again and, yelling, descended the ladder into the cabin.

"I'm going to kill you!" he shouted, staring around the dark interior. "I can see you." But he couldn't. He was shouting to cover his own nervousness. A felini, however—with those catlike eyes—could see *him*.

"You wouldn't kill me, would you, Pegman?" said a soft voice.

He dropped the ax. "Where are you, Karina?"

"Sitting on your bed."

"Why?" He forced his mind away from the mental image of warm limbs, a slim body dressed in alpaca, and

21

said, "I don't need to kill you. Your father will do it for me, when he finds out where you've been. Now—what do you want?"

The car moved out of the trees and a pale glimmer of early daylight came through the porthole. Karina was a dark silhouette. She said, "Tonight I met a queer woman. She said she was the handmaiden of a *bruja* called the Dedo. You're a wise man, Enri. You know more about the world than I do—and you're a True Human too. You know the legends, and you sing songs of the past. Why would that woman have said I would become famous? And she did heal my leg; she really did."

The Dedo. . . .

The word struck a chord in Enri's memory.

. . . . There was a dense jungle and the harsh screaming of birds, and he'd left the other trackmen and gone exploring. . . .

And a monster had charged him, bursting out of a thicket.

Huge it was, and terrible, carrying an aura of unspeakable evil. Not jaguar, nor bear nor caiman, yet possessing the most fearful characteristics of all three, and bigger than any of them, bigger even than the mythical thylacosmilus, about which he'd sometimes sung songs. But he never sang songs of this monster, in the years which followed.

So he ran until he collapsed sobbing with fear and exhaustion beside a stream, and while he lay there a girl came to him—a girl beautiful beyond measure, more beautiful even than Corriente, his love; but cold.

In a voice without expression she had said, "Don't be alarmed. Bantus will not harm you now. You are outside the valley, you see. . . ." And they had talked for a while, of Time and happentracks.

I am the Dedo, the beautiful girl had said. *You will never forget me.*

22

"What else did she say? Can you remember the exact words?"

Surprised at the tenseness in his voice, Karina said, "I didn't understand a lot of it. She used strange words. The Greataway—that was her word for the sky, I think. Ifalong. . . . Other words. That's it—she said, 'In certain tracks of the Ifalong you will be famous.' Me, famous? What do you make of that, Enri?"

"If the Dedo's handmaiden said you will be famous," said Enri carefully, "then I think you will. I met the Dedo myself once, and I believe her." He tried to smile. "People will write songs about you. Maybe I should write one, to be first."

"But what are tracks of the Ifalong?"

"The Dedo says that Time consists of happentracks, all branching out from the present. So that at any moment your future might go one way or the other, depending on what you do. The Ifalong is the total of all these happentracks in the future, when there are a billion different ways things might have happened. One thing the Dedo can do, is to *see* all these happentracks in the Ifalong, and work out the course people ought to take."

Karina caught a glimpse of immensity. "Ought to take, why? What's the purpose? Why not just live?"

"I think she thinks there's more to life than that. But she didn't tell me what."

Karina was thinking deeply. "I wonder. . . . Do you think it might be possible to *change* things, by jumping onto another happentrack which had branched off some time before? Suddenly find yourself in a different world, where. . . ." Her voice trailed away. She was going to say: where my mother is still alive. . . . "No," she said. "You'd have to do something so strange that it was completely out of place in your happentrack, something which simply didn't fit

23

in with the way things are, something—"

"Yes, you would," said the man who thought coolly of murder, and was given to meaningless bursts of shouting, and who perched on rails flapping like a bird.

On Urubu's deck.

The southbound dawn sailcar was captained by the infamous Herrero so Karina hung about the station for a while, drawing curious glances from True Humans who wondered why she hadn't returned to South Stage with the other felinos.

She knew her father would be waiting for her and she couldn't face his rage, not yet. It was daylight now, and in the distance the sun was coming up over the rim of the sea. Rangua sat on a shoulder of the coastal mountains. Inland, the jungle crawled up the slopes and there were great cleared meadows where slow-moving tumps could be seen: huge mounds of flesh eating their way across the landscape in the care of the tumpiers.

The town was small, bright and neat, and the signs of wealth were everywhere. The stores were full of exotic goods and bright woven fabrics from the great southern plains, and the people, mostly True Humans, were well-fed and clean, busily getting the town ready for the day. West, in the distant foothills, stood the white Palace of the Canton Lord, with his private sailway winding through the tumpfields.

"Hey there, cat girl!" The greeting came from a grimy individual leaning against a wall; even in Rangua Town there were derelicts. Karina grinned at him with some malice, toyed with the idea of teasing, then realized that the slatting noise of the car's sails had ceased. The crew had hauled them tight and the car was about to depart.

She ran along the dusty street pursued by the ribald shouts of the bum, reached the trackside and, timing her moment, seized the guide-arm of the sailcar *Urubu* as it rumbled past. In one fluid movement she hauled herself up onto the arm, laughed into the amazed face of an elderly passenger who stared out of a nearby porthole, and swung himself to the deck above.

The *Urubu* was a two-master and the crew of four were busy. The wind was light and it needed all their skill to keep the car moving; they hauled on the sheets to the instructions barking out of a voicepipe on the foredeck.

Then the car reached the downgrade and began to accelerate, and the men relaxed and turned their attention to the young girl leaning on the after-rail.

"Captain Herrero will kill you," one of them said. "You know what he thinks of felinos."

"He'll never know," answered Karina. The captain controlled the craft from a tiny cabin in the nose of the car, under the foredeck.

"He will if I tell him."

"But you won't." She stared at him in some contempt.

He grinned, embarrassed by the certainty in her tone, at her knowledge that he couldn't bring himself to harm her. "You're one of El Tigre's grupo, aren't you?" Although deck crews were True Humans, they had a good knowledge of felinos and their ways and were often used as mediators in disputes.

But Karinas's attention had been caught by a shiny object, one of six set in a row of holes in a deck-coaming. "What. . . ?" She pulled one out and stared at it. "What are these?"

"Knives, of course."

"But. . . ." That smooth, shiny surface, cold to the

touch. . . . "They're *metal!* They. . . . Why do you have *metal* knives?" Suddenly the thing seemed to sear her hand and she dropped it to the deck. Touched by Agni. The metal was cursed by the Wrath of Agni. All metal was.

Now a larger man spoke, slow and deep. "We have metal knives to protect ourselves against bandit gangs of felinas."

"But it's illegal. It's heresy!"

"Let's just say that Captain Herrero's religion involves keeping his crew safe, and we like it that way."

"But. . . there's only one religion—the Kikihuahua Examples. And the Examples say that metal is cursed by Agni the Fire-God, and that people are happier without it." She was staring at the knife. "And that thing proves the Examples are right. The knife is for killing."

Now the first man said, "The knives were found in an old dwelling. They were not wrought by any Ranguan man. They're used in an emergency if a sheet jams in a gale and the car is in danger."

And the big man added, "And they're used in defence." He moved close to Karina. "How is your father, girl? Is he still plotting rebellion? Does he still think the felinos could run the sailways better themselves? Tell him this." He reached out and gathered up a handful of her tunic and, his fingers biting into her breast, he pulled her close. "Tell him we're ready. Tell him about the knives. Tell him we don't fight any fairer than he does." His face was a centimetre from hers and she could smell his breath, and feel the mist of saliva which accompanied his speech.

"Little Friends," she said to herself, blanking out her reaction to the man's presence, *"don't let me lose my temper."*

"Let her go, Antrez," said one of the crew unhappily.

26

"And I tell you another thing, cat-girl," said the big man. "If there's any trouble from you people at the Tortuga Festival this year, why, me and my friends have arranged a little surprise. I suppose you and your kind think you're the only ones who hunt in packs? Well, now, the next time you take it into your heads to attack a True Human, you'll be making one hell of a mistake. This time, cat-girl, you'll find us ready and waiting."

"Me?" said Karina, while the Little Friends held her in check. "*Me* attack a True Human?" Her eyes stared into his.

Her eyes like hummingbirds, amber and alive. . . .

"You people. . . ." Now he was unsure of himself. "You eat meat. That's your problem. You use the Examples when they suit you, but you eat meat." His expression changed as he watched her, and he blinked. He realized he was holding her breast and he let go, ashamed. Suddenly she was a girl—a very lovely young girl, whom he was bullying. He wondered what had got into him; whether some of Captain Herrero was rubbing off on him.

He turned away and left her standing there. As he went, he mumbled something that sounded very much like *sorry.* . . . The *Urubu* rumbled on down the slope. Karina stood trembling with rage and disgust while the morning sun began to warm the deck. Another crewman approached her and said, "Don't mind Antrez—he takes his responsibilities seriously. He's in charge up here. And let's face it, girl, your father has no love for True Humans. And a lot of sailcars have been raided recently."

"The good ones are never attacked." But the Little Friends were soothing her and this True Human meant well. She tried to smile.

"That's better." He grinned at her. "Friends?"

Then the voice of Captain Herrero rasped from the pipe.

"Stand by for South Stage—and if any of those animals try to steal a ride kick them right off the deck. Pay out the mizzen sheet and brake for the curve—now! Watch out for that brute to starboard—looks like he has a rock in his hand. By Agni—it's El Tigre! Right—haul in all sheets now and away we go!"

Karina leaped from the deck, rolled in the dirt, and stood.

The *Urubu* gathered speed, sailing rapidly away across the coastal plain in the bright morning sunlight.

"And just where in hell have you been, girl?"

El Tigre towered above Karina. In one hand he clutched a rock. In the other he held a mule whip, which he slapped ominously against his thigh.

Meeting of the revolutionaries.

It was a bad morning for El Tigre and it had been a bad night before. He'd called a meeting for sundown in the big community hut at the north end of the camp near the bachelor vampiros. It had not been well attended. He'd suspected this would happen, because people had been avoiding his eyes during the day.

At sundown he stood alone in the hut, waiting for the others. It was quiet outside, and the last wisps of cooking smoke faded away; nobody can cook in the evening, when the sun is gone. It was a moment of peace which the anticipation of the coming meeting could not destroy. As he stood there, El Tigre thought: *I love this place. I love the people and the things, the bright sun and the ever-cooling winds. I love the tall, slow men and the noisy vicious bands of fighting girls. I love the sounds and*

the peace, the day and the night. I love the women. . . . His
mind dwelt kindly for a moment on the women he'd
known; the grupos he'd fathered. There had been Belle-
za and Tanaril, Amora and Serena. . . . And others. His
musings slowed. Serena, the mother of Teressa, Karina,
Runa and Saba. Serena, who was gentle in an unusual
way, and very loving, and strangely devoted. Serena,
who was dead. . . .

And his whole being rose up in a moment of supreme,
overpowering hatred for the True Humans, who had
killed Serena.

"El Tigre! Is anything the matter?"

His lieutenant, Torch, had arrived and was regarding
him in concern. El Tigre's face was corded with veins
and his fists were clenched in the air. He looked
murderous, and somehow doomed.

"No, I'm fine." The voice, after a moment's pause,
was deep and slow. "Where is everybody?"

"I saw Ligero and Manoso on their way, and others.
Maybe," suggested Torch with deference, "maybe it's
not the best time for meetings, El Tigre. The Festival is
near. People have other things to think of."

In the end there were about a dozen men in the hut.
Big broad men, bigger than most True Humans, heavy
of shoulder and haunch, with a slow, graceful way of
moving. They were uneasy in one another's company;
felinos are solitary creatures. Only the powerful presence of El Tigre could bind them together; and tonight,
even he was to have his difficulties. As Torch had said,
it was not the best time. The sky darkened outside and
the female grupos moved silently about their business,
some of them slipping away into the bush, others gathering around the cooling sun-ovens to tell stories.

The grupo which bore El Tigre's name because it had
no mother passed by the door of the community hut,

and Teressa called, "See you later, father!"

El Tigre growled, feeling embarrassed yet proud that his daughter had called to him, and began to address the meeting.

"Friends! I speak of revolution!"

"What, again?" came the audible comment and El Tigre, with that excellent night vision of his race, saw the lips of Dozo moving. Dozo, the elder sage, the fat bachelor who had never sired a grupo; the witty, lazy cynic who always seemed to be laughing at the ways of men.

Torch supported his leader, advancing on Dozo. "If you don't want to hear of revolution, then get back to your quarters where the young bachelors are. You might find it more interesting!" This was a reference to Dozo's rumored sexual preferences—a rumor which had never been proved. Or disproved, for that matter, since Dozo had an infuriating way of suggesting that the affairs of men were of little significance and that sex was possibly at the bottom of the list.

"I wouldn't miss the sight of El Tigre making a fool of himself for all the tortugas in Rangua," said Dozo, folding his arms across his ample paunch and lying back against the wall.

"Well, just be quiet, will you," said El Tigre. Then he raised his voice again. "I have called you together to hear some important news which was brought over the hill today by one of our people from North Stage. He told me about developments in the delta which are a threat to us all. It seems—and our informant was sure of his facts—that a secret establishment has been set up. Now, this place is as closely guarded as the tortuga compounds themselves and the North Stage felinos have not been able to get through. However—"

"They have it on the word of certain howler

monkeys," interjected Dozo, mimicking El Tigre's style perfectly.

"They had it from the tortuga guards—Specialists like ourselves—"

"What!" Dozo scrambled to his feet, seriously annoyed. "You compare us with the tortuga guards? Do you know what they are, El Tigre? Have you ever actually seen them, yourself?"

"Of course I have. They're Specialists. All Specialists are brothers. We are all human beings of the Third Species, the Children of Mordecai."

"They're *crocodiles*, for God's sake," snapped Dozo. "They have crocodile genes in their make-up and by God, it shows. They're untrustworthy, stupid and vicious. They lie instinctively. If you're calling this meeting on the word of a crocodile, then I suggest you save your breath. Me, I've heard enough."

Saying this, he lumbered out of the door and into the night. He left a silence behind him. His abrupt departure had had far more effect than any of his usual sly asides.

"Was it really the crocodiles who told your informant, El Tigre?" asked the tall, stooping Diferir.

El Tigre spoke with barely-suppressed rage. "They are *not* crocodiles. They are cai-men. It is contrary to the Examples to refer to human beings by animal names. It is as bad," he said slowly, "as calling us jaguars."

"But that's exactly what they call *you*," murmured Manoso, the tricky one. "El Tigre. The jaguar."

"That's different!" roared El Tigre, aware that he was losing his audience. "Listen to me! While we're arguing trivialities the True Humans are massing to attack!"

"Attack?"

"Yes, attack! And what better time than the Tortuga Festival, when our women are drunk and copulating and unable to fight!" Now he had their attention again.

He continued in tones of quiet menace. "In the delta the True Humans are constructing sailcars. But this is not the usual spate of building we see before the Festival, when the Cantons and the Companies compete to supply their captains with the biggest and swiftest cars. That's happening as well, of course. The tortuga loading yard is buzzing with True Humans and their apish carpenters. It's no secret.

"But deep in the mangroves of the delta they're building a different type of car—lighter and carrying more sail than anything we've ever seen. The first of this new breed has already been tested. My spy tells me it flew down the rails like the wind itself. He said he'd never seen such speed—and mark this, my friends. He said the car was virtually soundless. It flitted past him like a white ghost. It was a moonlit night, and he got a good look at the captain and crew. The captain was Tonio. The name of the car is *Rayo*—the Thunderbolt!"

Now Arrojo spoke excitedly. "Let's send the grupos in! I can raise three—that's fourteen women—for this kind of fight. It's a time for cooperation!"

"It's too late tonight," said Diferir. "The grupos are scattered all over the place. Anyway, a thing like this needs careful planning. We must define our objectives: what, after all, are we trying to achieve?"

"I may be stupid," said Torpe, a lolling felino, slow of speech, whose mouth tended to gape like a yawning llama and who was, in fact, stupid, "but surely El Tigre made it plain that our objective is the destruction of this *Rayo*."

"But I'm not stupid." The voice came from the doorway and El Tigre groaned. It was Dozo, who'd been unable to follow through with his grand exit and who'd hovered about outside, listening. "And I need to know a bit more. What exactly is the threat in this *Rayo*,

El Tigre? Why do you say the humans are massing to attack? Surely the Rayo—if it exists—is just one more fast car. If it's faster than the others, this means Captain Tonio will reach the southern markets before the other cars, and will get the best prices for his tortugas, and earn a bonus. And since he's employed by Rangua Canton, the Lord will profit too. It's an affair of True Humans. Why should we care?"

"Because *Rayo* can travel faster than a man on galloping horseback," said El Tigre quietly. "Just think about that for a moment, Dozo."

And Dozo said, "Oh."

The others, standing and sitting around in the darkened hut, chewed this over. Nobody spoke. In a short while, even Torpe had worked out the significance of the True Humans' technological advance. . . .

"So now," said El Tigre heavily, rubbing it in, "a car full of soldiers can be transported anywhere on the coast before warning of its approach can be given. We would know nothing until the car appeared and unloaded. All our work—the scouting system we've built up over the years—will be useless."

"But the Signalmen . . . ?"

"They've never been on our side. Don't kid yourself."

"But we are not at war," said Diferir mildly.

"We've always been at war. Ever since the great Mordecai created the first Specialist, we've been at war with the True Humans."

"This is quite a moment in history," said Dozo in calm tones. "Do you realize, it's probably thousands of years since humans have been able to travel faster than a galloping horse? I'd hate to think that war was the only purpose of this step forward. Perhaps we should make sure of our facts before we do anything foolish. If True Humans had wanted to attack us, they'd have found ways of doing it before now. Sometimes I think you're blinded by your hatred, El Tigre."

"Make sure of our facts," echoed Diferir the cautious.

"There are better ways of finding things out than talking to crocodiles," said Manoso. "This Captain Tonio, for instance. He passes by most days. While I'm sure he would tell us nothing, he often has his son with him in the car. Now a young boy, gullible, engaged in conversation on the long pull up to the Town, well. . . . Need I say more?"

"True Humans are frightened of felinos," Ligero objected. "We're too big for them."

"Who said anything about men?" Manoso chuckled. "I had in mind a young girl from the camp—beautiful, sexual. . . . True Humans are not scared of solitary women."

"So long as there was no suggestion of a grupo." Now Ligero laughed. "Even I am scared of grupos."

"A solitary girl, in innocent conversation with Captain Tonio's boy Raoul. . . ." Manoso's insinuating tones whispered through the hut, firing their imaginations. "A girl about his own age, pretty, friendly. . . ."

"Who are you suggesting, Manoso?" asked El Tigre in ominous tones.

"I'm sure you'll think of someone, El Tigre."

The meeting degenerated into idle chatter. El Tigre stood silent and sombre. Nothing had changed. He doubted that the felinos would ever take concerted action against the True Humans. Felino males are solitary and independent, and that factor alone meant that the True Humans would always stay on top. And yet the felinos had what ought to be the deciding weapon, in the grupos. Nobody fights so bravely, so skilfully, so cohesively as a grupo of felinas. Yet if a weapon cannot be coordinated and properly deployed, its value is limited. . . .

El Tigre's dream.

The True Humans came like locusts, pouring out of an endless succession of fast sailcars and swarming into the camp, consuming everything and leaving only the bones of vampiro tents behind like corn stubble. The grupos fought to the death while the big males roared orders from strategic points until, themselves beset by enemies, they seized their ironwood swords and laid about them. But the True Humans came on, irresistible, superior, well-organized. The grupos fought in little knots of snarling fury and went under, one by one. The males were beaten back to the bachelor quarters and in the end, acknowledging defeat, melted away into the bush. . . .

El Tigre stirred in his sleep.

. . . . Yes, there had been talk of a raid, but it had been a small thing; just a few drunken True Humans stumbling down from Town, seventeen years ago. Chuckling, whispering, out for mischief, nothing more. The felina dwelling they chose was a vampiro tent right on the edge of camp. Inside was the newest mother and her four infants, all asleep. In time they would have been a matriarchal grupo to be reckoned with. Apart from one sickly baby they were unusually big children and the mother had been unusual too—with beauty, grace, swiftness and courage which had set her apart and destined her for mating with the finest man in camp. . . .

El Tigre, rolling over, uttered a small cry.

She'd taken three True Humans with her. Their bodies lay disembowelled, almost dismembered, nearby. Serena had paid for their lives. She was only marked on breast and thigh, but she had paid heavily, because after the remaining True Humans had had their fun they'd taken her sword—a fine thing of stone-chiselled ironwood—and they'd driven it up her, killing her that way.

El Tigre awakened to a nightmare vision and spent a moment staring around the interior of his dwelling, re-orienting himself in the first glow of daylight, telling himself that the horror had been a long time ago.

Now he arose and dressed, and walked out into the morning. People were stirring, turning the sun-ovens to catch the first rays. An aroma of broiled tumpmeat lay on the breeze. El Tigre, his stomach rebelling, strode towards the sailway track. Here was a scene of activity and in the shouts of felinos and the rattling of harness he hoped to lose the night's memories.

Serena, transfixed. . . .

The southbound dawn car came into view, rumbling down the hill from Rangua Town. A carload of humans. . . . Almost without thinking, he'd bent down and picked up a large, jagged rock. The car drew level and he saw the saturnine Captain Herrero—certainly the least popular of the captains—eyeing him from the forecabin. Somehow El Tigre restrained himself and the car was past, lumbering away across the plain.

And his daughter Karina was rolling in the dirt, then standing and making a playful gesture to the receding deck crew.

Dropping the rock he seized her arm, jerking her towards him. Their eyes met, and a thrill of fear went through Karina; she'd never seen her father look so . . . *mad,* in an animal way, like a wounded jaguar finally taunted into attacking. And he, El Tigre—he saw in her face all the betrayal of years; all the timid deals made between felinos and True Humans, all the selling-out, lies and mistrust; the broken treaties, the skirmishes, the haggling over prices, the cheating and stealing. So long as people pretended to this sham truce, it would always be like this. . . .

Karina's smile was gone, but her fear had faded quickly too, because she understood this huge person before her. He was not *loco*. Things had gone wrong for him again, that was all—and if he was going to beat her because of it, she couldn't stop him. Her muscles tensed, she regained her balance and stood foursquare, prepared to do her best. Her hands were open, her fingers hooked.

El Tigre saw her expression change, and felt her weight shift into a fighting stance. He was looking into her eyes as her fear faded, and he'd seen that fear replaced by an understanding which, for an instant, caused rage to throb even more violently in his brain.

The girl is pitying me. . . .

Others arrived, moving into the perimeter of his rage. Idle spectators. And—not so idle—Teressa, Runa and Saba. They stood near, waiting for him to make his move, waiting to move themselves. They would not allow a member of their grupo to be beaten, not even by their father. So it was going to be a full-scale fight. Now he, too, moved into position. He would feint towards Karina and then take Teressa as she came in. Karina would be last, because she couldn't be hurt, so she never knew when to stop fighting.

Karina, *her eyes. . . .*

And suddenly he found his mind dwelling on something which had happened long ago, up in the mountains. *He was lying on the forest floor and didn't know where he was, or how he'd got there.* A girl had come up to him and said, "I am the Dedo. Don't be frightened. You've come a long way, and you've been sick. You will never remember anything which happened before this moment. Now, come with me and meet the woman who will be your mate, and *remember her.*"

She'd taken his hand and led him among a system of

interconnecting lakes and there, lying on the bank of the broadest lake, they'd found a girl with auburn hair. Although her eyes were open she seemed to be asleep. He'd looked a long time into those eyes, seeing something living behind them—not just a human mind, but something else—something . . . alien. "Go and make your life in the felino camp," the Dedo had said, "and always remember this sleeping woman, whose name is *Serena*. Get out of this valley as quickly as you can, because your very presence unbalances the scales of nature here, and may result in your death."

So he'd run, hearing a great crashing in the bush behind him. He'd lived in the felino camp, sired children there and become leader of his people. And when, some years later, Serena arrived, he'd loved her. . . .

Karina, *her eyes*. . . . They watched him with a life of their own.

They were Serena's eyes, reborn in the daughter.

El Tigre's own eyes filled with tears and he turned away, saddened and awed. He began to walk back towards the camp. Teressa, Runa and Saba moved away among the shrugleggers who shied and watched them with rolling eyes.

Karina ran to catch her father, and took his hand.

The morning meat car had stopped nearby and the crewmen had watched the incident with interest. One of them said,

"That's a good-looking girl. And just look at the size of that male!"

"El Tigre and his daughter," said another, knowledgably. "For a moment I thought there'd be a fight. She's quite a girl, but she hates our guts. Funny, though —felinos hardly ever fight among themselves. They're as vicious as all Agni, and yet they leave one another alone. They hardly ever challenge their own pecking order."

"Like animals," said the first speaker. . . .

So the two humans of the Third Species walked away holding hands, and there had been no victory, no defeat. They knew the strengths and weaknesses of each other, and they each had an inner knowledge of the value of each other to their people—and, possibly, to some other great Purpose. . . .

"I met a funny woman last night," said Karina. "She told me some strange things. She was a True Human, and I needed to talk to the Pegman about her. I'm sorry, father."

The lion of a man beside her, his temper soothed by her presence, growled, "I love you, Karina—always remember that. There is not much real love in the world. True Humans are murdering bastards, and it shames me in front of our people when you're friendly with them. I don't need to remind you what happened to your mother."

Karina said quietly, "Don't ever worry about my feelings for True Humans."

They passed vampiros where women cooked, laying strips of tumpmeat on the blackened rocks of the sun-ovens, then aligning the concave hemitrexes so that they caught the sun's rays and focussed them on the raw flesh. The felinas were slow and lazy, and they talked sleepily to one another as they worked, recounting stories of the night's prowling and hunting-games. Soon they would eat, then drowse the rest of the day away.

El Tigre sat on the ground outside Karina's vampiro while she cooked meat for him. Later the other members of the grupo joined them and, after a while, Torch. The young felino's eyes burned with excitement.

"Last night, we told them, El Tigre!"

"Dozo told us, I thought."

"No—all we need now is for Karina here to. . . ." His

voice trailed away as he remembered it was El Tigre's job to brief Karina on the seduction of Raoul, and maybe El Tigre had not seen fit to broach the question yet. He watched the girls with his hot eyes: Teressa, Runa, Karina and, well, Saba. It would be fun to mate with them. They lay around lazy and replete, and Karina's tunic barely covered her hips. They were a prime grupo —suitable mates for the future leader of the camp. . . .

"Manoso doesn't tell me what to do," El Tigre growled.

"Eh?" Torch dragged his thoughts away from warm flesh. "Of course not, El Tigre!"

"Neither does Karina consort with True Humans."

"What's this?" asked Karina.

"Of course not, El Tigre! I just thought—"

"It's a degrading thing to suggest of a girl such as Karina. A woman's job is hunting and fighting, not wheedling secrets out of True Humans!"

Karina was fidgeting with impatience. "Hunting? The Examples forbid real hunting with a kill at the end of it. We only play. And fighting? We play at that, too." She was now thoroughly awake again. "Father—let me wheedle secrets out of a True Human! It sounds like fun."

"Ah, by the Sword of Agni," grumbled El Tigre. "No!"

"But I want—"

"No!" Real anger flashed in El Tigre's eyes, and Teressa's and Runa's eyelids cracked open in curiosity. Saba slept, snoring gently. "I will not have you associating with True Humans, neither with that crazy Pegman, nor with Captain Tonio or his son Raoul, nor with any other of that damned breed. You may think they're weak, and you may hate and despise them now, Karina —but they're crafty and you know little of their ways.

Any kind of association could be dangerous for you. So long as I'm chief of this camp, you'll stay away from them until the day comes when I give the word to attack!''

Princess Swift Current.

Raoul held onto the forestay and watched the sun burn off the coastal mist. He was a big boy for his age, and he had a grace and economy of movement—unusual in True Humans—which caused some people to regard him oddly, and to speculate behind his parents' backs. And he was a dreamer, given to long solitary rambles in the foothills.

The *Cadalla* rumbled across the plain. She was a heavy car holding some forty passengers, heading north for Rangua, sails full of the morning breeze. The crewmen adjusted the lines in accordance with the clipped commands issuing from below, but there was little real work to do in this steady wind. In the distance Raoul could see a car approaching on the southbound track.

He indulged in one of his frequent daydreams, picturing himself in charge of the *Cadalla* in his father's place, barking orders. He saw the leaves in a grove of trees brighten suddenly, as a gust of wind took them.

"Ease the sheets," he whispered.

And the voice snapped from the pipe nearby, "Ease the sheets!" as his father, the alert Captain Tonio, anticipated the gust from his vantage-point in the car's nose.

Raoul smiled to himself. He'd given the right order and saved the car from harm. The gust hit the car. There was a slight lurch and the lee wheels screamed against the guiderails, but the sails had been let out a fraction

41

and the strain on the masts was eased. Nodding to the crew, Raoul descended the ladder to the main cabin. The passengers sat in two rows down each side of the tubular, planked hull. Some dozed, some stared out of the ports, others glanced at him. They all rocked to the rhythm of the car.

"All is well," said Raoul to himself. *"We hope to be in Rangua by noon, given a fair wind."* He ducked under the beam which supported the mainmast and entered the forecabin.

Captain Tonio sat there, eyes flickering over the scene through the open nose port. The wind blew in, swallowed by the *Cadalla*'s speed, ruffling his hair. A tall, austere man, he sat with knees bent to his chest, crouching forward, eyes slitted with concentration. He sensed rather than saw Raoul. "Everything in order on deck?"

"Fine, father." Leaning against the bulkhead, swaying to the motion of the car, Raoul indulged in one of his favourite fantasies: The Rescue of Princess Swift Current.

The stories and legends of the sailways are many, dealing with every conceivable type of disaster. Simple songs were often woven around such incidents which would later be incorporated into the Song of Earth: that great History of Mankind which came into gradual being through the songs of the minstrels during the Dying Years. The story of Princess Swift Current would begin thus:

"The *Cavaquinho* flew away beyond her crew's reclaim.

Her sails were stitched with cinders and her hull was forged of flame."

The *Cavaquinho* was a small craft, but fast. Built a quarter of a century before Raoul was born, she was an elite Company-owned car specializing in swift transport of wealthy and important people. She had an unusual privilege: the signalmen flashed a special signal to other traffic when *Cavaquinho* was on the track, warning them to pull off into the next siding to allow the faster car to get by. Signalmen also flashed codes to each other, up and down the line, warning that *Cavaquinho* was in the vicinity.

As an added luxury the craft carried guards; huge decorated Specialists of uncertain genetic origin chosen from a remote mountain tribe, who swaggered about the deck with ironwood swords to deter any bandit grupo.

The minstrels sing of *Cavaquinho's* last voyage, when she sailed south to Cassino Canton carrying the Lord of Green Forests, ruler of Portina Canton, and his daughter the Princess Swift Current, who was to be married to Lord Avalancha of Cassino.

The legend also mentions that the Princess Swift Current was already in love with a humble minstrel from Jai'a, although this detail is omitted from the later Song of Earth.

The car approached the Rio Pele estuary, passing through a heavily-wooded region. Without being told, the crew sheeted in the sails. This was standard practice in order to maintain speed in the more sheltered airs of the forest. Far above the car, the treetops danced in a fierce gale.

A heavy bough, falling end over end from a lofty tree, struck the *Cavaquinho* on the foredeck.

Two guards were swept over the side. One was hit by the guidewheel arm and died instantly, the other fell five metres into the mud of the estuary and, stunned, died more slowly as the crocodiles moved in. The branch then slid along the deck, tipped, and one end jammed between the guidewheel and the rail. The other end whipped around. One crewman was flung from the deck and crushed by the guidewheel, the other fell into the river and was never seen again.

The full force of the wind hit the *Cavaquinho* as she ran onto the bridge. Normally the crew would have eased the sails out—but there was nobody on deck. Neither was the main brake manned. Unable to spill wind, out of control, the *Cavaquinho* gathered speed as the gale came roaring up the estuary.

The bridge was about a kilometre long and rickety, because the water had attacked the pilings. Worse, there was a sharp bend about three-quarters of the way across where the track turned to follow the shore to Pele North Stage. The felinos saw the sails of *Cavaquinho* racing across the estuary. Afterwards, they said she sped 'swifter than a stooping eagle.'

Captain Cuiva applied the brakes from his cabin, but without avail; indeed, the small emergency forward brake caught fire within seconds and flames spread into the forecabin.

The *Cavaquinho* hit the curve. The guiderail split and collapsed. The sailcar left the track and leaped out across the water. The jagged end of the rail tore away the lath and fabric nose of the forecabin. Captain Cuiva was pitched into the river, suffering a broken leg and a broken back. He was picked up by the felinos but died within the week.

The main cabin of the *Cavaquinho* together with the deck, mast and sails, by now a streaming comet of flames, skipped some distance across the water before settling. The sail remained full and the craft, aided by the incoming tide, drifted rapidly upstream until it disappeared into the mangroves, where a pillar of smoke marked its presence for some moments.

The search for survivors was delayed. The felinos refused to enter the mangroves due to a local superstition concerning a *bruja*. That evening the wreckage drifted past the Stage on a falling tide and was pulled ashore. There was no sign of bodies, but later the same evening The Lord of the Green Forest's body came ashore, mutilated by caimans. The remains of Princess Swift Current were never found. . . .

In Raoul's imagination she had escaped, and lived on as his wife, a delicate creature with porcelain skin who sat quietly in the beautiful house he'd built for her. Like a lovely painting she was, never speaking of her ordeal, in fact never speaking at all. Having saved her, Raoul's mission in life was to look after her.

How did Raoul save the Princess Swift Current?

He swung from a tree and snatched her out of a porthole, like an ape kidnapping a baby. He dropped to the deck, beat off the guards, knocked out Captain Cuiva and led her to where he had two white horses waiting. He'd hidden himself under the car, clinging to the running wheel struts, and at the right moment he appeared in the cabin and. . . . He emerged dripping from the river, fighting off crocodiles as he. . . .

Such was the imagination of Raoul. The sailcar rumbled on, slow, prosaic, with a cargo of uninteresting True Humans on their way to meaningless destinations. Was the age of excitement dead?

"How fast will this car go?" he asked his father. *Swifter than a stooping eagle.*

"It would take a good horse to outrun us," replied Captain Tonio.

"You call that fast?"

"I can't understand why you kids are so impressed by speed." The journey was nearly over; Rangua Stage was in sight. The southbound car went by. Soon Tonio would be home; Astrud would be waiting, and she'd mentioned early tortugas for supper. Tortugas. . . . Content, Tonio felt he could indulge the boy. "Maybe one night I'll show you a really fast car."

"As fast as the *Cavaquinho?*"

"That was forty years ago. I'd like to think we've progressed since then."

He began to bark commands into the voice pipe, and Raoul heard the crew running on deck. The car lurched, and a rasping squeal announced that the brakes had been applied for Rangua South Stage.

The brawl on Cadalla.

The shrugleggers were creatures of little consequence. In the year 83,426 Cyclic Mankind was still lumbering about the Galaxy in his three-dimensional spaceships and although he'd already met the kikihuahuas and absorbed some of their culture, their mode of travel was too slow for him, and the Outer Think was over a thousand years in the Ifalong. So he rode his metal ships and he suffered the unaccountable accidents to which such crude transport was prone.

The tender from *Spacehawk* crash-landed on Ilos III.

Ilos III was known as the Mud Planet because much of its surface was covered with a suppurating volcanic ooze much prized for its cosmetic properties. Its only inhabitant of any consequence was a human-sized armless biped with gigantic thighs which spent its time foraging in the ooze and had been ignored by exobiologists, until the crash.

The tender's commander, his ship gradually sinking in the mud, watched by open-mouthed shrugleggers, was struck by an idea. Using morsels of reconstituted fish as bait he tempted the shrugleggers near, then slipped ropes around them, harnessing them to the ship. Twenty shrugleggers were enough. They had enormous strength in their legs, and soon the tender began to glide towards dry land.

The Captain of *Spacehawk* was interested in his commander's report. It represented a co-operation between Man and beast very much in accordance with the spirit of the Kikihuahua Examples which were becoming popular back on Earth. Those days, the spaceships with their prodigious energy consumption were attracting adverse publicity. The Captain saw a chance to show that space captains, too, were working towards the eventual partnership of Man and Nature.

In the name of the Examples he shipped a hundred shrugleggers back to Earth for use as beasts of burden in rural areas. The experiment was a failure—Earth's civilizations were not ready to embrace the Examples quite so readily—and the shrugleggers were banished to a remote corner of Lake Titicaca where they strode the shallows in peace for almost forty thousand years, until the coming of the sailways.

Then, at last, their value was realized.

The bargaining was over. Grumbling, Captain Tonio returned to his cabin. "Damned bandits," he was muttering.

Raoul watched from the foredeck as the shrugleggers were hitched on. The head felino was a large young man who seemed to have a good opinion of himself; Raoul heard the others call him Torch. He was competent, Raoul allowed that—conscious of a twinge of jealousy that this Specialist, little older than himself, held a position of some authority among his own people.

Whereas he, Raoul, was regarded as a child. . . .

Torch yelled, the felinos cracked their whips, and the

car began its slow ascent to Rangua Town. Raoul sat on the rail, dreaming, watching the plodding movement of the shrugleggers' haunches, when an astonishing thing happened.

A felina swung onto the car and sat on the foredeck.

He stared at her, resenting her intrusion into his domain. She was about the same age as he, with wide slanting eyes and, like all felinas, an air of barely-suppressed violence.

"You're not allowed up here," he said.

"Then throw me off," she answered, looking directly into his eyes in a way which caused a sudden emptiness in his stomach.

"Listen," he said after a moment during which nothing happened. "Get off here, will you?"

"I know your name," she said. "You're Raoul. You're Captain Tonio's son."

He thought he'd seen her before; but then, all felinas looked alike. He glanced behind him, but the crew were immersed in a game of Rebellion on an improvised board scratched into the deck; they muttered together, clicking counters. His father and the passengers were all below. The girl was cleaner than most of her kind, and quite beautiful in an animal way.

Cautiously he asked, "What's your name?"

"It's Karina. El Tigre is my father." Now she smiled, and something of the sun entered Raoul's body.

"El Tigre? He's a *bandido*."

Karina tensed and her fingers curled instinctively, and the nails itched for action. Just in time she recalled the reason for her presence here on this goddamned sailcar with this goddamned True Human brat. She was going to discover the secrets of the delta, and prove to her father that she was capable of looking after herself among True Humans. She was going to kill two rheas with one rock.

She would *captivate* this kid. True Humans couldn't resist felinas. And then, when he was crazy for her, he would tell her about the delta, the *Rayo,* his father Tonio, his mother, what he ate for breakfast, everything.

She glanced at him slyly, smiled, and wriggled where she sat so that her tunic rose up towards her hips. Then she stretched catlike, arching her back and clasping her hands behind her neck. She tilted her head back, relishing the sun on her face and his eyes on her body.

"What in hell are you doing here, Karina?"

It was Torch. His face dark with fury, he swung himself onto the deck. He stood scowling down at her, not unnaturally misunderstanding what he saw.

Karina swiftly assumed a demure attitude, hands folded in her lap, sliding backwards so that her tunic was stretched down to her ankles. Unfortunately this had the effect of exposing most of her breasts. Raoul was still staring at her, hardly aware of Torch's intrusion.

"Just taking a ride, Torch," she said sweetly.

"Well, get off and get back to the camp! This is directly against El Tigre's orders!"

"I'm happy where I am, thanks."

"I can see that! You'll be in big trouble when your father hears about this, Karina!" His eyes were hot with rage and lust. "By the Sword of Agni, you need to be taught a lesson!"

"You're not my father, Torch."

"Maybe not, but I'll be squiring your grupo before long!"

Karina gave a short laugh of incredulity. "*You* squire our grupo? *You?*"

"Your father is in agreement."

"Yes, because you suck up to him, agreeing with everything he says. But what about me? Do I agree? What about Runa and Saba? What about Teressa,

Torch? She'd claw the face off you, and more besides. Think about Teressa, Torch, before you start getting ideas about our grupo!"

"When the squire is ordained, all grupo members must concur," said Torch loftily, his desire temporarily forgotten in the niceties of cultural argument. "Your grupo has no mother, therefore your squire will be ordained by El Tigre. It is the custom."

"Piss on the custom," said Karina.

"What did you say, Karina?" Torch could hardly believe his ears. Karina's contempt for felino culture had genuinely shocked him. "Did you say piss on the custom, Karina?"

Raoul gave a shout of laughter. Torch glanced at him, hardly seeing him.

"That's what I said," said Karina. "Those were my exact words."

"Would you care to explain them further?" Torch took refuge in his dignity.

Karina opened her mouth, Raoul regarding her with respect and delight, and was about to expound her views on customs in general and Torch's sexual desires in particular when there was an unwelcome interruption.

"Just what in hell are these felinos doing on my deck, Raoul?" said Captain Tonio grimly, emerging from below.

"Come on out of here," snapped Torch, dragging Karina to her feet.

Furious, she aimed a swift kick at his crotch. Torch saw it coming, sidestepped, grabbed her foot and heaved. Karina turned a rapid midair somersault and landed lightly on all fours. Snarling with rage, she hurled herself at Torch's throat. He seized the ratlines above his head and met Karina's leap with the full force of both feet.

"Animals . . . !" Tonio was shouting. "Where in hell are my crew?"

Karina rolled end over end and fetched up against the deck railing with a crash. Torch dropped into a crouch and awaited her next attack.

Raoul kicked Torch violently in the buttocks.

Now Torch, caught completely by surprise, pitched forward onto the deck. Karina pounced on him, threw an arm around his neck and began to drag his head back. He uttered one strangled grunt, then began to fight grimly for his life. Unable to shake Karina off, he rose unsteadily to his feet, lurched across the deck pop-eyed and throttled, and began to climb the ratlines with Karina affixed to his back like some infant primate. When he judged he had enough height he let go.

They hit the deck with a crash, Karina underneath.

The crew, appearing belatedly, saw their chance and moved in. The contestants were pried apart and pinioned. Karina was gulping for air, hardly able to stand. Reaction hit her and she urinated uncontrollably, wetness streaming hotly down her legs.

"Get her off my deck!" shouted Captain Tonio, outraged. "There are passengers below!"

Torch was in little better shape, but he was able to shake himself free from his captors. He took Karina by the elbow. "Come on," he said. Leading her to the rail, he bent down, seized her thigh, and pitched her unceremoniously over the edge. Then he turned to face the True Humans and, summoning the tattered remains of his dignity, said, "I must apologize for her behavior, Captain Tonio. It will not happen again, I can assure you. You must understand, there is no mother to teach discretion to her grupo. All this will change when I am ordained as their squire. . . ."

He was already bigger than any of the True Human

crew despite his youth, and the figure he cut hovered uncertainly between strength and pathos.

"That's all right," said Tonio unhappily. "Forget it, forget it."

"All the same," said Torch slowly as though the words were forced out of him by the pressure of his own pride, "If I hear you refer to me as an animal again, Captain Tonio, I will kill you."

With a final venomous glance at Raoul he vaulted over the rail and was gone.

Astrud.

"He's such a big boy," said Astrud. "It's difficult to discipline him. This felina—how friendly was she? What was she like?"

"Like any other felina," said Tonio. "Pretty and aggressive, and she fought like a tiger. Red-haired, though. That's unusual. Her father's El Tigre."

"*The* El Tigre?" Astrud regarded her husband in some alarm. "He's the revolutionary, isn't he?"

"He'd like to be a revolutionary, but there simply isn't going to be a revolution." Tonio felt the need to explain. "Right now, True Humans and felinos are dependent on each other—we have this mutual interest, the sailways. From Portina right down the coast to Rio de la Plata we and the felinos operate the sailways together—that's nearly a thousand kilometres of track covering eight Cantons. If it wasn't for the sailways, we'd be a string of warring coastal tribes, the way we were centuries ago. But the sailways have joined us together so now we have trade instead of wars, and everyone's better for it.

"And now, a few of the felinos are saying they want their share of the trade. They say they're not satisfied with the fees they earn from towing. They want their own sailcars. And we can't let that happen."

"Why not?" Up here in Rangua hill country she was sheltered from politics—and Tonio rarely discussed his work.

Tonio walked to the window. He could see the Atlantic bright in the sun, with the grassy downs rolling to the beach, and the guanacos grazing. The sailway ran across the downs and a car was passing, sail brilliant with sunshine and bearing the emblem of its owner: the whale of Rio Pele. Squat, powerful crewmen were hauling on ropes and Tonio cocked a practiced eye at the wind indicators relative to the sails; and he decided the captain knew his business. To the south he could see the lower boundaries of the tumpfields, and one of the gigantic tumps was in view, like a great gray slug with the tiny figure of the tumpier perched on its back. This was his life; this was his place in the hill country and he wouldn't want anything to change.

He said, "The felinos control the hills. There are over thirty hills on the coast which are too steep for the cars to climb unassisted, so we have to use shrugleggers. Only felinos can make shrugleggers work. Why? Because the shrugleggers are scared of the felinos." He checked off the points on his fingers. "Because the felinos have jaguar genes in their make-up and by Agni the shrugleggers can sense it!

"Now, just imagine if the felinos could operate their own cars. For a start, they wouldn't have to pay towing fees, which is one of the biggest items in any voyage, believe me. So they'd be able to undercut the Canton and Company rates, and get a big share of the trade. Not only that, but there are certain prestige runs where they could block our craft."

"Like the Tortuga Races?"

"Exactly. They'd make a killing on the tortugas. Our craft would never get past Rangua North Stage. They'd hold them up while they let their own cars through, and they'd get all the best prices while our own cargoes went rotten and started exploding. No. The one thing we can't let happen, is for the felinos to get their own sail-cars." He sighed. "The felinos think we don't like them —and God forgive me I called them animals today. But it's not that. It's simply a matter of survival. We can both survive if we stay apart and stick to our separate jobs. But if we let the felinos in on our job when we don't have the physical characteristics to do theirs, then we cut our own throats."

Astrud made her way slowly up the stairs towards the bedroom of Raoul, her son the stranger. Her mind was in the past, remembering that bewildering, hurtful day when Tonio had mocked her barrenness by bringing a baby into the house and assuming, without question or explanation, that she would bring it up as if it were her own.

She'd tried, as a devout follower of the Examples must try, and as the years went by she'd learned to love Raoul because, after all, the situation was no fault of his. But she could never understand Tonio's attitude, or give any credence to his ridiculous story that some woman had *given* him the child one day. It was like a legend told by an old man at the inn, or one of those odd songs the Pegman sang. No—she was morally certain the baby was Tonio's, and she felt he ought to have the decency to tell him who the mother was.

And yet Raoul bore no resemblance to Tonio and sometimes, when some trick of the light threw his cheekbones into relief and shaded in the hollows of his eyes, he didn't look like a True Human at all. Even his

54

hair was a strange color, and she regularly anointed it with a dark resinous oil to tone it down.

Thrusting the disturbing image aside, she knocked on Raoul's door.

He opened it and smiled at her. He looked the way he always did, and she reprimanded herself for her fancies.

"How's father?" he asked. "Has he come down from the trees yet?"

"Your father is understandably upset by your behaviour, Raoul," she heard herself say woodenly. "And there's no call to compare him to some monkeyish Specialist. Sit down. We have to talk, you and I."

"Oh?" He put aside a model he was carving with a shell knife; a fine replica of a sailcar of the historic *Cavaquinho* type. He was clever with his hands, she had to allow him that. Like a monkey. . . . He smiled again, divining her hesitation. "What do you want to talk about, mother?"

"Oh . . . !" She uttered a small noise of exasperation and sat down on the bed. "You know very well what, Raoul. That Specialist girl. El Tigre's daughter. You were talking to her."

"Nobody said there was anything wrong with talking to Specialists. The Examples say we share the same world. They say we're all humans."

She watched this boy, knowing that he was playing with her, wondering how she could beat him at his own game. In the end he could always shock her, she knew; because she was a devout Believer. She decided to get her shock in first.

"Karina was showing her body to you, Raoul—inviting you to have sex when she knew perfectly well you wouldn't be able to do that on the deck of a sailcar in broad daylight. So she wasn't being fair to you."

He looked away. She'd got through to him. She

thought he even flushed at hearing those words come from his saintly mother. "It's just her way," he said. "The Kikihuahua Examples say—"

"Raoul, don't keep throwing the Examples in my face just because I'm a better Believer than you. The Examples say that people shouldn't eat meat, but the felinos eat meat. They've built up a whole bartering system with the tumpiers over the centuries, just to satisfy their craving."

"Only because it's been proved they get sick if they don't have meat. They're naturally carnivorous, mother—like the jaguar."

"Raoul! I will not have you calling human beings naturally carnivorous!" And now she was shocked, as he'd known she would be, and he was winning again.

He said quickly, not wanting to hurt, "But it's not the same thing as eating meat which has been hunted and killed. The tumps feel no pain. The meat's taken from the parts of their body which can spare it, by skilled flensers. I've seen it. They're really big walking vegetables, mother. They were bred that way, thousands of years ago."

"They're unnatural creatures, Raoul. They can't breed."

"But they don't get old and die."

She was sidetracked onto a subject which had given her much cause for thought during her lifetime; an ethical problem to which she could see no answer. "But they get sick and die occasionally. And they commit suicide. There are only fifty-four tumps left in Rangua, Raoul. The stories say there were hundreds of them at one time. In the future there will be none. What will the felinos do then, if they're truly carnivorous? What will they eat, Raoul?"

The First Kikihuahua Allegory.

Astrud *believed* in the kikihuahuas and their Examples although, by now, they were only a legend. They dated back to an encounter in Space in the days of the three-dimensional spaceships—which is to say forty thousand years before Astrud was born, before the Age of Regression began and Mankind retreated into himself. The true story of the first encounter is in the Rainbow.

The *real* story is known as the First Kikihuahua Allegory, and it is a legend, and it runs like this:

It seems there was once a space captain named Watt, and he was a True Human because this was nine thousand years before the Specialists were created by Mordecai N. Whirst. So Watt had no tiger genes, no extraordinary reactions like the legendary Captain Spring who drank from the river of *bor.* He was just an ordinary man who made an ordinary error of judgement, and he crashed on an uncharted planet.

He got clear from his ship just before it exploded into flames. The fire spread, and consumed a large tract of virgin forest.

Agni, the God of Fire, saw this and was offended. He appeared as a small devil, red and immensely strong, and he strapped Watt to a rock and left him to die in the burning sun.

No matter how Watt struggled and twisted, he could not free himself because the bonds were tight, and worse, there were no knots. Agni had fashioned the entire length from a continuous thong, so that they could not be loosened although Watt's hands were free.

The days were hot and the nights cold, and soon Watt was weak with hunger and thirst. He could not struggle any more, but lay back and waited to die. His senses began to slip away.

Then he heard a sound.

He opened his eyes. A small cavy sat nearby, eating a leaf. Carefully, slowly, Watt slid his hand across the ground until it lay beside the animal. The cavy didn't stir. It watched him with bright beady eyes, and it never stopped munching.

Watt grabbed it.

He killed it, and he drank the blood and ate the flesh. The food nourished him, and for a few hours he felt better. He fought his bonds again, but couldn't loosen them. He shouted aloud, and prayed to Agni to release him. But Agni cannot undo what he does—such is the way of the demon of fire.

The next morning another cavy came by.

Watt killed it and ate it.

The next morning the same thing happened again.

And so it went on for twenty days. A cavy would appear and Watt would eat it, and thereby gain just sufficient strength to lament his predicament, struggle with his bonds and pray to Agni.

On the twenty-first day a small furry alien came by.

"Release me!" shouted Watt.

"I cannot," said the kikihuahua. "There are no knots in your bonds for me to untie."

"Then cut them!"

The kikihuahua said, "We do not have knives, nor chisels, nor saws, nor any other thing which is *bent.*"

"But I'll die if you don't help me!"

"I cannot help you. Help weakens the species. If you cannot help yourself, you deserve to die. I will give you advice, however. The next time a cavy approaches, remember that you both have the same enemy—Death—and that you should perhaps respect his fears as well as your own." And with this, the kikihuahua went away.

58

Watt sat against the rock and thought. The day went by and no cavy came, and his hunger seemed to consume his very soul, but he remembered what the kikihuahua had said. And when in the morning a cavy came, Watt had gathered nearby leaves and set them in a pile for the cavy to nibble.

So the cavy ate and Watt watched it and his mouth watered at the sight of the plump flesh, but he kept his hands to himself. By the time the cavy had eaten, its fear had gone and it stayed with him for much of the day. The next day it came closer, and on the third morning it sat right beside him, eating leaves from his hand, unafraid.

During the night Watt wrapped the last remaining leaves around his bonds.

And the cavy came in the morning, and nibbled with strong teeth.

The bonds parted, and Watt was free.

He stood, very weak with hunger, and looked down at the cavy.

Suddenly the cavy trembled, and was afraid.

"Don't be frightened," said Watt. "I'll go and find food elsewhere. You don't want to die any more than I do, but there are other things around which don't have the sense to fear death, so I'll seek them out and eat them instead."

So he ate fruit and yams and milk, and even the eggs of birds which had laid too many to raise. But he never again ate flesh.

The kikihuahua, watching from afar, was pleased. It seemed that humans were beginning to understand.

Raoul had smiled at her when she finished the story, but it was a smile of love and tolerance; there was no belief in it.

"You tell the story better than a priest," he said.

. "The kikihuahuas are *real*. They were here on Earth once, and they'll come again."

Above Raoul's bed hung a small hardwood board, and into the wood someone had laboriously scratched characters with a sharp stone. The writing was in the imprecise, abbreviated hieroglyphics of those times, and roughly translated it said:

THE EXAMPLES OF THE KIKIHUAHUAS

"The kikihuahuas do not command or even instruct, for that is not their way. Rather, they set an example and leave others to follow or not follow as they think fit. The Kikihuahua Examples are great and complex and involve many creatures throughout the Greataway. They are a way of life and death, and it is the Will of God that human beings of all Species and Varieties work towards achieving their state; in particular the Prime Examples:

I will not kill any mortal creature
I will not work any malleable substance
I will not kindle the Wrath of Agni.

In this way you will take a step towards living in accord with your world and the creatures in it, which will be a step nearer to the Example of the kikihuahuas, and the Will of God."

In more simple terms, the Examples were translated by the irreverent as 'don't bash, bend or burn.' Naturally, it was the humans of the first variety of the Second Species—the True Humans—who had appointed themselves keepers of the faith. Periodically they sent priests into the felino camps and onto the tumpfields, and even into the mountains, to ensure that the Word was kept.

So Astrud stood, ruffled Raoul's hair—a thing he wished she wouldn't do—and went downstairs to prepare the supper.

Tonight they were having early tortugas, baked.

The grupo without Karina.

The El Tigre grupo, minus Karina, had stalked Iolande's grupo into the foothills. The huge sighing of the tumps hid any sound they might make. Above, the tumpiers dozed on their mounts; tiny human figures against the night sky.

"They went south, I think," said Runa.

"I really think I heard them heading west," ventured Saba breathlessly. She was having trouble keeping up, as usual.

"What can they be doing?" asked Runa.

"Poaching tumpmeat," Teressa stated positively. "There's been talk about this at the camp. Somebody's been creeping into the fields at night and stealing slices from the tumps. The tumps can't feel it and the tumpiers are asleep. Then in the morning they find fresh wounds."

"I'm hungry," said Runa. The talk of flesh was getting to her.

"Forget it, sister. We're going to catch them in the act, so you'd better make up your mind whose side you're on."

"But raw . . . ?" Saba was disgusted.

"It's better that way," said Runa with relish. "Haven't you ever tried it? Cold and juicy and full of flavor."

"Runa!"

"They frown on it at the camp, of course. They think if the True Humans ever saw us eating raw flesh, it would really convince them we're animals. But so what? If it tastes good, eat it, that's what I say." Runa's eyes shone in the moonlight.

"I think I can smell blood," said Teressa. She sniffed the air and smacked her lips. "The wind's from the east. That's where they are—they must have circled behind us." She swallowed. Her mouth was watering.

"Raw. . . ." said Saba thoughtfully.

"Hold it!" Teressa decided this had gone far enough. "Tonight we're on the side of law and order, for a change. We suspect Iolande's grupo is guilty of anti-social behavior, and we're going to confront them."

"Confront them?"

"Sneak up on them—" A vast sigh like the exhalation of a whale sounded from almost overhead, interrupting her "—and confront them. Point out how they're cheating the whole camp—in fact how they're cheating felinos everywhere, giving them a bad reputation with True Humans."

"Personally I don't give a shit what True Humans think of us," said Runa.

"Well, no. But it makes us look good in front of our own people. I mean. . . . Torch will probably put in a good word for us at the next meeting. We have a few things to live down, you know."

"Torch? To hell with Torch!"

The scene was set for one of those frequent clashes between Runa and Teressa.

"You'd better not say that when he's heading up our grupo!"

"He'll never head any grupo I'm a member of!" snapped Runa.

"You won't have any choice in the matter, sister!"

"Who's going to make me? You? Are you sweet on that swaggering goon, Teressa?"

"By Agni, I'm going to kill you, Runa!"

Runa sprang. Teressa sidestepped and Runa found herself clawing uselessly at the tough hide of the tump. As she turned, Teressa's kick caught her full in the stomach and she dropped, the air whistling out of her.

"You'll have to be quicker than that!" Teressa taunted her. "Torch is a big man. He'll kill you on the first night!"

"Stop it! Stop it! shouted Saba. "I wish Karina was here!"

"What's going on down there?" came a sudden shout from above.

"Now you've done it, you two," Saba whispered. "The tumpier's woken up."

"Let's get out of here."

They crept away, Teressa supporting the staggering Runa who was having difficulty breathing; and headed east, downhill. Far below them the sea glittered coldly and the polished hardwood of the sailway showed as a silver thread across the plain. The wind was cold, and bore the strengthening scent of blood.

Suddenly, Runa fell.

Instantly Teressa was kneeling beside her. "Are you all right?"

"I'm . . . fine." She tried to struggle up.

"No, lie there a moment. Saba! Go and scout out that smell. Don't let anyone see you. Just keep your head down and find out what's going on." When Saba was out of earshot, Teressa said, "I wanted to say I'm very sorry I hurt you, and I'll try not to let it happen again."

"I . . . I . . . ." Runa gulped, snuggling her head against Teressa's breasts.

"Tell me."

"It's so *hard*. The other grupos often have mothers or boys leading them and they know so much, and they just seem to run rings round us. I want us to mate well but Torch drives me insane, always creeping round father. . . . But he's well thought of in the camp. I don't know what to think."

"Well, we're well thought of too—you know that. We're pretty much the top grupo of our generation."

"A lot of that is due to Karina," said Runa.

"So where is she now?" It had been annoying Teressa for hours. "A grupo should be together. That's what grupos are all about. Suddenly she keeps going off on her own."

"We all need one another, I think," said Runa pacifically.

When Saba returned, she found Runa and Teressa curled up together like kittens, half asleep. "I'm glad you've settled your differences," Saba said with some asperity, "because Iolande's grupo's down there feasting on a tump like they haven't eaten for months, and if we don't hurry up they'll strip it to the bone and start in on the tumpier."

Teressa stood, "Right. Runa, you circle south around that knoll. Saba, north through the gully. I'll take them from the front—you'll have to keep your head down; the moon will be in our faces. Don't move in until you hear me yell."

Saba said, "I wish Karina was here."

The Purpose.

Many years before, the handmaiden, then a young girl, had asked the Dedo, "What is the Purpose?"

The Dedo walked across the bare floor of the cottage and laid her palm against the Rock. Since the Rock gave access to most areas of the Greataway, it followed that much of the knowledge of the Rainbow could be tapped into. After a moment the Dedo nodded.

"You will need to know," she said. And she told the handmaiden the story of Starquin, the Five-in-One. . . .

"Starquin passed near Earth a long time ago and, sensing that interesting events were going to happen, he decided to stay for a while. Life had begun on this planet, and life is always fascinating to an itinerant scientist such as Starquin. The small creatures walked on Earth, and the great land-mass of Pangaea was beginning to split into the smaller continents we know today. Starquin watched.

"Then he sent down extensions of himself—fingers, or *Dedos*—in the form which is now known as the First Variety of the Second Species of *homo sapiens*. The Dedos had two purposes: to keep Starquin informed of happenings on Earth, and to attend to the Rocks, which are used for Greataway travel.

"So the Dedos watched Mankind develop. Civilizations came and went and finally a crude three-dimensional space travel was achieved, and humanity began to colonize the stars. Then, in the Cyclic year 91,702, over 250 million years after Starquin's arrival, a crucial event occurred.

"A certain Captain Spring became host to an alien parasite, which she brought back to Earth. The details are unimportant, but as a result of this and other factors Mankind discovered the Greataway. He could travel in all dimensions now, even unknowingly stealing rides on the broad-band routes established by the Dedo's Rocks. They called this the Outer Think. By this means, humans spread throughout the Greataway—and inevitably met their match. They came into conflict with the inhabitants of the Red Planet.

"The Red Planet had a Weapon against which humanity was almost defenceless—you don't need to concern yourself with the nature of that weapon. But its existence forced Man back into his own corner of the Galaxy, and to protect himself he created a frightening group of pseudo-humans who became known as the Three Madmen of Munich. These creatures seeded the Greataway with the so-called Hate Bombs—an effective defense, because the Greataway is very fragile and travel depends upon emotions as much as dimensions.

"This kept the Red Planet's warriors out. But it cut humans off from many of their colonies, too.

"And worse, it imprisoned Starquin in a small area some sixty light-years across. . . ."

The cabin was silent. The Dedo gazed at the play of light on the Rock. Outside, a coughing roar signalled the presence of a huge beast. It was getting cold. The Dedo walked over to the fireplace and did something; flames trickled over the surface of a small pile of kindling, smoke disappeared up the blackened chimney.

"That was almost thirty thousand years ago," said the Dedo. "Starquin is out there still.

"Our Purpose is to work towards freeing him. To aid us in this Purpose, we have the resources of Earth. That's all. It's not much. But our knowledge of the Ifalong tells us it can be done."

A quarter of a century later, the Dedo said to the handmaiden, "You saw her, then. She is prepared?"

"She is a willful girl, like all young felinas. But she has a strong sense of loyalty towards her race, and she will suit the Purpose."

The Dedo said, "I hope so. She is the only chance Starquin has. I've monitored all the Ifalong and on just one happentrack I see a slender thread running through Time, carrying the seeds of *bor* through a thousand generations without a break, until a young man named Manuel is born. That is the happentrack we must bring about. That is the happentrack on which Starquin is freed."

"What must I do?" asked the handmaiden.

"You must prevent Karina being killed by the caimen," said the Dedo, whose name was Leitha.

"For how long must I guide her?"

"There will be a time when the conception and birth of John is inevitable," said the Dedo. "Our work will be finished, then."

**HERE ENDS THAT PART OF THE
SONG OF EARTH KNOWN TO
MEN AS
"THE GIRL BORN TO
GREATNESS"**

**"IN TIME,
OUR TALE WILL CONTINUE
WITH THE GROUP OF STORIES
AND LEGENDS KNOWN AS
"SUMMER'S END"**

Where True Humans and others
join the happentrack
on which Karina sails towards her destiny,
guided by the handmaiden.

Tortugo

"To seek purpose in the millenia of human existence is as futile as asking God the reason for the tortuga."
—*attr. to Ilos, 115,614C–115,701C*

Karina crept through the jungle, following her quarry by scent as much as by sound.

It was strange to be alone. All her life she'd been used to the strength of the grupo; and now here she was, unprotected, following two True Humans into the secret recesses of the delta.

Why?

Because of her stubbornness. Because she was loyal to her people. Because she wanted to prove to her father that she was capable of looking after herself. Because she was sure there was something in the delta which the felinos ought to know about.

But basically because she was a felina, born to hunt but condemned by her religion to play hunting games—until now.

Tonio halted his horse before a group of mouldering huts near a tall fence of vegetation and spun silk.

"Wait here, Raoul," he said, dismounting. "I won't be long."

"Can't I come?" It was an unpleasant corner of the delta, and Raoul thought he saw monstrous things in those huts. Certainly eyes watched him from the shadows.

"I said wait. It's Canton business—no affair of yours."

Tonio paddled through the boggy ground, not allowing Raoul to see his own uncertainty and slight fear, and ducked into the largest hut. "Cocodrilo?"

A supine figure opened an eye, opened a huge mouth in a yawning grimace and hoisted itself off a low bed, standing in a threatening crouch. "Yes?"

"I've come to inspect the crop."

"It's not convenient."

"Listen, I'm not going through all that again." It was the same every year. Of all the humans of the coast, the delta people were the most surly, the most unobliging. But then, they had to be strange, to live in a place like this. "Open up the gate and let me through!"

Grumbling, Cocodrilo shambled to the gate, brushed away a cluster of black widows with his horny hand, and tugged at the fastenings.

Suppressing a shudder, Tonio passed through. The black widows looked as big as puppies, and they could kill. He hurried across the farm, seeing Siervo in the distance. His mood changed to pity as he watched the man, emaciated almost to the point of looking skeletal, digging away at an endless dyke like a man possessed. He remembered his own childhood when they'd tested him, breaking the skin and touching the wound with a smear of brownish venom—and he'd been sick for days. It was one of his clearest memories—everyone said the same. A child never forgot his black widow test. . . .

"I've come to see the crop, Siervo."

Siervo hadn't noticed his approach. He dropped his shovel with a small scream of fear, and stared at him, hollow eyes guilt-ridden. "What's that? What's that? What do you want? Who are you?"

"Sorry—I didn't mean to startle you. It's me, Captain Tonio. You remember me—I'm contracted for your crop."

"Ah. . . . Yes." Pulling himself together, Siervo climbed out of the ditch and led the way to his hut.

"What are they like this year?"

"Fine. . . . Very good-looking animals."

"What did you say, Siervo?" Cocodrilo had sidled up, barking the question.

"An excellent crop. Excellent."

Cocodrilo laid a scaly hand on Siervo's shoulder as they walked among the shells of dead male tortugas. Tonio avoided the shells but it seemed that Cocodrilo took pleasure in stepping on them, crunching them and squeezing out stinking, decaying flesh. "Always remember this, Siervo," said Cocodrilo softly. "Tortugas are *not* animals. Not in any shape or form. They are vegetables which go through a mobile stage before maturing. Now, how many times have I told you that, Siervo?"

"Many. . . . Many times." The hand was biting into Siervo's shoulder like a claw.

"So, say it to me, Siervo," hissed Cocodrilo.

"That's enough!" Tonio found himself shouting. "Leave him alone!"

"He's a True Human and I'm a Specialist, is that it?"

"Nothing of the kind." They halted at the pens and Tonio took his chance to change the subject. "They'll be ready in time, will they?"

"Of course."

Tonio bent down and examined the tortugas. They were becoming torpid now, gazing around with lack-lustre eyes, scarcely moving. Meanwhile Cocodrilo had moved off, jaw jutting, sidling towards Siervo's hut. The tortugas were prime specimens. Tonio picked one up, imagining himself in one of the southern towns, haggling with a merchant over the price of his cargo. Then he looked at Siervo, the pathetic creature whose life was devoted to the tortuga. . . .

Siervo's eyes were wide. "No!" He was staring at Cocodrilo.

"You shouldn't let them get into your hut, Siervo," called Cocodrilo from the entrance. And he tossed a tortuga out; a thong trailed from its hind leg. It fell among the pregnant females.

"No!" Siervo was scrabbling on his knees, sorting among the animals in the pen.

"Well, if you can't tell one from another, it hardly matters." Cocodrilo gave a sharp laugh.

Tonio resisted the urge to hit him. It would do no good. Cocodrilo was immensely powerful; short thick arms, legs and neck; muscular torso. He sighed and turned away, saddened. He heard Siervo utter a cry of triumph and assumed he'd found his pet, but it didn't make him feel any better.

In the jungle clearing.

After the unwholesome atmosphere of the tortuga pens, the shops of the Canton engineer were a welcome change. Tonio and Raoul stood in a wide grassy clearing about two kilometres north of the loading yards. Here the sun shone, gleaming from the leafy roofs of a cluster of workshops, reflecting from the length of the test track.

At the near end of the track stood *Rayo*. . . .

She was tall, beautiful and two-masted. Probably around thirty meters long, her hull was fabricated from the lightest timbers of balsa, covered with fabric.

74

"Will it be strong enough, Maquinista?" asked Tonio. He could dig his fingernail into the wood quite easily.

"Certainly it will." The Canton engineer, a tall, stooping True Human, glanced at Tonio from under heavy brows, then winked at Raoul. "I've made a few modifications recently, too. Added a bit to the speed, I'd say. She's not a bad car. Not bad at all." His understatement barely concealed a deep pride in his work, and he regarded *Rayo* as a mother regards a new-born baby. "The strain's all taken by the masts, the keel and the guidewheel arms. The hull's just a shell for people to sit in. We've been building them too heavy for centuries."

Rayo looked clean and fast, like a killer whale. Raoul took his eyes off her with some difficulty and watched the odd little Specialists who swarmed about the yard, chattering interminably as they worked on similar cars with nimble fingers and great agility. *Rayo* stood proudly alone on the test track, ready to go.

They climbed aboard. "I'll stay on deck," said Tonio. "I want to see the effect of your modifications. Raoul—you go after and look after the brake. Maquinista, you ride with me on the foredeck. The rest of you look after the sheets."

The small Specialists, well-drilled, took up their positions.

The brake was a heavy handle projecting from the deck; a system of levers below pressed a heavy block against the running rail. Raoul worked it to and fro, getting used to the play.

"Haul in the sheets!" came Tonio's shout. "Ease off the brake!"

The wind was light, but as the crew drew the flogging canvas tight it freshened, and *Rayo* took off like a startled tapir. Raoul had never known such acceleration. He hung onto a stanchion as the ground flew past. He heard the rumbling of the running wheels on the rail, the squeal of the lee guiderails—but that was all. The axle bearings—usually a source of much rasping and groaning—were silent.

And *Rayo* gathered speed.

She sped across the clearing and Raoul found he was shouting with joy and excitement. This was what flying must be like. He leaned over the rail and yelled to the people below. Work was forgotten; they stood and watched with wide eyes in their little monkey-faces. One or two shouted back.

"Take care. . . ."

A small group of ponies shied at their approach and began to gallop alongside, but *Rayo* soon left them behind and they veered off, snorting, eyes rolling. Now a pitching motion developed with the combination of speed and rough track. Raoul clung on. The crew fought for balance as *Rayo* began to porpoise.

"Ease off sheets!"

There was alarm in Tonio's voice. The crewmen had been surprised by the rapid acceleration and the ropes were cleated down. They staggered about the deck, unable to get back to their posts. Some crawled, hanging onto projections and dragging themselves across the deck.

"Brakes!"

Raoul lurched towards the lever, grabbed it as he fell, and pulled. There was a scream of wood on wood. Sitting on the deck with his feet braced against the lever bracket, he put all his strength into it. *Rayo* streamed a trail of smoke as the brake block heated up. A Specialist rolled across the deck, bringing up against Raoul.

"The track ends—" His shout ended in a grunt as the deck bucked and flung him against a post.

"Let go those goddamned sails!" Now Maquinista was struggling aft, swinging on the shrouds, kicking the crew out of his way, lurching heavily against the mainmast.

In his hand was an ax which glittered like no stone ax ever did.

Bracing himself with legs astride, crablike figure in a semi-crouch, he swung the ax. *Rayo* pitched, and unbalanced him. The blade thudded uselessly into the deck. He yelled an incoherent string of oaths and swung again. This time the mainsheet parted with a sharp report. The end, whipping away, caught a crewman around the waist and plucked him overboard. His scream was lost in the roar from the overstrained lee guiderails. The boom swung out, spilling wind, and the motion steadied.

Maquinista charged onto the afterdeck, swinging the ax as he came, and Raoul ducked as the blade swished past his face and thudded into the mizzen sheet. Again the rope parted and the boom swung free.

Now the engineer hurled himself at the brake, biceps knotted, dragging at the lever. Ahead, Raoul saw the forest rushing towards them. He seized the brake and added his strength to that of the engineer. They stood side by side, hauling at the lever while smoke poured from beneath the car, and the crew began to jump overboard.

In those last moments before the crash Raoul noticed small things. Maquinista's shirt hung open and a livid scar was slashed across his stomach—or what was left of his stomach. At some time in the past the man had suffered a terrible injury. Gulping, Raoul looked away and saw his father standing beside the mainmast, mouth open in a frozen yell. The main boom hit a tree and came swinging back across the deck, carrying away the shrouds. The mast toppled, so slowly. The track ended, Raoul saw the butt end of the guiderail whip past, and *Rayo* leaped into space.

Then Raoul jumped.

Afterwards, he couldn't remember how it happened. He remembered seeing the trunk of a huge tree passing beside the deck—just a half-glimpsed impression. The deck was beginning to tilt forward and he knew that when *Rayo* struck she would probably go end-over-end —unless she piled into a tree. . . .

He found himself clinging to a thick bough ten meters from the ground. *Rayo* was gone, buried in the undergrowth. A tunnel of smashed brush showed where she had passed. He looked around, seeking a way down. There were no branches; he lay on the lowest. He would have to wait until someone brought a ladder. He wondered how his father was.

Little Specialists began to arrive on ponies, galloping across the short grass, leaping from their mounts, plunging into the bush. As they ran, the uttered small cries of desolation. Were they mourning the injured, or the loss of *Rayo?* Raoul couldn't guess.

He wondered how he'd reached this branch. It was much higher than *Rayo's* deck had been, and quite a way from the trackside too. He examined the trunk below him.

He saw a series of deep scratches in the bark, where his fingernails had stabbed into the wood. He'd climbed almost five vertical meters with fingers and toes alone. He examined his fingers. The nails had always been thick, but. . . .

Not for the first time, he began to wonder about himself.

Karina wondered, too.

She watched from the trees; first in astonishment as *Rayo* accelerated, then in anxiety as it rocketed towards the end of the track. She saw Raoul hauling on the brake, and she saw the smoke.

She saw Raoul jump.

He ran to the rail and leaped sideways and upwards, arms outstretched and fingers hooked like claws, and smacked into the trunk of the great tree. As he hit, he was already climbing, and he almost *ran* up the trunk into the crook of a branch. The toppling mast, swinging, slashed past his back, missing him by a centimeter.

At least he has some sense of self-preservation, thought Karina. True Humans were notorious for dying in the face of danger. *Rayo* raised a fountain of broken branches and flying leaves as she ploughed into the jungle. For a moment there was silence, then people began picking themselves up, crawling out of the bush, yelling; and a mob of wailing monkey-people leaped onto their tiny mounts and galloped towards the scene of the accident.

It occurred to Karina that Raoul had probably died on many happentracks; his escape had been nothing short of miraculous and she glanced around, half-expecting to catch sight of the handmaiden. But the jungle was empty, and after a while a procession began to move back to the huts; the injured limping, some being carried on stretchers, one motionless form laid over the back of a mule.

Karina sighed, then caught herself in some surprise. Why did she feel sad because the True Humans' fast car was wrecked? Her own father had said that *Rayo* could be used as a weapon against the felinos.

But the car had been a beautiful thing. . . .

She began to work her way around towards the village. She would find out more about this secret place in the delta, carry the news back to El Tigre, and bask in the admiration of the felinos.

The beast in the valley of lakes.

"When will you be able to let me know?" asked Tonio.

"Let you know what?"

"I have arrangements to make. I'm going to need a fast car for the Races—the Lord gave his orders." His expression was stony. A bandage was wrapped around his head; blood already showed through. He sat in a rough chair in the Engineer's hut. The walls were hung with antique mechanical devices—and the nature of some of those devices did nothing to improve Tonio's temper.

Raoul had rarely seen his father so furious. Maquinista stood in the centre of the room, arms dangling limply by his sides, eyes blank and dazed, his shirt hanging in rags around his waist so that the cavern of his stomach was clearly visible.

"Oh . . . that. I'll see what I can do. Right now I have other matters to attend to. You'd better go."

"Go? I want to hear your intentions first."

Maquinista walked to the doorway, looked out, walked back. "Give it a rest, will you? One of my men was killed. I have to make arrangements."

"One of your *men?*" Now Tonio was standing too, white with rage. "You have the impudence to call those Specialists men? You've been living in the delta too long, Maquinista. It wouldn't surprise me to find you were friendly with the felinos, too!"

"The felinos?"

"We've had word they're aware of developments here. They've had spies in the trees—probably your own mechanics. They know about *Rayo*, Maquinista!"

"There are no spies among my people."

"God, man, you talk as though you're some kind of

father to them! They're Specialists, just like the felinos! Can't you see that? You can't trust them. They have different values!"

The engineer shook his head slowly. "You can't class all Specialists together. My mechanics will do anything for me. They're loyal and they're trustworthy. But maybe you wouldn't understand that, living up in Rangua."

"Have the felinos approached you? Have you seen any of them sniffing around?"

"Probably. I don't know. Does it matter?" The engineer rubbed his eyes. He looked exhausted.

"It sure as hell matters if they find you're building cars which can climb hills without felino help!"

Raoul stared at his father. Cars which didn't need felinos? *Rayo*, certainly, had moved fast enough to climb most hills. So the felinos would be obsolete. What would they do? Would they run wild, hunting meat in order to survive? Would they sabotage the sailways? Would they march into Rangua?

"I obey the Lord's commands," said Maquinista quietly. "The felinos will find out eventually."

And now the real reason for Tonio's rage boiled up, boiled out. "The Lord didn't tell you to use *metal*. *Rayo* has metal axles and metal bearings. She's an offence against the Examples! You've sought out metal from old dwellings, you've kindled the Wrath of Agni and you've worked the metal. Why didn't you tell me? You tricked me into piloting that abomination. How in hell do you think you could have got away with it? Did you fail, was that it? Did you find you couldn't build a proper car fast enough, so you had to resort to *this?*" He strode across the room, snatched something from the wall and flung it to the floor.

It made a sharp ringing noise, startling to the ears.

It was metal. There was metal all over the place.

Raoul huddled nervously back in his chair, staring fascinated at the thing on the floor.

"You wanted a fast ship."

"Not at the expense of our beliefs!"

"Are you quite sure of that?"

"What in hell are you trying to say, Maquinista?"

"I'm saying we all bend the Examples when it suits us."

"I'm damned sure *I* don't."

"And how about your colleague Herrera?"

"Herrera is *wrong*. I know that, and so do you, Maquinista!"

"But I don't know that, Captain Tonio." Suddenly the engineer's voice was quiet, intense. "I was taught that, certainly. When I was a child, and lacked the experience to argue back. But I *know* differently. I know the Examples are wrong, for me. What may make very good sense to a kikihuahua flying through space in the pouch of a marsupial bat, may make nonsense when applied here in the jungle.

"Look at this." He picked up the curious article from the floor, hefted it in his hand, selected a rod from a shelf, pushed it into the cross-shaped object and pulled a lever.

Then he pointed the thing at the wall.

Wang-whack!

The cross jerked, the rod quivered in the wall. Raoul stared. He hadn't seen the rod move. One moment it had been sticking from the end of the cross, the next moment it was embedded in the wall. Tonio tried to pull it out, but he couldn't.

"My God," he muttered.

"No," said Maquinista. "*My* God. Yours is a God of stupidity. My God is practical. I'd like to tell you a story, Tonio. It won't take a moment. It might help explain a few things to you."

And Raoul, sitting in that dim hut in the delta clearing, was aware that there was metal all around him; on the floor, on the walls, even hanging from the ceiling—and that this place was alien and terrible. A short corridor led from the room to another place, probably the engineer's workshop; and as the daylight began to fade it was replaced by an eerie glow from this other place.

In that place, someone had kindled the Wrath of Agni.

So he shivered a little as he sat back and listened, and he thought of his mother, who told stories with a point; stories he could understand.

But the gaunt engineer with the ruined body told him a story which made no moral sense whatever. . . .

"The jungle up beyond Palhoa is dense and I was a fool to leave the sailway track. But work was finished for the day and I was young and adventurous, and something in the forest seemed to call me. There was plenty of daylight left and talk during supper turned to witchcraft, and the *bruja* whom the Palhoa people had warned us about, who lived in those parts. I was young and I laughed. The mountain people are always nervous —they shy away from sudden noises like guanacos.

"An older man dared me to go and look for the *bruja*.

" 'She's pretty,' he said. 'About your age too, so they tell me. Lives all alone. Go and find her, Maquinista. Ask her to grant you a wish.' " The engineer mimicked this voice in a bitter falsetto.

"I climbed a ridge where the trees thinned out, and it was much lighter here. There was time to take a walk into the valley below. I started off, and suddenly things were different. . . ."

"Different?" Tonio's question was a sudden, startling bark. He was staring at the engineer. "I . . . I know those parts," he said lamely.

It had been a long time ago. The young girl had come up

83

to him saying, "Here, take this child. I have brought it for you."

He'd held the baby. It was light and warm. Somehow it was not in his mind to question why; not at that moment. "What's its name?" he asked.

"You will give him a name. The name is unimportant, although it is written in the Ifalong as Manuel, Joao, and Raoul. His son, however, will be called John in every happentrack in which he lives. John will be the most important human of his time."

Maquinista said, "It was very quiet. No birds sang—although birds were there, I knew. They seemed to be watching me. All different kinds, all together. Animals too—I knew they were there, even though I couldn't see them. It was as though I was being *escorted* into the valley. They were on three sides of me, so that it seemed I could only go forwards. I walked on until the nature of the forest changed and the ground became spongy underfoot. I wanted to turn back, but I didn't seem to be able to. I walked beside small lakes, and crossed streams. When I started to climb a path away from the water, a tapir stood before me, barring the way. It didn't run. It just stood there, and I knew it wouldn't let me pass. The other animals were all around me, waiting—and I could smell jaguar.

"By Agni, I was scared!

"I stood there, and after a while the birds and animals went. Then, at last, I heard a sound.

"It was a woman singing.

"She sang a song I'd never heard before—a song of old times, like the Pegman sings. But as I listened, the song became something different, and the words changed and became strange, and somehow I knew the things she sang of were not old happenings any more. She sang of the future, of all of Time and the

Greataway, and the place of the world in all this vastness. It was a song about everything we ever knew and ever will know. A song of Earth.

"Then she stopped singing, and spoke. She didn't say much, but I'll never forget those words. Her voice was queer and flat and dead, quite unlike the song. And all she said was,

" 'Hungry, Bantus?'

"And something sighed.

"It was a huge sound, like stormwater blasting from a blowhole. And I was alone on the path. I took out my knife. It was a good knife with a keen blade chipped from the hardest stone. The handle was mahogany, bound to the blade with horsehair twine. It was a strong knife, and yet when I heard—*felt*—the creature moving down the path towards me, I knew it wasn't enough.

"I turned and ran. I ran so fast my legs couldn't keep up with my body, and I fell. I fell into soft wet ground and I lay there, too frightened to rise, screaming into the grass. The creature came for me. I felt the earth shake to its footsteps, then I felt its breath on my neck. I couldn't turn. I couldn't look at it. It touched my hip. Hard, sharp claws; I felt them. My eyes were shut. It rolled me over and began a huge sniffing, and at last I dared to look at it.

"I could only see its muzzle, a handsbreadth from my face. Warm fluid dripped on me. I've never seen jaws that size before or since—far bigger than the greatest crocodile. Then the muzzle tilted and I saw the eyes of the beast. They were quite small, and all the more frightening because they were not savage. They were curious, inquisitive like a bear looking at a hole in a tree. The face of this beast was hairy, but it wasn't warm. Wherever it touched me, I felt coolness. It looked at me as though I was a plate of food, not a living man. And I found the knife was still in my hand.

"I drove it upwards into the brute's throat.

"And I felt the blade snap like a stick.

"The animal didn't even blink. It sniffed its way down my chest, straddling me, seeking out the softest parts.

"Then it began to eat me."

There was a moment's silence in the hut. The air was keen and cool, blowing through the open doorway, and bore with it the sad singing of the little Specialists who were mourning the loss of their comrade. Maquinista regarded Tonio and Raoul, then turned away and disappeared into the dark recesses of the hut.

When he returned, he brought *light*.

It flashed from his hand, brightening the hut and glittering from the metal things on the walls. It dazzled Raoul and filled him with fear. He heard his father groan, saw him cover his eyes so that a black shadow fell over his face. But Raoul couldn't shut out the terrible sight. He had to look. The light held a dreadful fascination as it swung and flickered from Maquinista's hand. It was hot and fierce, like the eye of a cyclops. It stared at him, burning away his will to resist.

It was the Wrath of Agni.

"You'll kill us all," Tonio groaned.

And the engineer laughed. He set the little fire on a shelf, and it showed no sign of consuming the hut. It blazed alone there like the evening star. Unbelievably, the engineer seemed to have *controlled* it.

"That's your answer to the felinos," said Maquinista. "Fire. They're scared of it, even more than you are. It's the animal blood in them—a race memory of forest fires. If it wasn't for the damned Examples, the True Humans would rule the world, instead of going in fear of every Species they live with."

Raoul spoke. "But it's wrong to rule the world. We must live in accord with the world and the creatures in it."

"Tell that to the creatures. . . . No. Just forget about the Examples and take a fresh look at things as they really are. Explain it to me, Raoul. Explain to me why I was better off with a stone knife which broke, when I could have had a metal knife like *this!*"

And he sntached something from the wall and threw it. It struck the floor beside Raoul and stuck there, quivering.

Raoul flinched, pressing himself against the wall and shivering.

Maquinista turned, and the light fell across his stomach, and the scars were like rose petals, and Raoul thought he could see the outline of the spine in there.

As if from a long way off, he heard his father saying, "Maybe. . . . Maybe it isn't my business to judge, Maquinista. Maybe my business is to pilot sailcars the best way I can. Maybe the exact nature of those sailcars is none of my business. Wouldn't you say that's the case?"

"I can have *Rayo* repaired and ready for trials in two weeks," said the engineer.

Raoul saw the Wrath of Agni kindling a light of greed in his father's eyes, and felt some of his childhood crumbling away from the core of his belief, leaving him exposed and naked in this adult world, while outside the hut the monkey-men sang a slow lament.

And as he mourned, the sounds of the Specialists changed. There were little squeals and shufflings, and a deadly barking. Suddenly things were different, Maquinista was cocking his head, and the dream of glory faded from his father's face to be replaced by a questioning look.

Then came the trampling of heavy footsteps.

A solid body of cai-men burst into the hut. They were bunched about something, corralling it with their scaly bodies. They flung short-arm punches at it, barking and grunting in excitement. The air was fetid with their fishy stench and as they milled around one of them knocked over the lamp. A trickle of fire ran across the floor. Maquinista threw a sack down, snuffing the flames.

"Get the hell out of here, you bastards!" he shouted, "How many times do I have to tell you to stay away from my camp!"

Cocodrilo detached himself from the others and stared coldly at the engineer. "If you had the sense to take proper security measures I wouldn't have to waste my time on your part of the delta, Maquinista! Just take a look at what we found out there!"

He reached among his men, seized a pale arm and dragged out a struggling figure which he flung to the floor.

"A felino spy, Maquinista," he said softly. "Now, what do you think of that?"

Karina looked up at them, bleeding, her tunic hanging in rags.

"What were you doing out there, girl?" asked Maquinista quietly.

"Spying, that's what!" snapped Cocodrilo. "Now you've seen what can happen around here, Maquinista, I'll take her away for disposal. I'll report this to the Lord, of course. I don't suppose he'll be very pleased."

"You tell me, girl," said Maquinista.

Karina was silent, staring at them with blazing eyes.

"Disposal?" echoed Tonio uncertainly.

"Well, she can't go back to the felino camp now, can she?"

Tonio regarded Karina. "Who is she, anyway? She looks familiar."

Raoul said, "She's Karina. You remember, father— El Tigre's daughter. She came up on deck the other day." There was a bitterness in him. He'd liked Karina, but now he suspected that her apparent friendship on that occasion had been a ruse to pump him for information. So here she was, caught. A dirty spy. She deserved everything she got—except disposal. That was taking things too far.

"El Tigre's daughter?" Tonio's expression was worried. This presented a political problem.

"There's no way we can let her talk to El Tigre now," said Cocodrilo, jerking Karina to her feet. She lashed out at him but her fingernails had no effect on his horny skin. He laughed coldly. "You've met your match, girl."

"And there's no way you're going to dispose of her, either," said Maquinista.

"Talk!" Cocodrilo suddenly shouted, wrenching at Karina's arm. She winced, blinked back tears of pain, tossed her head so that her hair flew like spun copper, then slammed her elbow into Cocodrilo's stomach. The man-creature grinned toothily, tightening his grip so that Karina gave a little mew of pain.

"Easy, Cocodrilo," said Maquinista. "We'll keep her out of sight for a while."

"Won't her people come looking?" said Tonio.

"I doubt it. They'll probably assume she's gone brute. They often do, around her age. Then after a while they snap out of it and go back to camp."

"They'll follow her trail," objected Cocodrilo.

"I don't think so. There were guanaco clouds blowing in from the sea today. The rain will wash away her scent." In fact they heard a light patter on the roof at that moment, and the wind gusted cooler.

Cocodrilo's jaw was set stubbornly, tips of the teeth showing against his lips. "I still say dispose of her."

"Maybe. . . . Oh, I don't know." Tonio looked from Cocodrilo to Maquinista helplessly. It was a complex situation. "Where can we keep her? How can we be sure she won't escape?"

"She wouldn't escape from the tortuga pens," said Maquinista."

Cocodrilo's mouth opened in a slow grin. "I'll say she wouldn't."

"Now, *I'm* going to report this to the Lord," said Maquinista, eyeing Cocodrilo closely. "And if any harm comes to her, he'll have your hide, Cocodrilo. He wants no part of murder."

Tonio said, "But what happens when we release her in the end? She'll still tell them everything."

"Ah, but it'll be too late," said Maquinista. "Can't you sense it, Tonio? Don't you feel the gathering unrest in the camps, in the jungle and the foothills and on the plains, everywhere? Can't you feel that the climax will come this Tortuga Festival? After that, I think we're going to see a different situation on the coast. A different relationship, one way or the other. . . ."

And Raoul shivered, only half understanding the deliberations of his elders but knowing, somehow, that the existence he'd always known was threatened.

"Take her away, Cocodrilo," said Maquinista.

The heavy bodies clustered around Karina again, pawing her, pinioning her. She was dragged struggling from the hut. As she passed Raoul her eyes met his and she said viciously, "Don't you have anything to say, brat? Don't you have any say in what goes on around you?"

Then she was gone, out into the curtain of rain.

Nobody spoke for a long time. Nobody looked at

anyone. The rain grew heavier, and big drops began to force their way through the roof and splatter to the earthen floor.

The maturing of Mariq

It was unseasonable, the rain. Usually heavy rains came a month later, after the Festival, washing away the debris and cleaning the coast ready for the winter. But that year, the Year of Nodal Conception, freak depressions in the South Atlantic brought early storms.

It was a year of changes in many ways. Locally, the relationship between Specialists and True Humans would never be the same again. Climatically, it marked the onset of a new Ice Age. Historically it was marked by a new calendar: the Johnathan Years. In some remote parts this calendar is still used; but elsewhere it is just a memory in the Rainbow, along with various other ancient calendars.

So they dragged Karina into the new Ice Age, through swamp and jungle which would be cool dry pampas twenty thousand years later, when the Triad would come together and free Starquin. They dragged her brutally, because they were little more than brutes, and they tripped her often because they enjoyed seeing her fall; and they enjoyed seeing her get up again, with her mud-soaked tunic clinging to her body. The rain fell ceaselessly and the cold wind blew, and Karina fell again.

Cocodrilo bent to pick her up this time, his sharp fingers probing at breast and groin.

"She's weak as a kitten, this cat-girl," he grunted, setting her on her feet. "Soft and weak, like a fungus."

His companions muttered agreement as they

ploughed through mud and water, their bodies well adapted to this kind of travel.

Siervo had watched the first clouds sweep low over the treetops but he'd anticipated rain long before that, with the first cool breath of wind and rustle of leaves. Maybe even before that, during the steamy summer, he'd known this year was going to be different—the year which, to him, was the Year of Goldenback.

Last year had been the Year of Mariq. He'd named the creature Mariq after a child he'd once known, in Rangua. As the years passed he'd found, to his dismay, that he'd stopped thinking about Mariq. So perhaps the tortuga had been an attempt to perpetuate her memory.

It had failed.

The mating of tortugas is as inevitable as the branching of happentracks.

Although he'd taken every precaution to keep the males from Mariq he'd reckoned without the female's own persistence. The mass mating had taken place and the males had wandered off to die, and he'd untied Mariq so that she could forage in the mud. She had a particular fondness for the tiny water-snails which abounded in the stagnant waters of the dike.

She found a male there, stuck, unable to climb out and take part in the mass coupling. So they mated down there in the green water; slowly and, presumably, enjoyably.

"You bastard! Son of Agni, you bastard! Where in hell did you come from?"

Siervo scrambled down into the ditch and kicked the male tortuga away. The creature skittered across the mud, spun on its back, and was still.

Siervo picked up Mariq gently, cradling her in his arms. "Oh, my pet. . . . What did he do to you?" She regarded him with bright button eyes, passive, fertilized, replete. He didn't release her. He kept her in his hut, talking to her, telling her his plans for the trench he was digging. Autumn closed in and the leaves blew about the farm and whirled into the gray sky.

And the carts came, drawn by llamas and led by dumb mountain people with their prancing walk and timid eyes—the first humans Siervo had seen for a year, apart from Cocodrilo. They loaded the female tortugas into the carts, never speaking to him, tossing their heads if he attempted to strike up a conversation. They despised him—him, a True Human of the Second Species!

They left the breeding stock behind—like the marketable females, these were becoming plump and their legs short. The carts trundled away down to the yards where the tall-masted sailcars would carry the cargo down the coast. They left Siervo with his mad plans and his tame tortuga.

Mariq grew fatter until her shell was almost spherical and her head was barely able to emerge from the narrowing orifice. One morning Siervo awoke to find her balanced on the curve of her undershell, legs paddling at the air, unable to reach the floor. He untied the thong, satisfied that she could not leave him. He talked to her a lot, while she watched him gravely until her shell grew over the neck orifice and the transformation was complete.

In the late fall there was a brief Indian summer and the sky cleared.

And Siervo heard the first of the explosions.

He carried Mariq out of the hut; by now the tortuga was almost perfectly spherical and about the size of a human head. He took her to a special place, chosen because of the wind direction and the thickness of the silken fence, and he set her on the ground. She was an almost featureless globe, dark golden in color, with slight fissures in her surface tracing the lines of the original shell plates.

And the words of an ancient philosopher came into his mind. Without realizing it, he was speaking them aloud. "To seek purpose in the millennia of human existence is as futile as asking God the reason for the tortuga."

Mariq exploded.

Siervo staggered back, temporarily deafened.

The air was filled with tiny gossamer-borne eggs. Caught by the wind, they drifted towards the fence and hung there for a while until the gossamer deliquesced. Then they fell to the wet ground, winking like little eyes in the unseasonable sunlight. Siervo kicked water, washing them into deeper puddles.

The shell of Mariq lay shattered.

He picked up the pieces and slung them over the fence.

He walked quickly back to his hut, fetched the shovel and began to dig his trench with uncontrolled vigor. When Cocodrilo next came he teased Siervo:

"Only a fool would want to befriend a dumb thing which can't decide whether it's a reptile or a plant, and which dies just when a man would be starting to live. Fix your hut—it's a disgrace! Live for the day, Siervo. The future is no better than the present, you can take my word for that. Look at that drainage trench of yours. You've almost finished it, so now you have nothing left to live for! Can't you see what's wrong with your philosophy?" Cocodrilo had yawned hugely, showing rows of sharp teeth.

Death and freedom.

And so another year, another crop. Goldenback

chosen from Mariq's offspring. Sometimes Siervo wondered, in those moments when his thoughts made sense, what he was trying to breed. Did he have some crazy idea that it was possible to produce a real, empathetic companion?

The rain hammered the mud around him and the trench began to fill, flowing out under the east fence. He hurried back to his shack, avoiding the carcasses of the males, anxious to see Goldenback again. He was shivering, and it wasn't simply the cold and the wet. He was running a slight fever. He was seized with a spasm of coughing as he entered the hut, so it was a moment before his mind registered what his eyes told him.

Goldenback was not alone.

A male tortuga crawled away from her, his slow movements telling the story. . . .

When Siervo awakened he felt refreshed, as though he had slept a sickness away. The rain still slashed at the roof but the sky was brightening outside; a new morning was beginning. In the first waking moments he forgot what had happened to his tortuga, and rolled over to speak to her.

He gulped, a sudden shock hit his stomach, and a shaft of pure madness lit his dim brain.

Goldenback had turned into a girl.

She lay on the floor with her knees drawn up under her and her head pillowed on her hands, asleep. Her hair spread across the dirt like a tawny fan. Her clothes were in rags, so that one breast rested across her forearm, the nipple pink and bruised. Her legs were encrusted with gray mud streaked with blood.

Somebody had mistreated Goldenback.

The remnants of reason were ebbing away from him as he rolled to the floor and knelt beside the girl, stroking her hair and mumbling, "Everything will be all right, my pet. You'll see."

She opened her eyes.

Her eyes, so hurt. . . .

"Everything will be all right," he said numbly.

She was on her feet in one movement. She stood panting, staring down at him. Her eyes were pools in which hatred swam. Her belly contracted, muscles bunching above the matted triangle of hair. Dry mud fell away from her toes and he saw the nails, tough and pointed. The toes curled and flexed. There was a sudden animal stink, and when he looked up at her face he saw murder there, and her lips drawn back over sharp teeth.

Sanity returned to him in a flash.

He rolled away.

Her foot lashed out, toenails grazing his shoulder with sharp pain. She recovered her balance instantly and dropped into a crouch.

He rolled under the bunk, whimpering with terror, pressing himself into the angle of wall and floor. He heard her cough with rage and fling herself on the bunk. He saw her fingers hook under the rough wood, clawing for him. He shrank away. The fingers grasped the wood, seeking to wrench the bunk from the wall. The retaining pegs creaked, and one snapped.

"Get away!" he was screaming. "Get away, you bastard!"

Beside him, the rotting timber of the wall sagged. The bunk began to shift. A sudden cool breeze blew in through the new gap. With a final rending the bunk came free, and a portion of the wall with it.

He dived through the hole and rolled in the mud. He heard a crash inside the hut. He stood, his breath sobbing in his throat. The flat mud of the farm stretched in all directions, giving no cover, no refuge. Scarcely pausing to think, he jumped, got a grip on the eave, and pulled himself onto the roof.

He lay on the wet mat of leaves, his heart pounding. Below him, all was quiet.

Later, Karina walked out of the hut.

She gazed at the mud, and sniffed the air. It smelled of decay. Spherical things lay around. They almost looked like tortugas, except that they had tiny legs which waved aimlessly. In the distance a tall fence separated the muddy compound from the jungle. Ignoring the pain in her body, she ran towards it.

Hideous spiders hissed at her. Through the thick, translucent screen she could make out guards, lying in the mud like driftwood.

She walked back to the hut, and saw a sallow little man lying on the roof, watching her with scared eyes.

She felt herself flush with embarrassment. "I'm sorry."

He didn't reply. His lips moved, but he seemed temporarily bereft of speech.

"I won't hurt you. You can come down now."

He uttered a faint moan, clinging to the ridge.

"Listen, if you don't come down right away, by Agni I'll come up and get you!"

Now he slid to the edge, hung for a moment watching her imploringly, then dropped to the ground. His legs slipped from under him and he fell on his back, flinching as though he expected her to pounce on him.

"That's better," she said. He was a True Human, but a very puny one. She couldn't think why she'd been scared of him before.

"Who are you?" he asked, getting up.

She told him the story. As she talked, his eyes grew wide; and when she spoke of Cocodrilo and the journey through the jungle he made little noises of sympathy, and bobbed his head. They sat together on the step while

97

the rain washed the mud from them.

"He hurt you, this terrible man-thing? I'm not surprised—I know him well. What did he do?"

She pulled aside the remains of her tunic, showing him her scratched and bitten body.

Siervo said slowly, "He is the cruellest creature I've ever known. And yet. . . ."

"What?" Karina was suddenly discomfited. Siervo's eyes had filled with tears.

"I look forward to him coming," he said in a low voice. "There's nobody else, you see."

"Well, why don't you go into Rangua sometimes? You don't have to stay here. You're a True Human, aren't you?" There was some impatience in Karina's tone. The man was more feeble than Raoul, even.

So Siervo told her his history.

They talked all day as the rain fell and the waters rose. It was one of the days Karina would remember best from that year; the rain, more gentle now, and the gentle voice of this strange True Human who'd known more unhappiness than she'd have thought a person could bear. It was the lack of freedom which affected her most, of course. The thought of spending twenty years penned in the same place was unthinkable to a free-ranging felina.

And now she was caged, too.

The fences seemed to march towards her as evening came, imprisoning her with walls of claustrophobia.

"I've got to get out of here!" she cried suddenly.

Siervo watched her pacing to and fro. "We can leave in the morning, if you like," he said diffidently.

"How? We can't get through the fence for the spiders, and you say Cocodrilo's men are guarding the outside anyway!"

"I've had a long time to think," said Siervo. "I have

it all planned. I hadn't intended to leave until after the Festival, but since the rains have come early, well. . . ." He shrugged rapidly and glanced around with a sudden, sly grin which was so close to madness that Karina doubted him.

"Maybe we should talk about it in the morning," she said.

. They slept together on the narrow bunk but Siervo was restless, twisting and turning for a long time before he relaxed and his breathing became regular and even. Karina was a light sleeper like most of her species, and she was awakened in the middle of the night by Siervo's hand sliding over her body and cupping her injured breast. She pushed it away gently, but Siervo awakened with a start, realized what he was doing, and crawled out of bed, mumbling with shame. He spent the rest of the night on the floor, muttering to himself, mortified by the involuntary actions of his own body. Karina was sorry he'd gone, because the warm proximity reminded her of the grupo.

When morning came the rain had ceased and the sun was filtering through the roof. Siervo was up and about, arranging a row of breeding tortugas outside the door, clucking over them. Karina awakened, stretched, and sat up in bed watching him.

"Tell me about getting out of here," she said.

He didn't meet her eyes. He'd been peeping at her waking up, and her wild beauty scared him. It was many years since he'd seen a pretty girl, and he'd never known how they could affect a man. He'd been very young when they'd brought him here. And Karina was a Specialist, apparently. He shouldn't even *think* of her as beautiful.

But she was.

Suddenly he didn't want to leave. He was scared of

the world outside, and he was scared of losing Karina out there.

"Maybe the time isn't right yet."

"Oh. . . . I don't think I could face Cocodrilo again," she said quietly. "He told me he would be coming, today. To see how I was settling in. He'll probably bring other guards."

After a pause, Siervo said, "We'll go. First, we'll eat." He cracked open a tortuga by banging it against the doorstep so the shell split, then handed it to her. It was not quite ripe, and there were clear indications of flesh and blood inside.

The ripe tortuga is filled with delectable tiny eggs, like caviar.

Karina regarded it with distaste. "This isn't a tortuga. This is some kind of animal."

"Of course it is. Tortugas are animals."

"But. . . . What about the Examples? True Humans don't eat meat."

"Most people think tortugas are plants."

"But what if they found out? If True Humans eat meat, why are felinos forbidden to hunt and fish? Why do they say it's the animal in us, that makes us need tumpmeat?"

Siervo said, "Why do you think the tortuga farms are kept secret? Why am I a prisoner here?"

"Well. . . . Why?"

And the True Human, with no loyalty to his race—how could he have, after a lifetime's imprisonment?—said, "Only by regulating the food supply can True Humans keep Specialists under control."

"But why do True Humans grow tortugas? Why take the risk?"

"It's a profitable crop. I don't suppose the True Humans down south know the tortuga is an animal. It can only breed here in the delta. The eggs would never hatch in the drier lands—in fact the shell would get too hard to explode. The Rangua Canton Lord, the sailway captains and the other True Humans have gotten rich on tortugas. They'll make sure nobody finds out what tortugas really are."

Karina looked at him, her eyes widening. "But I've found out."

"So they can never let you go."

She gulped. "I don't want any of this tortuga. I don't like the look of it. Let's hurry up and get out of here."

"All right."

Now this mild, timid True Human did a series of things which surprised Karina.

He took a strong hardwood staff and jammed it into a crack in the outside corner of the hut. Feet planted firmly in the mud, he threw himself against the end. The hut groaned, swayed and finally collapsed; one long wall falling outwards and the other walls piling on top of one another.

"Help me with this," said Siervo, and together they carried a long wall across the mud, laying it beside the fast-flowing trench. Then they took the two short walls, leaving only the wall with the door in it, and Siervo placed these upright on the long wall, then leaned the two top edges together and formed a triangular shelter. Pegs slid smoothly into place.

"As I said, I've had a long time to think," said Siervo drily, noticing Karina's astonishment.

Now they had a raft with a small chalet-shaped cabin. Siervo brought tortugas and other food which he placed in the cabin. He ran back to the wreckage of the hut and collected the hardwood staff, jammed it under the raft and levered.

"Push," he said.

"Wait a moment." Karina was bewildered by the swift events, the imminent plunge into unknown dangers. "Where are you taking me?"

He paused, leaning against the staff. "I've no idea. But I know that if we don't go now, we'll never get out of this place. We'll die here."

"Yes, but. . . ."

"HAH!"

Cocodrilo was running towards them, followed by a number of his men.

"Push, Karina!" Siervo leaned on the pole. Karina got her fingers under the raft and heaved. It slid a few centimeters, then stuck. "Push!" Siervo jerked at the staff.

It snapped.

Cocodrilo had pulled ahead of his men, skittering across the wet ground in a low-slung run, using his hands from time to time so that, horribly, it looked as though he was scuttling on all fours. As he came he uttered harsh cries.

Karina and Siervo stood shoulder to shoulder, lifting and pushing, feeling the raft move, but too slowly. Siervo was sobbing. After twenty years of subservience the enormity of his actions was almost too much for him.

"Stop!" shouted Cocodrilo.

And Siervo stopped, his body sagging, the raft falling back into the mud.

Karina said, "He's going to kill us if we don't get away." She siezed Siervo's arm, swinging him round to face her so that he couldn't see the monstrosity bounding towards them. "Do you really want me to die?" she asked, trying to get him to meet her eyes.

Her eyes were like mountain lakes. Siervo stared.

Her beauty was more important than life itself. It was

a gift placed in his care. It was. ... .

He hurled himself at the raft.

It slid forward into the trench. The current seized it. They jumped aboard. Cocodrilo, arriving seconds too late, trotted alongside, gauging his leap. The raft moved faster, the mud flats slipping by. Cocodrilo, yelling to his men, plunged into the channel and took hold of a corner of the raft. The vessel tilted and swivelled, touching the bank and slowing. The cai-men were yelping like hounds, closing in.

Cocodrilo, his head protruding from the water, snapped, "Stop. Get off this raft."

Karina could see Siervo shaking as he dropped to his knees and, with trembling hands, tried to pry Cocodrilo's fingers away. The raft tilted further, water swilling over the deck.

"We daren't stop." Siervo's tone was pleading. "Your men are out of control, Coco. They'll kill us. Look at them!"

There were six of them. They scurried along the bank, level with the raft, uttering fearsome coughing sounds, their mouths snapping at air, their coarse lips dripping fluid. They were crazed with the ecstasy of the hunt. They began to roar with anticipation, seeing a shallow place ahead where they could easily drag the raft to a halt. They scuttled on, arms pumping, overtaking the raft and getting ready to jump into the trench.

"You . . . asked for it," gasped Cocodrilo, water washing over his face.

Karina found she was holding the shattered end of the staff. She stepped forward. The raft heeled and Cocodrilo disappeared underwater.

"Go to the other end," she told Siervo.

He glanced at her, uttered a little moan of despair, climbed to his feet and scrambled away. The fence loomed less than fifty meters ahead—but Cocodrilo's men were waiting for them in the shallows. As Siervo reached the other end, the raft balanced itself.

Karina crouched.

Cocodrilo emerged from the water, gulping air.

Karina rammed the jagged end of the staff down his throat. As he screamed, blood sprayed over her legs. Karina laughed, a harsh yell of pure delight. He let go and drifted away, twisting and turning in the water like a gaffed fish, seaming the surface with pink threads.

Karina ran to the other end where Siervo was struggling with a cai-man who had got a grip on his ankle. She kicked, and ripped the man's throat open with her toenails. Blood welled out, bubbling as he fought for breath, then he was gone somewhere under the raft.

Then someone grabbed her leg, scaly fingers digging deep. She kicked out, slipped and fell, sliding towards the edge of the raft. Another hand gripped her thigh just as she caught hold of the cabin front and checked her slide. The fingers were like steel, inhumanly strong, and although she kicked with all her strength she couldn't shake them free. She caught sight of Siervo in a similar predicament, being dragged off the raft; then two of the men began to climb aboard, grinning, crawling towards her.

The raft tipped.

Karina floundered in deep, icy water. Something struck her a smashing blow across the head, then the grip on her legs slackened and she rose. Surfacing, she found the raft beside her and pulled herself half onto it, gasping for breath. Other heads bobbed up, Siervo's among them. They began to drop astern as the raft sped over the shallows. Karina stood, preparing to dive to Siervo's aid.

"No!" The little True Human shouted. "Leave me, Karina!"

She couldn't do that. But his cry made her pause, and in that instant the raft swept past a tall figure dressed in black, standing motionless beside the ditch. The ruined face turned to Karina, the scarred lips formed just two words.

"Leave him. . . ."

And Karina hesitated, just for a second.

Then a fetid blanket enveloped her and she fell.

Siervo had designed his escape route well. The gathering momentum of the raft across the shallows was sufficient to carry it through the fence, and a hundred spiders hissed their fury as the raft smashed through their handiwork and sped on past the guards, across a shallow tributary and into the deeper waters of the delta.

She lay still, wrapped in a dense, translucent web, using every last part of her self-control to summon her Little Friends against the spiders attacking her body, while the floodwaters hastened her towards the sea.

In later years the Escape of Karina formed an important part of the Song of Earth, being celebrated in the stanza beginning:

"Karina fought the crocodiles with courage and with might,

Then called upon the power of *bor* to dull the spiders' bite."

But there was another Karina on another happen-track, who refused to heed the command of the Dedo's handmaiden, and who dived into the swift water to swim to the aid of her True Human friend. Now *that* Karina fought the cai-men bravely, killing one and mortally wounding another before her neck was broken by two of the brutes.

The minstrels of Late Earth do not sing of that Karina. They do not know of her, because her story is locked in some cold memory of some dying Rainbow on some remote happentrack. On that happentrack the Purpose was not fulfilled, Starquin was not freed, and in his eventual disinterest he allowed Mankind to rot in his Domes and villages. The Dedos were withdrawn into Starquin's body and Earth spun on its way, of no more use to him than the dead canyons of the Moon, while in the reaches of the Greataway the Hate Bombs circumscribed his eternal tomb.

The Canton Lord.

In the year 91342 Cyclic, Earth was threatened by a race of aliens known as the Bo Adon Su. This was during the Age of Resurgence when it seemed that nothing could stop humanity from populating the entire Galaxy, given time. His three-dimensional spaceships were everywhere and their navigational, drive and defensive equipment were wonders of physical technology. You will understand that this technology was to seem incredibly clumsy fifteen hundred years later, in the age of the Outer Think and the Invisible Spaceships; but at the time it was a thing to be marvelled at. And marvel was what the less-advanced races did.

All except the Bo Adon Su. Refusing to accept the supremacy of Man, they scythed through the Galaxy in a series of clumsily-executed raids of little more than nuisance value, finally arriving at the Solar System itself —the very cradle of Mankind. They poised to attack Earth, trying to mass their fleet into some semblance of order for a concerted onslaught.

Suddenly, humanity woke up to what was happening.

They fed the Bo Adon Su's tactics into the Rainbow, to prepare their defences.

The Rainbow found the Bo Adon Su's tactics incapable of analysis.

The attacks had been utterly undisciplined, character-ized only by inventiveness and adaptability. Frequently the attacks had not been pressed home despite initial gains. The Bo Adon Su had apparently lost interest, or maybe proved their point, and taken off in search of fresh glory.

And now they were at the gateway to Earth.

The Rainbow had metaphorically thrown up its hands, so the defenses of Earth were as uncoordinated as the Bo Adon Su, who milled around somewhere out-side Pluto, filling Space with urgent but incoherent messages to one another.

The situation for Earth was particularly alarming since the Rainbow, by that time, had gained some repu-tation for foretelling the Ifalong. But if the computer couldn't even tell Earth how to defend itself, its Ifalong predictions must be meaningless. Some gloomy individ-uals even took this to mean that the Earth had no future.

Then, suddenly, the Rainbow emitted the message:

"Put the matter in the hands of the Whirst Institute."

The Mordecai N. Whirst Institute for Genetic Re-search had up to that time been involved in low-key im-provements to human stock, adapting humans to alien environments and, most controversial of all, creating new varieties of humans for specific purposes by adding a tiny proportion of appropriate animal genes to their chromosome structure. These were the Specialists, who became the Felinos and the tumpiers, and many others who lived and died outside the scope of our story.

The Whirst Institute rose to the challenge.

Calling upon its most distinguished geneticists includ-ing several who had to be summoned from outlying col-onies, the Institute commenced Operation Coun-terthink, a five-year crash program which culminated in the creation of the Us Ursa.

The Us Ursa was a triumph. It was a living, breathing

creature which combined the intelligence of a human with the social instinct of an ant, the reactions of a leopard, the intuition of an ultrapigeon, the planning ability of an architect-mouse of Chega IV and the strength and ferocity of a grizzly bear. In addition, it had an extremely high self-preservation quotient. It was a superb creature, well suited to its task of protecting Earth against the Bo Adon Su.

Unfortunately, by that time the Bo Adon Su had lost interest in Earth and were seeking adventure elsewhere.

Now the Us Ursa's instinct for self-preservation came into play. Realizing that their existence was now unnecessary they fled into the mountains where, for several thousands of years, they lived in tiny villages, hunting and growing crops and generally maintaining a low profile. In time their file at the Whirst Institute deteriorated and could not be recalled, but they remained in hiding, knowing full well that if the rest of Mankind learned what powerful creatures they were, they would be hunted down and destroyed.

Then the Inner Think came, and the Age of Regression, and Man drifted back into the Domes.

And the Us Ursa came down from the hills.

Captain Tonio received a summons to appear before the Canton Lord.

He trembled. He watched the back of the huge man who had delivered the message, and he resisted the temptation to cry after him:

"Why? Why does he want to see me? What have I done?"

His mind rifled through a casebook of imagined misdemeanors.

"It's quite an honor," said Astrud, unsuspecting, brushing his best vicuna jacket.

Raoul watched him thoughtfully, and Tonio wondered what the kid was thinking.

Tonio rode the deck of the Lord's private sailcar, aware that he hadn't been invited to use the cabin. The crewmen were reticent, handling the sails with quiet skill, saying little as they concentrated on a difficult, jibing run uphill.

And then, at the Lord's palace, the guards.

They were giants like the one who had delivered the summons. They carried weapons of unknown workings and like the crewmen, they hardly spoke, escorting Tonio through endless corridors, past exquisite statuary, paintings and tapestry, to a vast anteroom.

"Wait here," said the guard. He was a head taller than Tonio, immensely broad in the shoulder and thick at waist and hip; bigger than a felino male even, and more powerful. Tonio watched him depart with a heavy, shambling gait quite unlike the graceful walk of El Tigre.

Then Tonio waited. For at least an hour he stood in the anteroom, hesitating to sit, examining the tapestries until he knew every stitch. The books—thousands lined the walls—did not interest him. Like most of his contemporaries, he was unable to read the complex prints of the ancient texts. Forty thousand years later much of the substance of this library would be rediscovered and its contents keyed into the Rainbow to flesh out the history already recorded. By that time, some of the stories would already have found their way into the repertoire of the early minstrels, ultimately to be included in the Song of Earth.

The door opened.

"Enter," said the Lord.

Tonio knew that nobody had ever seen the Canton Lord—or maybe nobody had lived to tell the tale. It didn't surprise him when he entered the chamber to find nobody there. There was a chair, however, and the voice said, "Sit." Tonio sat facing a blank but translucent wall through which a shadowy form could be discerned.

"Speak," said the Lord.

This confused Tonio, since he was not yet aware of the purpose of the summons.

He said, "I regret to report that the experimental sail-car *Rayo* was severely damaged in a trial run. We shall have to develop new techniques for handling such craft. As we gain experience, we will pass on the knowledge to other Canton crews." Was the Lord going to tell him he was being replaced as captain of *Rayo?*

"I heard about the crash," said the Canton Lord.

"Maquinista used a revolutionary design of axle bearing. This, together with the light weight and altered sail-plan of *Rayo,* resulted in remarkable acceleration." Who would be given the job, then? Not Herrero!

"I know all about that, too."

"Well, then. . . ." Tonio's voice trailed away.

"There was a spy," prompted the Lord gently.

"Hardly worth mentioning. A young felina named Karina. I had Cocodrilo lock her away until after the races."

"Well, not quite, Captain Tonio."

"I beg your pardon, Lord Benefactor?"

"She escaped, didn't you know? She arrived back at the felino camp yesterday and had a conversation with her father, the redoubtable El Tigre, no less. He held an emergency meeting. His objective, so it seems, was to whip up dissension on the basis of his daughter's story and to lead the felinos into some kind of action against the sailways. He failed, due to that lack of cohesiveness so peculiar to the felino character. His daughter was not believed, and is being temporarily sent away from the camp."

"That's . . . that's *good*, Lord Benefactor."

"How much did Karina find out, Tonio?"

"Nothing. She couldn't have. She probably thought *Rayo* was fast, that's all. And the felinos already knew that. There have been other spies."

"That's all?"

Then it hit Tonio like a kick in the stomach. The tortugas. Maquinista told Cocodrilo to lock Karina away in one of the pens. Maquinista was an engineer. He had no thought for the niceties of religious belief—he'd already proved that. But now Karina probably knew the life cycle of the tortuga. Would she realize the significance—that True Humans were trading in *meat?* Probably not. Felinos ate meat. If Karina had thought the matter important enough to mention to her father, the Lord would have known, and said so.

Unless the Lord was trying to catch him out.

People who defied the Lord came to a bad end. The guards were sent for them, and they were never seen again. Fear of the guards was the whole basis of the Lord's rule. The guards were incredibly strong and efficient.

In the end, Tonio decided to play innocent.

"I'm sure she didn't hear our conversation after the accident," he said evasively. "I criticized Maquinista for using metal in the construction of *Rayo.*"

. To his disappointment, the Lord seemed unmoved by this sacrilege. *"Rayo* is the top Canton car. It is very important that Rangua Canton wins the Tortuga Race —not merely for financial reasons. The Companies have been troublesome lately, and I want it to be seen that Canton cars are superior."

The Companies were loose associations of True Humans who operated cars out of various coastal towns in competition with the official Canton cars.

"I have sent a reprimand to El Tigre," continued the

Lord, "recommending his daughter be sent away for a while. This will give matters a chance to calm down."

"Lord Benefactor, the felinos aren't fools. They will have guessed the capabilities of *Rayo*. There will be ugly scenes when we demonstrate these capabilities. The felinos will see *Rayo* as the first step towards their becoming redundant."

"As indeed it is. But I anticipated this. Guards will be posted at the Stages. All that remains now is for you to prove yourself worthy of the trust I've placed in you. You will win that race, Tonio. You understand?"

"Yes, Lord Benefactor."

The interview was at an end. He was still alive. His vicuna jacket was drenched in sweat. He rose, and left. His final impression was of the sheer size of the Lord, who rose on the other side of the screen like a thunderhead.

Karina in the tumpfields.

The ride into the foothills seemed endless. The shrugleggers plodded slowly uphill, following the sailway towards Rangua Town for a while, then joining an ancient trail which wound among the rolling downs. The short grass became streaked with a richer green—the sign that tumps had been here. The shrugleggers pulled on, dragging the crude meat-carts with their squeaking bearings, heads twitching to the bites of countless insects.

Karina seethed. She was in disgrace and her punishment was, to her mind, unjustified.

From time to time the other felinos grinned in her direction as she rode, bolt upright, beside her father. She ignored them. She despised them—particularly that fat

112

fool Dozo who had ruined El Tigre's meeting, calling her testimony into doubt and holding her up to ridicule.

"So Karina says *Rayo* is faster than the wind. . . . Well, she must be more trustworthy than our previous informant, the anonymous crocodile. Or wasn't it her grupo that Iolande caught stealing tumpmeat the other day? Dear me, I can't quite remember. . . ."

The El Tigre grupo minus Karina, having been beaten by Iolande in battle, had been presented to the camp as the guilty ones. Might, in the felino culture, is always right.

By the time the meat train reached the tump station, Karina was at bursting point. She stood sulkily by as her father bargained with Haleka, the head tumpier, and she refused to speak to the young felinos.

Haleka was a frail figure beside El Tigre, but he carried himself with pride. He had never kowtowed to the felinos and he wasn't going to start now, even though El Tigre himself had come. He bargained almost absently, while with razor-sharp shell he cut strips of meat from the tump.

Haleka prided herself on being the best butcher in Rangua. He cut strips a metre long and five centimetres deep, wedge-shaped so that the beast's skin was marked by a single cut which healed within two days.

And the tump lay there, making no sound, feeling nothing.

Haleka wore a simple robe of guanaco hide. His face was long and pale despite a lifetime in the sun; his eyes pale also, and deep-set. When El Tigre finally arrived at an acceptable price, he merely nodded slightly, saying nothing. The felinos carried the strips to the cart. There were other felinos, other tumpiers; but the best tump was Haleka's and the best meat went to the cart of El Tigre. The meat was ripe red and bleeding sweet blood.

Karina stood beside the tump. She touched one of the neat incisions. No blood flowed here, and only a faint indentation in the skin showed where the wedge of meat had been cut.

"And the girl will help you," said El Tigre. "She is my daughter, so you will treat her with the respect she deserves."

"I will certainly do that," replied Haleka drily, "but not because she is your daughter, El Tigre. Here in the tumpfields, respect must be earned."

"And each year there are less tumps. Perhaps there is something wrong with the tumpiers' code."

"When God wishes it, the tumps will breed. Maybe God wishes to cut down on the felino population." He referred to the felinos' dependence on tumpmeat.

"One day the felinos will hunt the jungle again," snarled El Tigre, "But without tumps there will be no tumpiers."

Haleka was preparing his next sally when his gaze fell upon Karina. She stood beside the tump, swallowing heavily. As he watched, she brushed a finger along the wound and raised it to her lips.

"Get your dirty hands off my tump!" Haleka shouted. He stepped forward and slashed at Karina with his tumpstick, then picked up a bundle of herbs and began to rub them gently along the length of the wound, chanting in a sing-song voice:

"Spirit of the herb make the tump live long.
Spirit of the herb make the muscle strong.
Spirit of the herb make the man belong,
All one with hills."

And as he sang, he nicked his own forearm with the shell, and rubbed the herb into that wound, too.

"Damned fool," said El Tigre.

114

Karina stood by, fingers hooked, restraining herself with difficulty. The tumpstick had missed her by several centimeters, but the indignity had struck home.

When the meat was all loaded the felinos returned to their carts. Seven tumps lay in a great circle, their keepers ministering to their wounds, their chanting borne up the foothills into the trees, where the monkeys heard it and yelled back with animal derision.

"Goodbye, father," said Karina, feeling suddenly alone.

El Tigre looked at her for a moment, then turned away with a growl. The felinos shouted. The shrugleggers threw themselves against the harness. The carts squealed, and the long procession moved off downhill, El Tigre in the lead, hopeful vultures circling overhead, Rangua a clutter of little boxes under the noon sun.

Iolande rode in the last cart with her grupo trotting alongside. Karina's final impression of the meat train was Iolande's malicious grin.

"You will learn to respect the tump," Haleka stated from his lofty perch. "You will always walk on the uphill side of him, because it is from the forest above that the danger comes, when the jaguars walk at night. You will match your pace to his, because he dislikes being hurried or held back. His very life depends on steady movement across the grass because he cannot move his head."

Karina paced slowly along in the late afternoon sun. The other tumps had diverged on their separate paths, the tumpiers sitting on their backs, the apprentices walking alongside. The apprentices were the lowest of the low.

Karina, for the time being, was one of them.

"The sun and the grass are all the tump needs," Haleka droned on. "When God created the tump, he created the perfect meat producer."

"If the tump is so goddamned great, how come it's got no goddamned legs?" Karina shouted in sudden temper.

"The tump has no need of legs, because it can move by flexing its ribs. There have been tumps on these hills for many thousands of years, and they'll be here for thousands more."

But even as he said this, a sadness took Haleka. The tump numbers had dwindled alarmingly in recent years. The trouble was, they didn't breed. At one time this didn't matter, because they didn't die, either. But increasing felino demands on them had resulted in some overflensing, and recently there had been the occasional death through disease.

More worrying, though, was the increasing incidence of suicide. Disturbed tumps—those who had been attacked by jaguars, for instance—were subject to a mental disorder known as *loco*. The symptons were a tendency to travel downhill until the tump's progress was halted by the sailway track. It would then butt against this structure, endlessly, unable to feed, until it died. A few tumps had even been known to smash their way through the track and to disappear into the sea, presumably to drown.

It was a serious problem. It was also degrading for the tumpier who was obliged to stay with his mount, subject to the jeers of the True Human passengers on the sailway.

Was that why they had sent Karina?

El Tigre's story was that Karina was in disgrace for some reason, but there was a rumor rife in the tumpfields that the Canton Lord had commanded her presence here. The Lord must be worried about the falling tump population. He might look on sailway-butting as evidence of tumpier incompetence—the felinos always said the tumpiers were too gentle with their charges. The tumpiers' methods contrasted sharply with those of the felinos, who simply *terrorized* the shruggleggers into obedience.

Perhaps the Lord intended the felinos to take over the tumpfields, and had sent Karina as an experiment.

Haleka shot Karina a glance of intense suspicion. The girl paced alongside like some big cat, nostrils twitching at the scent from the still-fresh wounds. Granted, she was a beautiful creature—even old Haleka could not help being stirred by her—but she was dangerous and the tump sensed it. Its path across the hillside—the wide wake of cropped and fertilized grass—showed a definite curve away from the side on which Karina walked.

It was beginning to head downhill.

It might be going *loco*.

"Get on the other side of the tump!" shouted Haleka.

"But you said. . . ."

"I don't care what I said. Do what you're told!"

The path of the tump straightened out over the next few minutes, but soon showed a marked tendency to the right. Haleka knew a moment of sudden fury, unusual for a tumpier.

How could he drive a tump when a wild animal walked beside it?

Night in the foothills.

The foothills were exposed and, although Haleka halted the tump in a shallow declivity, the air was cool and breezy.

The tump did not halt readily. It edged relentlessly forward, its jowls chomping, while Haleka leaned against its nose and shouted tumpier oaths. Karina watched him with contempt. He was frail, and slant-eyed like all tumpiers—more like a True Human than a Specialist—and she wondered what creatures had lent its ineffectual genes to his make-up.

There were legends of a sea-going race of similar appearance to Haleka, who populated the floating islands of Polysitia and helped provide the continents with life-giving oxygen. In the Dying Years the minstrels would sing of Belinda, the most famous Polysitian, who was pursued and imprisoned by the black rider Or Kikiwa, blown ashore in a gale and loved by Manuel of the Triad before the Great Blue took her back to her people.

Haleka looked like the Polysitians of legend. . . .

Karina stepped forward and laid her hand on the tump's nose.

The tump's tiny eyes blinked, and it stopped moving.

Haleka glanced at her without expression. He reached into his robe and took out a handful of dried herbs, which he crushed in his palm and held under the tump's nose. It was a mild narcotic—*falla*—to deter the tump from moving off during the night. Then Haleka gathered grass and leaves from the fringes of a stream. He took two rocks from a hempen bag hanging from the tump; a large flat rock and a smaller spherical one. With these he pounded the vegetation into a paste. This he ate with apparent relish, sucking his lips afterwards. Then, without having suggested that Karina satisfy her own hunger—indeed, without having uttered a word since she'd immobilized the tump—he unrolled his blanket on the ground, lay on it and closed his eyes.

I was only trying to help, thought Karina.

She lay down too, but the ground was hard and she was cold. She had no blanket, and she felt alone and frightened. She longed for the companionship of the grupo. She didn't feel *whole*. She wasn't even sleepy. In her sorrow she began a soft whimpering.

She'd seen her sisters briefly after the meeting, when a

mysterious messenger had arrived and spoken to her father just before he propelled her through the camp to the meat train, his face like thunder. The grupo hadn't spoken to her. They'd avoided her eyes. They blamed her for their disgrace over the Iolande incident. They thought that if she'd stayed with them, instead of fooling around in the jungle, Iolande would never have got the better of them.

Karina whined.

"Will you stop that caterwauling!" Haleka was propped on one elbow, staring fiercely at her, the moonlight glittering from his slant eyes so that he looked like an alien creature.

After he'd settled back again, Karina crawled over to the tump and nestled up against the rough hide which provided some small warmth and shelter. She lay awake for some time, swallowing heavily and continuously and wondering whether she was sickening for something—her whole throat seemed to be choking up.

Then she realized that the proximity to the tump was making her salivate . . .

It was a night of discomfort and strange dreams, and just before dawn she discovered, drowsily, that she'd been incontinent; and in her despair she thought: *this will surely convince Haleka that I'm some kind of wild animal.* . . .

But in the morning Haleka had other matters to worry about.

"There was another attack!" An apprentice stood panting steam in the cold dawn.

"Where?"

"Further up the gully. They got at Axil's mount!"

"Did he see them?"

"No. . . . We slept." The apprentice avoided Haleka's eyes.

"You were scared," said the tumpier. "You heard,

119

but you were too scared to do anything. By Agni, this is too much!" He stared around furiously. "Where in hell is that goddamned jaguar-girl? She's at the bottom of this, I wouldn't be surprised. It's insane, letting her loose among the tumps. As if the big cats in the forest aren't enough for us to contend with, every grupo in the Canton will home in on the smell of her! This attack—was it felinas or jaguars?"

"There was a lot of damage. Jaguars hunt alone. I think it was a felina grupo."

"And I know which grupo it was!"

Haleka sniffed the morning breeze, stiffened, then strode down the gully, splashing through the stream. Further on he came to a tiny waterfall spilling into a pool. Sitting beside the pool was Karina, naked and shivering, squeezing the water out of her tunic.

"Washing the blood off, eh?" He stood looking down at her, trembling with outrage.

"What? No, I. . . . What do you mean?"

"Explain what you're doing!"

Karina stood with downcast eyes, the tunic hanging from her fingers, dripping. "I. . . . I thought, maybe it would make the tump more easy for you to control, if I. . . ." She swallowed. "If I washed myself and my clothes, so that. . . . So that the tump wouldn't be so sure I'm a felina, and wouldn't be so scared of me."

"That would make a better story if you and your grupo hadn't attacked Axil's tump last night!"

"My . . . grupo?"

"Yes, your grupo. The famous El Tigre grupo. Or are you saying you've disowned them suddenly?"

Karina said quietly, "I think perhaps they've disowned me."

"What do you mean?"

So she explained. And as she stood there, shoulders

drooping, defeated, something of her sorrow transmitted itself to Haleka. She'd scrubbed herself until her skin glowed in the thin morning sunlight, her wet hair captured this sunlight like glowing copper and her figure was beautiful beyond belief. All this touched something in Haleka which took him right back to his youth, returning to him a strength and compassion which had been leeched away by the lonely years on tumpback.

"No doubt you brought it on yourself," he said eventually, gruffly. "Get dressed and I'll find a slice of meat for you." He turned away abruptly.

She smiled like the sun itself. "Thanks, Haleka."

When they got back to the tump, Axil was there. "I see you've caught her," he called. "That's good. Now we can deal with her. One thing I know—she won't pull a trick like this again." He held a tumpstick with which he took a practice swing, making the air whistle.

"She didn't do it, Axil."

"Tell that to the howler monkeys!"

"I said she didn't do it." He faced the man squarely. "She told me so, and I believe her."

Now Axil got his first good look at Karina. The cat-girl met his gaze and for a long moment held it, and during that moment two minds met: the mind of a girl whose race had been created thirty thousand years ago in a laboratory, and the mind of a man whose race went back to the Paragonic Years, which had lived for millennia on remote islands before undertaking a duty which took it around the world and deprived it forever of a permanent home. The two minds met and recognized each other as human. And a third mind was there too—an alien mind, a catalyst.

"No, Karina didn't do it," said Axil.

He walked away slowly, as though sleep-walking.

Moving camp.

Saba said, "I wish Karina was here. She was good at this. The vampiro liked her."

All over the hillside the vampiros were rising into the afternoon sky like leaves in an autumn wind, trailing thongs. There was excitement in the air and the felinos were singing as they set off northwards, an old felino song:

"My house is like a warm cocoon,
And shelters me from fear.
But when the Festival draws near,
My house is like the Moon."

And the vampiros soared on membranous wings, filling the air with their shrill piping.

"You fed it too much," Runa accused Teressa.

"I never fed it."

"Well then, you starved it. It's too weak to fly."

"What about you? What about you? Why blame me?"

All around them the vampiros were taking off, the felinas gripping the ends of the thongs and hurrying away. Teressa was tugging at the giant bat's claws which remained obstinately fixed into the ground, like the roots of a very old tree. The vampiro watched her with baleful eyes. It had folded its wings so that the grupo's furniture was uncovered, but some unknown grudge caused it to remain sulkily earthbound.

"Get moving, girls!" called El Tigre, passing by.

"Mordecai!" swore Teressa. "All the best sites will be taken!" She jumped up and seized the vampiro around its scrawny neck. "Help me!" she shouted to her sisters.

"What are you trying to do, strangle it?"

"I'm trying to knock it over, you fool!" The vampiro

122

had straightened its back, lifting Teressa's feet from the ground. She hung there kicking. "If we can get the weight off its legs, we stand a better chance of unhooking its claws from the ground!"

The vampiro, a creature of great stoicism, ignored her. When crouched with spread wings to form the traditional shelter, vampiros are bell-shaped and not much taller than a man. In the standing position, though, they are of impressive height, and Teressa's feet were a good meter from the ground. The vampiro gazed stolidly at the distant ocean, as though reflecting on the timelessness of it all. Its face was small and mouselike with a curious harelip but its neck was comparatively long, and bald. This gave the whole creature the appearance of a giant and dignified condor.

Runa flung herself bodily at the animal.

It absorbed her momentum like a leathery pillow.

"Oh, God!" shouted Saba in mortification, glancing frantically at the grinning faces which were beginning to turn their way, then taking a short run and hurling her own slight frame against the resilient vampiro.

Dull Torpe drew near, blinking. "I may be stupid," he said, "But I can't understand what you girls are trying to do." His mouth dropped open again, his face resuming its characteristic expression of doltish surprise.

Teressa dropped to the ground, turned, and in her frustration attacked Runa. "It's all your fault! It's all your fault! I hate you!" They rolled to the ground in furious combat while Saba backed off hastily.

Now the cynical Dozo appeared, smiling enigmatically as Teressa and Runa hammered each other and the gathering crowd hooted encouragement.

"This would never have happened if Karina had been here," said Saba by way of an excuse, as Dozo cocked an eye at her.

"Grupos always fight," he replied. "It's in the nature of things. It strengthens the bond, although God knows how. Karina would make no difference . . . or would she? She certainly has a presence, that girl."

"We hardly ever fought when she was around. Oh!" cried Saba in sudden despair, as Teressa straddled Runa, got a handful of her hair and began to pound her head into the dust, "I wish she was back!"

"I'll have to speak to El Tigre," said Dozo. "For what it's worth. We can't have our top grupo falling apart. Have you seen much of Torch lately?" he asked unexpectedly.

"Not since Karina left. . . . Anyway, it's no use talking to father. Teressa's the one who doesn't want Karina around. She still blames her for running out on us."

"I do. With good reason." Teressa stood before them, panting, the tunic ripped from her breasts and hanging in rags around her waist. "A grupo is no grupo if one goes off alone. We're supposed to share adventures—and Mordecai knows, adventures are hard enough to come by." Runa lay in the dirt, shaking her head dazedly. There were a few delighted catcalls from the bachelors concerning Teressa's state of dress, but the crowd was beginning to disperse, the fun over. "You'll never see that traitor back in this grupo," Teressa said.

The vampiro still stood there with folded wings, like a huge and dignified patriarch watching the squabblings of children.

"I wonder," said Dozo.

"Ah, get out of here, you old faggot," said Teressa in disgust. She dragged Runa to her feet. "Go and get a rope, Runa. We'll lasso this stupid bat. Then we can pull him over with a couple of shrugleggers."

"She wishes Karina was back, really," said Saba to

Dozo, but very quietly, so that Teressa couldn't hear.

It was dark by the time the El Tigre grupo arrived at Rangua North camp. The other vampiros were all in position, replete with food, snoring softly while the grupos chattered under the domes of their wings. After a change of campsite the vampiros were always fed well —otherwise a grupo might awaken to find open sky above, and the giant bat winging across the rain forest, never to return.

Karina, hiding nearby, heard the creaking of cart wheels and the familiar, loved voices. She waited behind the curve of a tent for her chance.

Then, "Saba," she whispered.

"Who's that? Is that you, Karina? Oh . . . !"

Saba rushed into her arms and they hugged, pummelling each other in affection, stepping apart, then wrestling with soft growlings.

At last Karina asked, "Where have you all been? All the other felinas are here. I got worried."

Saba explained the problem.

Karina laughed, then clapped her hand over her mouth.

"Saba? Saba, is that you, for God's sake? For the love of Mordecai, where is that girl?" Teressa's voice was tight with frustration. "Come and help hold this bastard down, Saba, otherwise he'll take off for the hills the moment we untie him!"

"Maybe we shouldn't untie him, Tess," they heard Runa say. "Maybe we should leave him there until morning."

"And let him meditate on the error of his ways, I suppose. God damn it, Runa, he's just a dumb vampiro. A good whipping is what he needs!"

"No, I meant it would be easier in daylight. We could—"

"If you think I'm spending the night out in this cold, you're dumber than this crazy vampiro."

"Listen, Tess, I wish you'd stop calling me dumb. People can hear, you know. And anyway, I'm a sight cleverer than you. Everyone knows that. You're just a quarrelsome brat. That's what they all say!"

A scuffling broke out, and the sound of heavy blows. "I'm going to kill you, Runa!" Teressa screamed.

It was too much for Saba. "Stop it!" she shouted, rushing up to the dim figures thrashing in the dirt. "Karina's here!"

"Huh?" The fighting stopped. The combatants stood, dusting themselves off. "Oh, it's you, is it," said Teressa as Karina stepped forward.

"Want some help with the vampiro?"

"Wouldn't mind."

Teressa stood by sullenly as Karina examined the creature who lay, trussed as though ready for the sun-oven, on the floor of the cart. Karina placed her palms on either side of the vampiro's head. "Be quiet," she said to the others. The vampiro lay still.

The sounds of the evening seemed to fade away, leaving Karina and the vampiro in a private world, small and walled with silence. Karina waited, concentrating. *Little Friends.* . . . she thought.

She felt the strange force flow down her arms.

And later, a minute or a microsecond later, she felt it return.

And she *knew*.

"Well?"

"It's. . . . It's time for this vampiro to mate. He needs to be set free. We'll. . . . You'll have to get another."

"Yes, and what about tonight? What about that, huh?"

"He'll shelter you tonight, if you're kind to him."

"Thank you so much, Karina," said Saba. "You're so clever. Isn't she, Teressa?"

"Huh. Just a trick. She isn't getting round *me*. She deserted the grupo when we needed her most, remember?"

Suddenly, this ingratitude merged with her recent unhappiness, and Karina felt a flash of temper. "Oh, so I'm not getting round you, Tess? Want to bet?"

"None of that stuff," said Teressa nervously, backing away.

But Karina pinned her arms. "Want to bet?" She thrust her face close to the other, forcing her sister to meet her eyes. "Watch me, Tess. Watch me!"

"Let me go!"

"Look at my eyes. . . . That's right. Now. You don't really hate me, do you? Of course you don't. Keep looking at me, or I'll break your goddamned spine. . . . I could, you know. You love me, Tess. You don't believe I ran out on you. You love me. You always have. You'd do anything for me. Wouldn't you? *Wouldn't you?*"

"I'd do anything for you," repeated Teressa woodenly.

"Okay. Now, let's get this vampiro untied and set up." Karina let Teressa go and she blinked, then smiled.

"I've been a fool," she said.

"Wait a moment," said Runa. "Just wait a goddamned moment. You don't convince *me* as easily as that. Why the hell did you run out on us, anyway?"

"I didn't. It was important to the felinos that I found out what was happening at the delta. And if you don't believe me, then by Mordecai I'll convince you!"

"No, that's all right," said Runa hastily, edging away.

"Convince *me*," purred Saba, moving up against Karina and gazing at her round-eyed.

The tension broke, they laughed and hugged, and the

El Tigre grupo was united again.

"Now," said Karina after a while. "Let me tell you how we can get back at that lousy Iolande grupo. . . ."

The hemitrex and the victory.

"We are nothing," said Haleka into the afternoon air. "We are less than the mountain, less than the sea. We are ants, without understanding, without effect. We move through a brief instant of Time like a puff of wind, and are gone, leaving nothing."

"Aren't you glad I'm back, Haleka?"

"Gladness does not enter into it. You were sent here as a punishment, and since you have performed adequately I saw fit to allow you a brief respite. So now you're back. When do you leave us permanently?"

"Father says I can't go back until after the Festival. I really wanted to see the Festival, Haleka."

"Another example of your desire for corruption. El Tigre has more sense than I'd have given a felino credit for. The Festival is a disgusting bacchanal; a drunken, brawling exhibition of gluttony, lust and other pleasures of the flesh."

"What others are there?" asked Karina innocently; then, seeing Haleka's frown deepening, she said hastily, "I'm hungry. I haven't eaten all day. Can we stop, now?"

He looked down at her and found himself saying, "All right. But hurry. The tump must receive his full daily intake." He reached into a large sack and took out a portable sun-oven, handing it down to her.

"That's all right. I can eat it raw."

"Certainly not! I shall not encourage you to eat raw flesh except in an emergency. I took the trouble to have this oven made for you, and so long as you are in the tumpfields you will use it."

Karina set the complex of hemitrexes on the ground and focussed the sunlight on a strip of tumpmeat, which soon began to crackle and emit a delicious aroma. Haleka slid down the tump's flank and joined her, squatting on his skinny haunches. He watched her eat while he chewed thoughtfully on herbs and reflected on the unseemly coarseness of her nature. Feeling himself in the mood for lecturing, and judging Karina to be a worthy victim, he cast around in his mind for some parable fitting to the occasion.

"I am going to tell you a story, Karina."

"But won't the tump lose out on its daily intake?"

"Sit down." He directed a skeletal forefinger at her, and she resumed her seat with every sign of reluctance.

Haleka then told her the story known as The Dead People of Arbos—which, millennia later, passed into the Song of Earth as the Second Kikihuahua Allegory. . . .

The Isle of Arbos lies thirty kilometers off the coast, and people say it floated out to sea on the waters of the Rio Plata. It is quite barren, and uninhabited—although it was not always that way.

Once it was peopled by a tribe of Wild Humans some forty strong. They arrived by raft, having been driven from the mainland by a hostile tribe. When they arrived, the Isle of Arbos was covered with forest, much of which they cut down to build huts. The fishing was good, so although the trees did not bear fruit there was no shortage of food. In the mornings the men would depart in dugout canoes, and in the evenings they would return with fish. They would kindle the Wrath of Agni, and the fires burned into the night as the fish were cooked and eaten. The tribe grew fat.

But the trees became sparse. In a hundred years every tree had been cut, and since none were planted the island became a dusty waste. The islanders were reduced to eating their fish raw; and they became like animals as their art and culture declined.

A hundred and fifteen years after they arrived, the waters around Arbos turned red. A tiny organism, carried by the waters of the Rio Plata, had found salt water to its liking and had multiplied prodigiously. The fish ate the organism, and the shellfish ate it too, and they thrived.

But any humans who ate the fish, died.

They died slowly, over a period of months, but they died nonetheless—and in some agony at the end, as the organism ate into their flesh.

One day a kikihuahua came by.

He saw the people lying sick on the beach, and he guessed the cause.

"Our God has deserted us," said the chief. "He has left us on this barren island to die."

"No," said the kikihuahua. "That is not God's way. He is displeased with the kind of creatures you have become, and he has sent hardship your way so that you may improve. It is God's way of weeding out the people who do not use the wits he gave them."

"But there is nothing we can do! We have no fire and no food!"

"The time for burning and destroying is past," said the kikihuahua. "You must adapt—that is what God is telling you." He bent down, and from the beach he picked a small dish-shaped object. "You see this hemitrex? Millennia ago, the hemitrex was a different creature altogether. It was soft. It had no hard shiny shell. It was just a fragile mass of jelly floating in the ocean—in fact people called it the jellyfish. It was at the mercy of tide and current, and since it floated near the surface, it was at the mercy of the sun, too.

"And one day, the sun became terrible.

"Giant balls of fire exploded from its surface and sent evil rays shafting towards the Earth like poison arrows. Men and animals and plants died in the heat and sickness of its light. For ten thousand years this went on, until the fires died down and the sun was normal again. But the men and animals and plants were no longer normal. Except for those humans protected by the Sisters of the Moon, they were changed, because only by changing could they have survived the furious sun.

"The jellyfish adapted too. In order to protect itself against the rays, it grew a hard thin shell of a shiny substance which had the power of reflecting almost all the sunlight which struck it. The jellyfish adapted, and it lived. As did many other creatures. As you must."

The chief pointed out, "We don't have ten thousand years. We're dying *now*."

"Then eat something other than fish."

"There is nothing else. The land is barren."

The kikihuahua put its hand into a rock pool and drew out a handful of seaweed. "Eat this. It is not affected by the red tide."

"We've tried. It's too coarse. We cannot digest it."

"Then cook it."

"We have no firewood, remember?"

The kikihuahua sighed. "You haven't learned anything." He placed the seaweed on the rock and held the hemitrex over it, tilting it so that the sun's rays were gathered in the shiny bowl and focussed on the weed. After a while, steam rose. In a few moments the seaweed was cooked, tender and edible.

The kikihuahua bowed, walked across the island, climbed onto his vehicle-creature and disappeared.

At this point the Second Kikihuahua Allegory, as told in later years, ends. In Karina's day, however, people were more ruthlessly literal, and Haleka continued the story to its climax, as he knew it, like this:

The chief approached the pile of cooked seaweed, sniffed it and made a face of disgust. "We can't eat this muck. It may be food for a kikihuahua but it's no food for humans. We're a tribe of fish-eaters, and fish-eaters we will remain, and no alien with hairy buttocks will tell us otherwise."

"And anyway," said his woman, holding up the shell, "This jellyfish may have adapted, but it's dead all the same."

"There's a lesson in that," said the chief.

And from that day on they thought no more of the kikihuahua, but continued to eat raw fish, getting even sicker until they died, one by one.

Which is why the Isle of Arbos is uninhabited—and there's a lesson in that, too.

"So?" said Karina.

"You will obey the dictates of the Examples and not eat raw meat."

"Are you sure that's what the story means?"

"You will not question me, Karina!"

During the rest of the afternoon the tump browsed its way through the foothills and Karina walked beside it; first on the seaward side, then on the side of the mountains—and the tump always tended to shy away from her.

I'm not cut out to be a tumpier, she thought in some satisfaction.

Evening came and Haleka slid down, allowing Karina time for a small cooked meal before the sun dropped below the mountains. Then the coolness of night eneveloped the fields and Karina climbed onto the tump's back to watch for jaguars. Looking around, she could see the dim shapes of other tumps, each topped by its attendant. The moon slid from behind a bank of clouds and the scene was suddenly washed with cold light. Karina, alert, stared about her, hearing faint sounds from a nearby grove of trees. A night-hunting owl swooped low overhead, snatching some squealing rodent from the grass and startling her. From somewhere else came the metallic roar of a big cat.

There was something wild and elemental about the night.

It's a time for killing. The words came unbidden into Karina's mind, planted there countless generations ago by a forgotten technician at the institute of Mordecai N. Whirst.

A sudden scream cut through the night sounds.

Karina whirled round. The tump to her left gave a convulsive heave, and the attendant was missing from its back. Then there was a worrying sound; a grunting, and noises of a struggle.

Karina threw her head back and uttered an unearthly screech.

"Huh? Huh?" It seemed that all of nature had been shocked into silence—with the exception of Haleka, who was muttering his anger at being roused. "Is that you, Karina? What in the name of Whirst is—"

"Be quiet." Karina pulled him unceremoniously to his feet. "Come with me."

Karina dragged Haleka at a trot towards the riderless tump. When they got there, they found the apprentice lying unconscious on the ground. Blood seeped darkly from a wound at his temple. His tumpier was crawling from under a blanket, grumbling.

"What . . . ?"

"There's been an attack." Karina looked around. "Where have they gone?"

"They? Jaguars hunt alone, Karina."

"Felinas don't."

Others arrived; tumpiers and their apprentices, alerted by Karina's screech. Then, sliding from the backs of nearby tumps, three girls.

Haleka stared at them in surprise and suspicion. "Who are these felinas?"

"My sisters. I thought we might need some help tonight, so I replaced three of the apprentices. It was bad luck we picked the wrong tumps, or we might have had them. Did you see anything, Teressa?"

"Not a thing."

"I thought we'd catch them in the act. But it seems they've gone. Maybe I frightened them off," said Karina unhappily.

The apprentice on the ground groaned, returning to consciousness.

"Weakling," observed Teressa disgustedly. She pulled him to his feet, not very gently. "Who attacked you, huh?"

His eyes focussed and he saw her. Sudden fear showed. "A grupo! What's a grupo doing here?"

"Trying to help you, idiot. Who attacked you?"

"I was pulled off the tump from behind. I didn't see."

"Jaguars often attack from behind," said a tumpier wisely. "They run up the back of the tump and pick the apprentice off, clean as a mango."

"They don't club him across the head," said Runa. "This is human work."

"A goddamned felina grupo!" somebody shouted, staring in deep suspicion at Teressa.

"Shut up, all of you!" Runa shouted, as a babble of accusations arose. "Shut up! This may be a diversion! While we're all arguing here, they could be stripping a tump to the bone somewhere else!"

Karina raised her head, sniffed the air, and cried, "I smell blood! Over there! Towards the mountains!"

"But—"

"Be quiet, Saba." Karina allowed the main body of the hunt to move off westwards, then took Haleka by the arm and called to her sisters. "Come on—this way. The noise from that crowd is enough to scare a herd of crocodiles. We go east, and we have Haleka as our witness."

The five of them walked quietly downhill, and before long they heard the sounds of feeding.

"They don't know you're here," whispered Karina to her sisters. "They won't be expecting a full-scale attack. If it's Iolande's grupo, there'll be four of them. That's one each. Haleka—you help Saba."

But the tumpier was accelerating down the slope, skinny legs pumping. "That's my *tump!* For the love of Mordecai—it's *my* tump they're eating!" His voice was shrill with outrage, and the sounds in front of them ceased suddenly.

There was a low chuckle.

"Poor old tumpier. What a shame."

Dark figures moved against the moonlit bulk of the tump. A jagged gash wept black blood. No knives had been used; the felinas had simply slashed at the tump with their tough fingernails and chewed their way in.

"Now," said Karina.

She'd already picked out Iolande, the tallest of the grupo—the mother, skilled in battle. Iolande stood a little apart from the others, frozen in the act of cramming a chunk of meat into her mouth, her fingers dripping while she watched the oncoming grupo with narrowed eyes.

"So. . . . It's El Tigre's little girls. Go home, kids.

135

Find someone your own age to play with."

"Take the others!" shouted Karina. "I'll look after this old cow!"

"You'll regret your choice," said Iolande calmly, and jammed the wad of flesh into Karina's eyes as she came in, blinding her for one vital moment.

Karina felt a knee crash into her groin and she doubled up, pawing at her eyes. Instinctively she swayed aside as she fell, and felt the wind of Iolande's other knee as it swept past her head. This was for real. Iolande was fighting, if not to kill, at least to maim. On the ground, Karina grabbed for the other woman's knees. She caught one of them. The other foot slashed into her flank, cutting flesh. She let go and rolled away. The wind had been knocked out of her.

Little Friends. . . .

Her vision cleared and she looked up. Iolande was standing nearby, breathing normally, unmarked, a faint smile on her face. Behind Karina, a little way off, the battle rolled on.

"Had enough, pretty Karina?"

Karina hurled herself forward, the Little Friends driven from her consciousness by the sheer violence of her rage. Iolande jumped as she came in, pulling herself up by the trappings and hanging from the tump's back, and slashed at Karina with her feet—but she didn't quite allow for the strength and speed of the girl. Karina turned in mid-leap, caught Iolande's foot and, still turning, dragged the woman to the ground.

Iolande yelled as the ligaments of her knee tore, sending hot needles of pain through her leg.

Karina maintained her grip, twisting the foot back until Iolande screamed again. Then Iolande's other foot caught her in the stomach with devastating force, hurling her against the tump. She fell aside in the nick of time, barely avoiding Iolande's rush.

For a moment they stood face to face, recovering their breath. They hardly noticed the shouts and thump of flesh on flesh from nearby. They watched each other, and then they heard a male voice shout with pain.

And Iolande smiled.

There was a perfect confidence in her smile, a knowledge that her grupo was mother-taught in fighting, a certainty that they would win.

Karina watched her eyes. Karina's face was streaming sweat and her hair hung like wet kelp. The skirt of her tunic was missing and blood seeped from a deep wound in her side. Her eyes were wide and steady, and they watched, watched.

Iolande thought, *Mordecai, she's beautiful.* . . .

Her head spun.

And her smile became fixed; a grimace of twisted lips.

Karina said, *"Scream, Iolande."*

She reached out with hooked fingers and drew her nails deeply down that smiling face, gouging the flesh. She took her hand away, still watching the eyes, while parallel rivulets of blood trickled down Iolande's face, two on either side of the nose, flowing aside at the bow of the upper lip then entering the mouth at the corner, dribbling into the smile and forming a little lake in front of the teeth before flowing again, down the chin.

"Scream, Iolande."

Now Karina's hand fastened on the neck of Iolande's tunic and jerked downwards, exposing the breasts. The sounds of battle had ceased but Karina didn't notice. Iolande had suckled eleven children and her breasts were just slightly pendulous, in contrast to the trim muscularity of the rest of her body. Karina's fingers, hooked into claws, reached towards those vulnerable breasts. Iolande smiled her bloody smile, her mind emptied of thought.

"No, Karina!"

137

Saba had her by the wrist, tugging at her, pleading. "That's enough! Leave her alone! They're beaten— beaten, all of them!"

Karina blinked.

The spell was broken. Iolande crumpled to the ground.

"We've got them all." Teressa appeared, dragging another felina, and flung her down beside Iolande.

The tump was wriggling now, moving away as though the pain of its wound and the savagery of the fighting was too much. Runa pulled two more girls forward. They were crying; little mews of mortification. Karina said shakily, "I didn't think you could do it. I thought I'd have to get Iolande to surrender."

The tumpiers began to gather, coming from all directions to view the prisoners.

"Bastards!"

"Always knew it was a grupo. Jaguars don't do that kind of damage to the tump. Look at the poor brute— the pain's beginning to get through to him!"

"Well done, Karina."

Karina said, "How's Haleka?"

The elderly tumpier limped forward, assisted by Saba. "Pain is of little consequence," he said. "It comes, it goes. More important the effect upon the tump. I would like to express my gratitude to you and your grupo, Karina, but. . . ." His face was like parchment in the moonlight and suddenly he coughed, clutching his chest. "Would you . . . mind controlling the tump for a while? I am not quite capable at this moment."

So saying, he sagged against Saba. She laid him carefully on the ground. "He went to help me," she explained, "and he took a hell of a kick in the ribs. Maybe something's broken."

Leaving him there, Karina went after the tump. She

wanted to get away from them for a moment, to sort herself out. Events of the past few minutes had left her very frightened. *For the first time in my life,* she thought, *I completely lost control of myself. . . .*

And the words sounded in her head. *Lost control of myself.*

It was a horribly apt phrase. She had lost control, and something else had gained control, pushing her aside.

Just for a moment, the Little Friends had stopped being mere assistants, and had *taken over. . . .*

A fit of shivering took hold of her, and for a moment she thought she was going to be sick. She gulped, breathing deeply at the cold night air, and the pain of her wounds swam back. To divert herself, she turned her attention to the errant tump.

"Basta!" she shouted; the traditional cry.

The tump ignored her.

Suddenly concerned, she ran around to the front of the beast and laid her hand on its nose, leaning against it.

"Basta! Basta!"

The tump moved on, thrusting her aside. She peered into its eye as it moved past. *"Basta,* you brute!"

Still the tump undulated forward, an irresistible mountain of meat, moving relentlessly downhill, towards the coastal plain. Karina punched it, shouted at it, kicked it, climbed on its back and tried to guide it—but it was no use.

Haleka's tump had gone *loco.*

Bor.

"It is done," said the handmaiden. "She is in the tumpfields."

139

The walls of the Dedo's cottage were hung with animal remains; furs and skulls and skeletons of creatures which the handmaiden had never seen living. A giant pelt almost covered one wall; russet with the hairs running in an unusual direction. Behind it hung a big skull of a carnivore with two upper canines lengthened like tusks and fitted into curious sheaths which extended downward from the lower jaw. Next was a batlike creature with a considerable wingspan, a leathery skin, a long jaw with sharp teeth and an odd lump which extended back from the head and seemed to counterbalance the jaw. There were all manner of creatures, big and small, all carefully preserved and displayed, occupying two of the four walls and hanging from the rafters.

The Dedo said, "From there she will go to Torres. There are two possible deviations from our happentrack. Make sure they don't occur." She went on to give exact details.

The handmaiden said, "Who *is* she?"

"You sense nothing remarkable about her?"

"Well. . . . She seems to have a resistence to pain."

"That is caused by *bor,* the alien parasite consumed by the legendary Captain Spring. It was *bor* which assisted Captain Spring to achieve many of her exploits; otherwise she was an ordinary tiger-woman in charge of a clumsy three-dimensional spaceship."

"But how would a parasite help?"

"*Bor* has a remarkable sense of self-preservation. It permeates the cells and achieves a complete empathy with the host. At first it was thought to be a hallucinogenic drug, because it made the host feel good—and incidentally made him live longer. A technique known as the Inner Think was later developed to harness this property of *bor* and extend Man's lifespan to several hundred years. Even now, a few people with traces of *bor* in their genes are able to practice the Inner Think."

The handmaiden said thoughtfully, "So Karina has this *bor*. How does it help our Purpose?"

"I don't know," said the Dedo. "All I know is that Starquin will be freed by a descendant of Karina's possessing *bor*—if he is freed at all."

**HERE ENDS THAT PART OF THE
SONG OF EARTH KNOWN TO
MEN AS
"SUMMER'S END"**

**IN TIME,
OUR TALE WILL CONTINUE
WITH THE GROUP OF STORIES
AND LEGENDS KNOWN AS
"TORTUGA FESTIVAL"**

Where El Tigre strikes a bargain
which is not in accord with Starquin's Intent,
while Karina utters blasphemy
and the seeds of revolution germinate.

The frustration of Tonio.

"Haul the sails and grease the rails
As down the coast we fly!"
                                    —Traditional *carrera.*

One day before the Festival. . . .
You will win that race, Tonio.
He'd woken at nights sweating, dreaming of those words and the tone of infinite menace in which they were spoken. During the daytime, as he piloted his car along the sailways, the shadow of the Canton Lord seemed to loom behind him, watching his methods, assessing his skill and finding it wanting, so that he began to make mistakes and actually caught himself glancing over his shoulder.

He'd kept it from Astrud. She thought it was simply the gathering tension as the time of the Festival approached.

"Why don't you rest, today?" she said. "You don't have to work. You don't have a sailing until tomorrow."

But Tonio was pulling on his tough hide jacket and saddling up his horse. "I have to get down to the tortuga pens. They're loading today. I want to see nothing goes wrong."

Astrud sighed, watching with concerned eyes as he

rode away. Raoul was still asleep, and Tonio hadn't even asked him if he wanted to go too.

A scene of confusion met Tonio at the pens. Long-necked mountain people moved slowly around the farm, gathering up ripe tortugas in disinterested fashion while a cai-man harangued them with threatening barks.

"What's going on?" Tonio glanced wildly from the tortugas, scattered far and wide, to the cart. Loading hadn't even commenced. "We'll miss the start of the race! God, it'll take all day to get the cart loaded, at this rate. And where are the other carts?"

"Nobody thought to order the carts," the cai-man told him. "This one was all I could find. We'll have to make several trips—the other sailcars have reserved all available carts."

"But why weren't the tortugas ready for loading?"

"A tapir broke through the fence and ran amok."

"But Siervo . . . ?"

"Siervo is dead."

"Dead?"

"I killed him." The cai-man stared at Tonio and behind his eyes was something primitive and savage which caused the True Human to blink and change the subject.

"Where is Cocodrilo?"

"He is dead, too."

"Cocodrilo dead? I can't believe that." Siervo, yes. But there had been something indestructible about Cocodrilo.

"Are you calling me a liar?"

"No, no. Of course not. I'm surprised, that's all. And by the way, what happened to that felina we captured?" Tonio's fear turned into bluster. "I thought you people were going to look after her, and now I'm told she escaped. The Canton Lord told me that," said Tonio, making it clear he had friends in high places. "You're going to have to answer to him."

"It was I who told him," said the cai-man. "He seemed upset about it."

"So?"

The Specialist gave a cold grin. "I told him he was welcome to come to the delta and reprimand those responsible. I think he decided it wasn't worth the trouble." He glanced at the huddle of stinking huts outside the gate, where the children fought tooth and nail, and the elders lay on the wet grass watching the proceedings with sleepy menace.

Tonio shivered. "Well, just keep those mountain people moving, will you? I'm going to check on the yards." His words sounded high-pitched and scared to his ears. He turned quickly, annoyed with himself, and mounted his horse.

Things seemed to be going wrong rapidly, so he was mildly surprised when he reached the tortuga yards some time later to see *Rayo* sitting in her siding, apparently ready for loading.

Eight cars were participating in the race. Eight sidings ran parallel along the coastal plain before converging into two southbound tracks. The first two cars to reach these convergences would have a considerable advantage over the others. There was not much chance of overtaking, further down the coast. The usual procedure, if one car found itself seriously delayed by another, was to change lanes at the felino stages before the shrugleggers were attached for the climb.

But the first two cars would have a clear run, so speed off the mark was essential.

Behind the racers were the slower cars who would not be competing, some twenty of them flying the colors of a multitude of Cantons and Companies. These were the older craft, the big names of bygone years whose owners

147

had to be content with lower prices in the tortuga market. Many of these cars would take three days or more for the journey to Rio Plata, selling their cargo for what it would fetch along the way. The racers generally completed the course in two days.

And *Rayo,* not requiring assistance at the hills, could conceivably complete it in one. . . .

The Tortuga races were steeped in history. Each year added to the lore of famous deeds, crippling accidents, bravery and skulduggery. The Festival even featured a special type of song known as the *carrera,* which celebrated events of past races—and, like the Pegman's songs, were one of the roots of the great Song of Earth.

Groups of felinos ambled about the yards, singing these songs, chatting with the race crews and concluding agreements for shruglegger help at the vital hill at Rangua North Stage.

Not wanting to arouse suspicion, Tonio came to such a deal with El Tigre.

Later the first cartloads of tortugas began to arrive. Tonio climbed into the cargo hold of *Rayo*—the tubular space which would be fitted out as a passenger compartment after the race.

The hold was full of nimble-fingered moneky-Specialists, pulling things apart.

"What in hell is going on here?"

Maquinista followed Tonio in. "A slight setback, I'm afraid. One of the axle housings was weakened in the accident, unknown to us. It fractured during this morning's trial run. We must replace it."

"But how can we load the tortugas if your men are tearing up the floor?"

"Well, clearly you can't load the tortugas, Tonio."

"But the race starts tomorrow!"

"It's not likely *Rayo* will be ready for the race," said

Maquinista absently, as though the point was of little consequence to him—as, indeed, it was. He hated the yards; the panicky captains, the inadequate facilities. He looked forward only to tomorrow afternoon, when he could pack his tools into his cart, gather his mechanics about him, and return to his workshops in the delta. Engineering was a pure science and the design and production of a beautiful craft like *Rayo* was an end in itself. The scrambling, frantic atmosphere of the tortuga yards was a debasement of all he held dear.

"Not ready for the race! But—"

"Listen, Tonio. Would you rather a wheel had come off at the kind of speed *Rayo* can do?"

"The Canton Lord will be furious!"

"Refer him to me," said Maquinista sarcastically, echoing the earlier attitude of the cai-man. "Meanwhile, perhaps you should have the carters dump the tortugas beside the car, so we can load once the axle housing is replaced. And get out of the way of my men."

"When will you be finished? For God's sake, you must have some idea!"

"Maybe by noon tomorrow."

"The race starts at dawn!"

"You'll be able to sail with the slow cars, probably. You'll still get a good price, Tonio. Tortugas are a valuable commodity."

"It's not just a question of price. . . ." *You will win that race, Tonio.* The difficulties of the past days suddenly overwhelmed him, and he found his eyes filling with tears. He swung around and almost ran from the hold. Outside, a felino caught his arm.

"You know me, Captain Tonio—my name is Diferir. Now, I think we can do business—"

"Let go of my goddamned arm, you animal!"

"What did you call me?"

"Get away from me!" Tonio tore himself free and set off up the yards, almost running.

The big felino paced alongside. "Just what did you call me?"

"I have nothing to say to you." Tonio turned away and ducked under the rails of a siding. Captain Herrero stood there, tall and irascible, quibbling over prices with the crafty Dozo. "Stop following me!" cried Tonio.

"Maybe you should hear what the great Captain Tonio just called me, Dozo," said Diferir.

"Causing trouble again, Tonio?" asked Herrero, seizing his chance to put a rival down.

"Just get away from me!" Tonio was almost out of control, close to weeping. "All of you—leave me alone!"

"Well, now, this isn't what we expect from. . . ." Herrero's voice trailed away as the general hubbub of the yards was interrupted by an extraordinary commotion from the south. Beyond the convergence of tracks a crowd could be seen waving their arms, yelling and running. Rumbling along the track beside this mob came an ancient sailcar with patched sails. Swinging from the cross-trees was a bizarre one-armed figure who shouted:

"Hoooooo! Hoooooo! Make way for the Rangua express!"

"It's that crazy Pegman," said Diferir.

"If he doesn't climb down and use his brake he's going to cause an accident," said Herrero.

But the Pegman came rocketing in with sails tight until someone, with great presence of mind, flung himself at the pivot arm of a swinging guiderail and diverted the *Estrella del Oeste* to a vacant siding.

Still the decrepit craft careered along, outpacing the mob apart from a couple of excited children on mule back. Then, about fifty meters before he ran out of track, Enriques de Jai'a dropped to the deck and threw himself bodily at the brake. Wood squealed on wood, smoke trailed and, as the car shuddered to a stop, flames licked around the brake shoe. The Pegman stood at the deck rail with stiff dignity, waiting for a crowd to gather.

Tonio, glad of the diversion, joined the hurrying crowd. Within seconds, most of the people in the yard—True Humans, Specialists, and quite a few inquisitive mules—had assembled beside the *Estrella*. The mood was of amused impatience, but the Pegman seemed in no hurry to explain the reason for his precipitous arrival. He stood with eyes raised to heaven as though awaiting a sign. Children began to throw decaying fruit.

"That buffoon is an embarrassment to the True Human race," said Herrero.

The Pegman held up his hand for silence. An overripe mango smacked into his palm and he frowned in sudden puzzlement, examined it, sniffed it and, amid derisive cheers, punted it across the yard.

"People!" he shouted. "I regret that the race will be delayed!"

There was a chorus of disbelief.

"No—I tell the truth. There's been an incident south of Rangua and extensive track work will be required. I shall need twenty men—and you, Maquinista!"

"Pegman!" shouted El Tigre. "When will the work be finished?"

By now Enri had jumped down from the deck to avoid the mangoes. He leaped astride a mule and began to gallop wildly around the crowd, shouting, "Follow me, monkey-men! Follow me to the storehouse and fetch pegs and hammers! We have work to do, monkey-men!" He was probably the only True Human who could so describe the small, dextrous Specialists without causing a riot. Still yelling, he reined the mule in, dragging it to a halt beside Maquinista. "Bring strong tools," he said. "You know what I mean?" And he contorted his face into an exaggerated wink. "And we're going to have to work right through the night, so we'll need. . . . What's it called again? You know—something to see by."

Maquinista laughed aloud. "The Wrath of Agni, most people call it, as you know very well, Pegman."

"Hush!" Wide-eyed, Enri glanced around, finger pressed to lips in theatrical fashion. "Would you have my audience faint with fear? But yes—that is the Wrath we need."

"I'll see to it."

El Tigre had been pushing his way through the crowd while this was going on, followed by Tonio, Herrero and Dozo. "I said, when will you be finished, Pegman?"

"When the sun is at its zenith, when the shadows shrivel like burning flesh."

"Noon, you mean, for God's sake. All right, Pegman, we'll delay the start until noon. But then the cars will roll, and if the track isn't ready it'll be on your own head!"

The Pegman swung his mount and galloped for his ramshackle storehouse, followed by a rabble of small Specialists.

"You can't go," said Tonio to Maquinista, "You have to work on *Rayo!*" He clutched the Engineer's arm as the other turned to follow the Specialists.

"My men can finish the job." Irritably, Maquinista shook his arm free. Then he looked at Tonio and his mood seemed to change. "I probably won't be back in time for the start. Good luck, Captain Tonio." He gripped Tonio's shoulder for an instant, then walked away.

"Well. . ." said Herrero. "So the great Captain Tonio is saved. His car isn't ready, but the race is delayed.

Quite a coincidence. And El Tigre. . . . You've come to an arrangement with the captain.''

El Tigre frowned. "All the felinos have their arrangements, Herrero. I'm sure you and Dozo have a deal.''

"We certainly have. But here is a coincidence which I find even more remarkable. I've just heard that your daughter is involved in the . . . incident which damaged the track.''

"Karina?''

"Who else? Now, some people might call that a coincidence. Others would perhaps call it opportunism. And then,'' Herrero smiled coldly, "there are others who are using the word sabotage. . . .''

El Tigre took a quick step forward. His fingers hooked into claws.

Dozo caught his arm. "Not worth it, El Tigre.''

Herrero stopped smiling. "Meanwhile, El Tigre, I'll leave you with a thought. If you've taken unusual steps to help Captain Tonio in his present difficulties, that's your business. He will still have to beat me, to win the race. But are you sure you can trust him, this partner of yours? Will he return the favor?''

"I tell you,'' snarled El Tigre, "I do no favors for any True Human!''

But Dozo was watching Tonio, seeing the color drain out of the True Human's face, seeing his hands twisting together, the fingers white.

Dozo looked from Tonio to El Tigre, thoughtfully.

The second decision of Karina.

"When a felino's shruglegger dies,'' said Haleka, "he replaces it. If a captain's sailcar should be irreparably damaged, he builds another. If a mountain-man's llama

153

falls down a cliff, well, it will always leave the kids behind to take up the burden. But when a tump dies, what
does the tumpier do? It cannot be replaced or repaired.
And it certainly cannot have children. So the tumpier is
useless without his tump."

"Don't talk like that," said Karina. Evening approached, and she and her sisters sat beside the errant
tump. The animal had ceased its downhill crawl only
because it had reached the sailway. Now it pushed
against the southbound running rail, having already de-
molished the lee guiderail. Its body heaved with effort
and it snorted hugely from the nostrils near the top of its
head. Messages had been sent and traffic halted.

"I inherited this tump from my father, and he from
his father," said Haleka.

"And so on, back until the first tump crawled from
the Whirst Institute, mounted by the first tumpier," suggested Teressa with a hint of laughter.

"Shut up, Tess."

Haleka continued, "I have a son. He's an apprentice
over Torres way, and he would have mounted this tumo
when I died. But now—I have nothing to leave him, and
I have no reason for my own existence."

"This stuff's *good,* said Runa, munching on the
narcotic herb *falla.*

"There's a car coming," said Saba.

In fact two cars came rolling eastwards on the light
evening air. The first was *Estrella del Oeste* of the
patched sails, the Pegman swinging from the shrouds
and gibbering like an ape, then suddenly calling upon
Fate in a voice which carried across the plain: "I de-
mand that you change happentracks! I request an immediate transfer! Corriente, where are you?"

The second car was newer, a light passenger craft
bearing Maquinista and a number of Specialists. The

two cars drew up and the workers rushed for the damaged track, some gathering around the tump and trying to lead it away from the wreckage.

"You're wasting your time," said Haleka.

Meanwhile, Maquinista and Karina confronted each other.

Karina said, "You see, I'm still alive. Your crocodiles couldn't kill me—not for want of trying."

"Did they . . . hurt you?"

"Well, what do you think?"

He regarded her steadily. "But you didn't tell El Tigre. Why not?"

"I fight my own battles. And Cocodrilo is dead, isn't he? Perhaps you'll be next, True Human bastard."

Maquinista looked at her for a moment longer, just long enough for something behind her eyes to disturb him profoundly, then he turned back to the tump. "Pegman, dismantle both tracks. We're going to have to let the brute through, then repair the tracks behind it."

"We don't have time! Darkness approaches on leathery wings!"

"I'll provide the light."

"I hope you have your prayers ready," said the Pegman more seriously, "otherwise Agni may consume us all."

"I find a jug of water much more useful than prayers, in these situations," said Maquinista drily, and dispatched a Specialist to the beach. He then fetched a pot filled with a tarry substance from the sailcar, beat sparks from a pair of stones, and kindled a bright yellow flame and quantities of thick black smoke.

The Pegman and the girls sighed with superstitious awe, but the little Specialists were used to such marvels.

"No good will come of such heresy," said Haleka.

"The Wrath of Agni is good for cooking, too," said

155

Maquinista. "Cut me a piece of that tump, Haleka."

"Never!" The tumpier was trembling with outrage.

Work went on through the night, and shortly before dawn Haleka was able to ride the tump through the gap, while the Specialists lay in exhausted sleep. Teressa, Runa and Saba slept too, curled up together; but Karina stayed awake in case Haleka needed help, while Maquinista and the Pegman fashioned makeshift jacks for use in replacing the heavy rails in their gantries.

"I'm coming with you, Haleka," said Karina.

"That's entirely up to you." His voice was flat, his shoulders slumped.

Saba awakened. "Aren't you coming to Torres with us, Karina? It'll be fun there—much more fun than Rangua. Not so many people know us. It's going to be the best festival ever. The Pegman's taking us."

"I'll see you later," said Karina. She looked around the temporary camp. The black humps of the Specialists' tents were appearing in the first light of dawn. The Pegman slept, murmuring as he loved his lost Corriente in his dreams. Maquinista slept too, one arm thrown over his face, the tarpot smouldering beside him, spitting yellow sparks.

Saba had gone back to sleep, her arm around Runa.

Haleka dozed on the back of the tump which, as though realizing there was no longer any urgency, had slowed to a crawl.

Carefully, quietly Karina picked up the tarpot by its wooden handle and crept through the camp in the direction of Maquinista's sailcar. She would set fire to the car and it would burn there, blocking the track and delaying the race further. And Maquinista would be blamed for kindling the wrath of Agni, and the Canton Lord's guards would come and get him. And it would serve him right, for giving her to the cai-men.

She tilted the pot.

"No, Karina."

The voice was cold and familiar. Karina's heart gave a convulsive thump. She turned round.

The Dedo's handmaiden stood there.

Karina put the pot down and began to edge away. This woman was bad enough in daylight. In the half-light of dawn, standing tall in her black robes with the devastation of her face lurking unseen like a shadowed monster, she was the distillation of all the childhood nightmares Karina had ever screamed through.

"Stay."

"Well, I must get to Haleka. I'm worried about him. I think he needs me."

"I'm sorry, Karina. You can't go with him. You must accompany your sisters to Torres. That's the Dedo's plan."

"Why do I have to hurt someone I like?" Karina said. "You made me run out on that poor little man Siervo, and he died. Now you want me to run out on Haleka. What will happen to him?"

"He will die."

"And if I stay with him?"

"He will live a few years longer. Just a few years, Karina. It's nothing compared to the sweep of the Ifalong."

"But it's a hell of a lot to Haleka!"

"You gave your word, Karina," said the handmaiden.

Karina gazed down towards the ocean, where the slumped silhouette of Haleka could be seen atop his doomed tump, and her eyes filled with tears.

The race begins.

The tortugas had been stowed aboard the sailcars and

the mountainmen relaxed, lazing about the yard in the morning sun, waiting for the race to start. The little monkey-like Specialists were finished too; the rails greased, the wooden bearings likewise. Each car carried its own supply of grease for use at Stages. Resting quietly in that fringe of the yards where the low brush merged into the jungle were the cai-men.

Tonio saw all this through a frenzy of impatience as the Specialists worked on *Rayo*.

Things had gone badly in Maquinista's absence. When daylight faded the Specialists downed tools, refusing to work by the light of the Wrath of Agni because, they said, this would provoke hostility among the more devout people in the crowded yard. Astrud and Raoul had arrived and, finding themselves targets for Tonio's frustration, had spent the night in an empty cabin nearby while Tonio paced the silent deck of *Rayo* and muttered curses at the stars.

In the morning cat-girls had hung garlands of flowers around the captains' necks. Tonio had kept his on for appearances' sake, but the scent of the flowers was like a mockery.

At last Maquinista's sail showed above the low coastal scrub. Tonio seized the engineer the moment he stepped down.

"The car isn't ready. You assured me your men would finish in time, but they haven't. Now they tell me they'll be lucky if they finish by noon. And then we have to load."

There was no animation in his voice. He'd had all night to get used to the idea. His face was gray with exhaustion.

Maquinista was exhausted too. As he turned away without replying his arm was caught in a strong grip.

It was El Tigre. "Engineer," he said harshly, "Tell me about Karina."

158

"She's all right. It was a case of a *loco* tump and old Haleka happened to be the unlucky one, that's all. So Karina was there. She did nothing wrong. After we'd fixed the track, she went with her sisters and the Pegman to Torres."

El Tigre relaxed. There was even a glint of humor in his tawny eyes. "My girls can't enjoy themselves when their father is around. Ah, well. The Festival is a time when we shed our inhibitions. I wouldn't have spoiled their fun here, but they couldn't have known that."

"I never had any children," said Maquinista.

For a moment the two men, the Specialist and the True Human, stood in the silence of mutual understanding, then Tonio intruded.

"Yes, but what about *Rayo*?" The color was in his cheeks and he looked fevered. He still had a chance. He might not be among the leaders leaving the yards, but he could still catch them. Every second counted. "Come and speak to your men, Maquinista! Get them started!"

El Tigre said, "I'll see you at North Stage, Captain Tonio." He turned away and strode south, along the rutted path beside the track.

Tonio flushed and glanced at Maquinista.

The engineer said, "The race only lasts a few days. What about the rest of your life, Tonio? El Tigre is a powerful man."

"Not so powerful as the Canton Lord," said Tonio. He tried to laugh, but it came out as an asinine bray of despair.

"Between Bantus and the Behemoth, eh, Tonio?"

"What's that? Bantus . . . ?" The unfamiliar name struck a strange and fearful chord in Tonio's mind.

"Just a saying," Maquinista said, glancing at him. The engineer was becoming seriously concerned. Tonio showed every sign of cracking up. He hoped he was in good enough shape to handle *Rayo*. . . .

Now the sails were hoisted and the flags snapped, multicolored, in the breeze. The guiderails groaned and the sailcars shuddered with potential energy, held in check by big wedges jammed under the running wheels. Crews waited tensely on the decks. Captains and their families leaned nonchalantly on the afterrails, chatting to their agents, fooling nobody.

On the most westerly track, one car had not yet raised its sails. A frenzied crowd loaded tortugas into the hold, True Human working side by side with Specialist. A chain was formed, passing tortugas down the line; and Tonio was there, and Astrud and Raoul, a dozen Specialists, and Maquinista. A couple of cai-men watched, grinning widely but making no attempt to help.

Herrero shouted across, "See you later, Tonio. If ever!"

And a burst of laughter came from the other cars, relieving tension.

Then the Yardsman mounted his rostrum, and seven cai-men took hold of seven ropes.

"Ready?"

Each captain raised his hand.

The cai-men tensed. They were employed on this important task because they, of all men, were least likely to do any favors.

The Yardsman gave the traditional cry:

"Volad!"

The cai-men jerked the chocks away. The sailcars slid forward.

The annual Tortuga Race was on.

And now the most important people in the yards were two small Specialists known as Mountain Switcher and Ocean Switcher. Mountain Switcher is less important, and you rarely hear his name mentioned in the Song of Earth. He is there, certainly, but merely as a counterpart to Ocean Switcher.

Ocean Switcher was a small, brown-faced man of about forty years, who lived with his tiny wife and seven children of varying ages in a tree-house on the fringes of the delta. He was an independent mechanic, which is to say that after fifteen years of working under a True Human engineer he had branched out on his own.

Ocean Switcher, who was once called Da Para, prospered. It had become customary, whenever a crippled car arrived at Rangua, for the captain to cry, "Send for Da Para!" And Da Para would come, posthaste, a tiny figure bouncing on top of a galloping mule. He would fix the problem with nimble fingers and surprising strength, he was less expensive than the True Human engineers such as Maquinista, and he was never rumored to use the Wrath of Agni. In short, he was a good man.

Seven years before the time of our story he received the ultimate honor for a monkey-Specialist: he was put in charge of one of the complex switches at the tortuga yards. Although he exercised this duty only once a year, the position was considered so important that his name was officially changed, and Da Para became Ocean Switcher all year round.

So the sailcars rolled towards the place where eight tracks became two. Here stood Ocean Switcher and Mountain Switcher, each with a team of assistants, each team holding its heavy switching rail. The switchers watched the Mark—a gaunt windswept tree standing alone some fifty meters away.

The first sailcars past the Mark would receive precedence at the switches, and all other sailcars would have to reduce speed.

Ocean Switcher heard the cry, *"Volad!"*

"Ready," he said to his men, glancing down the row of intent faces. They nodded and he turned his gaze back to the distant sails. Beside him, the rails began to rumble.

The two switches were the most crucial points in the whole race, and rarely a year went by without some kind of incident. Perhaps the most spectacular event had occurred eight years previously, when two captains on adjacent tracks had reached the Mark simultaneously—or so they later insisted. Whatever the truth of the matter, the Ocean Switcher of that time made a decision and pegged the switching rail to favor the easterly car.

Neither car slackened speed and, neck and neck, they rumbled irresistibly towards the switch. The switching team scattered. The captains yelled at each other.

The sailcars reached the switch at the same instant and jammed there while rails splintered and flew. Ocean Switcher, who had stuck to his post until the last, was flung several meters away. The two captains, their craft locked in a reluctant embrace, continued to exchange their views while the crews, being of more forthright material, met on the fused deck to settle the issue with the bare fist.

Meanwhile Mountain Switcher's men were so intent on watching these happenings that they omitted to peg their own guiderail. It collapsed as the first sailcar arrived. The car lurched off the running rail and fell between the tracks, bottling up the only other route south.

The carerra songs tell of the eventual winner of that race, one Mario, who had the presence of mind to send a runner to Rangua North Stage. A team of shruggleggers arrived at the trot by which time Mario had removed a guiderail from the track beside his car. The shrugleggers then dragged Mario's craft down a jungle trail and re-railed it a kilometer past the yards at a short siding normally used for loading taro root. Mario went on to win by several hours and assure himself of a place in sailcar lore. Ocean Switcher, bruised and disgraced, resigned his post, and Da Para took his place and his name.

Three years later the race began in strong winds and it was the turn of Salvatore to become legend. Off to a flying start, he rolled towards the switches ahead of the field with all sails set and straining. Unfortunately the strain was too much for the lee guiderail which collapsed. Salvatore's car leaped to the ground, miraculously still upright.

Normal procedure would have been to drop sails and brake hard, but the Tortuga Race was not a day for convention. The hull slid along the guiderails of the adjacent track, holding the car upright, and Salvatore, standing on the poop deck, had an inspiration.

If he couldn't win the race, at least he could ensure that nobody else did. He shouted to his crew to haul the sails in tighter still.

The sailcar bounded through grass and scrub, scattering spectators and animals alike, and ploughed into the switches, demolishing the trackwork. Nobody could pass. Runners were sent to Rangua North Stage, shrugleggers came trotting and Salvatore, his car already on the ground, was the first to the taro siding. His craft had suffered considerable damage but, with a superb example of sailsmanship, Salvatore nursed it along and was finally credited with finishing third.

Such was the background to the start of the Tortuga Race in the year 122,640 Cyclic. A history of disaster, opportunism and greed.

"This year," said Maquinista as he turned from his

work to watch the sailcars gliding towards the switches, "I hope to God nothing goes wrong."

"My only hope is if nothing goes right," said Tonio, stacking tortugas in the hold of *Rayo*.

Joao was leading in *Esperanza*. This was unexpected, and Captain Herrero was watching in some astonishment as the car in the adjacent track began to pull away from him.

"Antrez!" he shouted to his chief crewman. "Sheet in the main and set the topsail. That bastard's getting away from us!"

It was unthinkable! He'd looked on Tonio as his only threat so he'd bribed the little Specialists to refuse to do night work, which put Tonio out of the way. He'd secured the services of Dozo who, although perhaps not so competent as El Tigre, was one of the better Rangua felinos. And he'd made a couple of other arrangements down the line. But in order to take advantage of them, he had to get there first. Who in hell was this Joao, anyway? Nobody knew him, and it had been a surprise when he'd qualified to be among the eight racers. He'd come from some obscure Canton down south; Rocha, perhaps. Damn the man!

Soon the *Esperanza* was half a length ahead. Herrero studied the set of her sails and gave further instructions to his crew. Sheets were hauled in and other sheets paid out, but without appreciable effect, Herrero left the poop deck and strode forward. Joao, ignoring the *Urubu* as though it was of no consequence, gazed steadily ahead from his casual stance at the stern rail. Herrero roared his rage, pushed a crewman aside and seized the mainsheet, sawing the boom to and fro in search of the optimum position.

Joao's crewmen relaxed, belaying the lines and sitting down.

The Mark approached.

Further down the track, Ocean Switcher, anticipating the result, gave the order to his men.

"Track three. All together, now!"

They lifted the guiderail into position and began to dog it down, setting the track to let the *Esperanza* through first.

"God damn you!" Herrero shouted. "He's not there yet!" It was that last load of tortugas. He should never have allowed it aboard. *Urubu* was too heavy, too ponderous for quick acceleration. Furious with himself and his agent, he watched *Esperanza* creeping ahead.

Esperanza passed the Mark.

Urubu reached the Mark a second later. Her bow, where Herrero stood, was level with *Esperanza's* stern, where Joao lounged with a crewman—and where the mainsheet was fastened tautly to a deck cleat.

So close that Herrero could almost have touched it. . . .

And now, at last, Joao looked at Herrero. There was a faint smile on the southerner's face.

Herrero, lips tightly compressed, snatched up a billhook—a long pole capped by a knife used for cutting vegetation free from *Urubu's* wheels and spars. As Karina had noticed previously, all *Urubu's* knives were fashioned from metal, wrought in the Wrath of Agni. The billhook was razor sharp.

Herrero raised it above his head and brought it down across the deck of *Esperanza*.

The mainsheet parted with a crack like a whip.

The boom swung out, carrying a crewman with it. The sail spilled wind, flogging uselessly.

As *Esperanza* slowed and *Urubu* began to pass her, Herrero uttered a roaring yell of triumph. So much for the goddamned foreigner. Then *Urubu* ran into the guiderail, smashing it aside and flinging Ocean Switcher to the ground. Lurching and wobbling, *Urubu* stayed on the running rail by virtue of Herrero's expert juggling of the sails, gained the undamaged track, and fled south.

The race leader was on his way.

At Rangua North Stage.

The sun-ovens had been going since dawn. They were huge, used only at this time of year, great bowls comprising countless hemitrexes and big enough to roast oxen. They were contained in heavy wooden cradles to which llamas were harnessed. Mostly the animals grazed, but every so often the sun in its movement across the sky would light up a single hemitrex above each oven, directing a hot beam of light onto the rump of the llama, which would take a step forward, thus correcting the sun-oven's solar alignment.

The kikihuahuas would have approved of this mechanism.

The sun-ovens were arranged along the beach and the wind bore the aroma of roasting tumpmeat inland, adding spice and anticipation to the festivities. Twenty meters inland the parallel tracks of the sailway ran above short grass and coastal scrub, turning inland at the Stage for the diagonal climb to Rangua Town. Rangua North Stage was similar to the South Stage where Karina lived, comprising a couple of sidings to accommodate crippled sailcars, a clutter of sheds for the shrugleggers and, on the hillside, a large community hut surrounded by the vampiro tents of both Stages.

The main activity of the Festival was concentrated in the strip from the community hut down to the shruglegger sheds, then east to the sun-ovens. Along this thoroughfare the pitchers of ale were set up, and the temporary huts erected for mating. The bards squatted here, singing of heroism and glory to the complex Carerra rhythms so different from the classic simplicity of the Song of Earth. There were True Humans from Rangua dressed in bright cottons, walking in male-female pairs. There were Specialists of all kinds, from the hawk-mothers and their chattering broods enjoying a day out while their menfolk manned the signal towers, to the grim-faced cai-men. Long-necked mountain people laughed nervously, sharp-faced little pygmies from the upper jungle twitched their noses at the cooking smells, felinos strode everywhere, big loose-limbed men and beautiful women dressed in tunic of the finest skins.

This was the time of waiting, when people walked about the Stage chatting and joking, drinking little as yet. The felinos saw to the shrugleggers, decorating them with ribbons and jockeying for advantageous positions at the trackside. Frequently teams would become tangled and the shrugleggers would begin to kick and plunge. Then the felinos would dive in, cursing and jerking at harnesses, occasionally coming to blows.

The time of waiting was an electric time, and this year it had lasted since dawn because of the accident to Haleka's tump.

Dozo had established his position early and defended it against all comers. His shrugleggers waited patiently between the tracks—so that they could take a car whether it arrived on the east or west track—a little further up the hill than the others. He reasoned that any captain, and particularly Herrero, would want to roll as far uphill as possible before taking on assistance. It was a question of calculating just where the sailcar would stop.

El Tigre had assembled his shrugleggers beside the inland track, level with Dozo.

"Too proud to fight for position with the others?" Dozo taunted him.

"*Rayo* was drawn on an inland track."

167

"There are other cars beside *Rayo*."

"I made an agreement with Tonio."

"Ha!" Dozo uttered a bark of derision. "Since when have we trusted the word of a True Human? Mark my words, El Tigre. If *Rayo* happened to come to rest beside Manoso down there, do you honestly believe Tonio would wait for you to bring your team down? Of course not. He'd tell Manoso to hook up. I'm surprised at you. You're the one who preaches revolution. You, above all, have reason to hate True Humans!"

"So far as we're concerned, Dozo, the Race is the climax of our year's work. I feel it would be sacrilege to disrupt it. I might cheat a True Human—or be cheated by him—at any other time. But not during the Race."

The track trembled, and bright sails came gliding along the beach.

Urubu rolled to a stop.

Dozo had overestimated, and his hindmost shruglegger stood twenty meters past *Urubu's* nose. Herrero stood there, sizing up a team directly beneath him. It belonged to a felino from Rangua North Stage named Peleante.

"My honor," said Peleante.

Dozo hurried up while an assistant undertook the difficult task of backing his team downhill to *Urubu*.

"Piss off," said Dozo to Peleante. To Herrero he shouted, "My shrugleggers are raised on the southern slopes, Captain. They're far stronger than these scraggy creatures."

Herrero glanced over his shoulder. Another set of sails was approaching, passing swiftly through the coastal scrub. "Hook up, Peleante," he snapped. "The fat man's lost his chance."

"I have three grupos to set on you," said Dozo quietly

to Peleante. "Look to your left."

Peleante did so, and saw a row of powerful women lounging against the guiderail, watching him with narrowed eyes.

"Look to your left, fat man," he said.

Another bunch of females stared through the tracks like caged animals. Dozo, recognizing a stalemate, changed his tactics. "Captain!" he called. "My price is reduced by the advance payment you made at the yards!" It was the ultimate sacrifice, allowing Herrero to apply the bribe against the towing charge.

Herrero's habitual expression of irascibility did not change as he rapidly checked out the economics. Then, after another glance over his shoulder, he said, "Couple up then, Dozo. Make it fast!"

Dozo's assistant was already fastening the harness to the towbar. Dozo named his price and Herrero tossed a handful of tokens at him. Meanwhile the car behind had arrived on the same track as Herrero and its captain, seeing a chance to overtake, was paying a gang of felinos to manhandle him through the crossover onto the other track. Peleante hurried across to haggle with this new arrival while his assistant reversed the shrugleggers. They became entangled with a team belonging to Diferir, and while they were sorted out Manoso's team was engaged for the haul to the summit.

Peleante shrugged and turned to watch for further arrivals. It was all in the game; all part of the bright tapestry of the Tortuga Race. There was no point in getting excited over a few hardwood tokens.

A short distance away, El Tigre had company. A woman, beautiful with the voluptuousness of the mature felina had approached him. "All alone, El Tigre? What are your plans for today? I have a tent with many cushions of the best skin over there."

"I'm sure you do, Iolande." As she raised her arm to point, her tunic had slipped a little, displaying a brown, erect nipple. El Tigre smiled, it had been artistically done; no wonder Iolande was the most sought-after of the felinas. "I expect you have plenty to eat in there, too."

"Everything a man could desire." She still bore the marks of Karina's nails on her face, but this imperfection had the perverse effect of heightening her desirability. "Anything you want, El Tigre."

"Including stolen tumpmeat?" He reached out and tweaked the nipple playfully. "Maybe later. Right now, I have a job to do."

"I may not be around later," said Iolande.

"A woman is a woman," he said casually. "There are plenty of opportunities on the day of the Festival."

Now she smiled, too. "And a man is a man. Only True Humans make commitments, and look at them." A True Human couple were walking past at that moment, arm in possessive arm, while their eyes wandered among the attractive cat people.

"Go away, Iolande," said El Tigre gently.

"Later, then. And. . . . El Tigre, I'm sorry it had to be your grupo we tangled with the other day." The theft of the meat was nothing; felinos' principles were different from those of True Humans and Iolande's punishment had been a mere reprimand. The framing of El Tigre's daughters was a matter of circumstance; no felino could condemn opportunism. But it was a pity, and Iolande recognized this. "Where are your little girls today, El Tigre?" she asked maliciously.

Before he could reply, Torch walked up. The young man was frowning, scanning the hillside. "Yes, where is the grupo, El Tigre?"

"They've gone to Torres."

"That's a pity. . . . I'd hoped that we. . . ." Torch's voice trailed away. He'd hoped that tonight, as the drink flowed free and dissolved petty objections, he might have consummated his relationship with the El Tigre grupo. . . .

While they'd been talking, four more sailcars had passed, drawn by shrugleggers amid much shouting and cracking of whips. Next came Dozo, riding downhill with his shrugleggers trotting behind.

"Herrero's away. Salvatore close behind. Four on the hill—that leaves two." As he talked, Dozo cocked an eye at El Tigre. "Ah, and that's Belin coming in now. Arrajo has him. So that just leaves *Rayo*. . . ."

Iolande said, "You've agreed with Tonio, El Tigre?"

"Yes."

"And you're an honorable man. You could have taken any of the others, but you didn't." She made a parody of sighing. "Ah, well. . . . I must get back to the fun. Maybe . . . ?"

"Perhaps."

She left them, walking slowly to disguise her limp—another legacy of her fight with Karina.

Dozo said, "Just a couple of weeks ago we were all getting heated about this *Rayo,* and how it was going to give True Humans all kinds of advantages—and where's *Rayo* now? Stuck on some siding, I'll be bound, with a broken spar."

"Rayo will be here," said Torch. "Or Captain Tonio will have El Tigre to answer to!"

"Loyally put," Dozo's tone was sarcastic, as the seventh car rumbled up the hill, the impetuous Arrojo flogging his shrugleggers and the captain yelling encouragement from the prow.

"Here she is!" The triumphant shout from Torch announced the flag which could be seen moving above the trees some distance away. Then *Rayo* burst out of the delta region and the white sails flitted along the flat lands behind the beach, taut and shining.

"She moves fast," said Dozo thoughtfully. "Very fast."

El Tigre took the harness of the lead shrugleggers and began to drag the team uphill, anticipating that *Rayo's* present speed would carry her much further up the bank than he'd thought. "Move, you bastards!" he shouted, and the shrugleggers obeyed, eyes rolling in terror. Dozo and Torch ran beside him.

"She's coming. She's coming so *fast*," gasped Torch, trying to look over his shoulder and run at the same time.

The hubbub of the Festival quietened suddenly. The only sound was the pounding of feet from El Tigre's team.

Then came a drawn-out, piercing shriek as *Rayo* hit the curve at the foot of the bank and the guiderails protested with the strain. Children scattered and felinos yelled in alarm, dragging their shrugleggers aside as *Rayo* swept by.

El Tigre ran on, hearing the running rail resonate beside him, knowing without looking that he still had a long way to go. The shrugleggers ran behind in an untidy file, beginning to balk, kept going at this unnatural pace by their fear of the big cat-man who led them. And then El Tigre's foot caught in a tussock and he fell. The shrugleggers halted, bunching and milling.

El Tigre stood. The shrugleggers would go no further. If Tonio passed this point, he would have to roll back to him.

The rumble from the rail was growing to a roar.

El Tigre looked back.

Rayo had barely slackened speed! Sails full and straining, she raced up the gradient towards him, passing shrugleggers and felinos, passing the cairn marking *Triunfo*'s record height of two years ago, passing Dozo as he toiled uphill, passing Torch who stood gazing in open-mouthed astonishment, passing El Tigre's shrugleggers. . . .

Rayo rocketed on and the wind of her passing pushed El Tigre aside. The shrugleggers were snorting and pawing in terror and El Tigre fell, still hanging onto a rein. As he lay there he caught a split-second image of Tonio's face, pale and staring fixedly ahead; then *Rayo* was climbing rapidly away from him and the sound of her passage, already unnaturally quiet, was fading to a murmur.

Seconds later, Dozo arrived. "I told you, never trust—" Then he saw the expression on El Tigre's face, fell silent, and began to think. A car had climbed the bank without assistance. The implications began to hit him, one by one. "Mordecai . . . ." he whispered.

El Tigre said, "Round up the men, Dozo. Saddle up the fastest mules."

Then he began to run up the hill.

Reaching the signal tower at the south end of the town he began to climb the ladder. From the top he saw *Rayo,* going like the wind, heading out across the plain. In the far distance he could see the hill at Torres and, as he watched, a winking light caught his eye. News of the race was coming through.

He threw open the signalbox door.

"Have *Rayo* stopped at Torres!"

Two signalmen worked in the box; small men but with a proud, upright bearing and a reputation for belligerence. As El Tigre entered, one had been watching the signal from Torres and transcribing it into charcoal symbols on a tablet. The other was working vigorously at the signal arms which projected downwards into the middle of the cabin, acknowledging the message and adding comments of his own. On the roof, a big battery of hemitrexes caught the sun and flashed the reply back down the coast.

The signalmen stopped work, staring at El Tigre in anger. Theirs was an exclusive guild, their codes were secret and the boxes sacrosanct. Even the Palace Guards never climbed the ladder. And now, here was this brutish man issuing orders.

"Get out! This is private property! Out! Out!" They shuffled towards him with mincing steps and peremptory gestures.

El Tigre stood his ground. "Send a message, now! Get that goddamned car stopped and have the felinos hold Captain Tonio at Torres North Stage!"

"Out! Out! Messages must be presented in the proper manner through the agent! Out!" They stood before him, small men barely reaching his shoulder, heads jerking with the violence of their speech. They pushed him in the chest; short-arm shoves of some force.

With a roar of rage El Tigre seized them and slammed them together. They staggered, blinking rapidly, then came back with whirling arms. One of them caught him a chopping blow across the neck and El Tigre took hold of them again, pinioning them.

"Listen to me," he growled. "Something's happened which threatens the whole future of Specialists on the coast—and that includes you. We have to act quickly. If we let Tonio get away with this, it will show the True Humans that Specialists can't cooperate even when our livelihood is threatened. We might as well take a long walk into the mountains! Do you understand me? Now send that message!"

"That can't be done," snapped one of the men. "The Guild rules are designed to cover all circumstances and *no* man, not even a felino, tells the Guild what to do. We're not frightened of you. You can't harm the Guild!"

The little man stared fiercely up at him and El Tigre knew he spoke the truth. Everybody knew signalmen were different from other people. Their society was like a hive. Individuals would willingly sacrifice themselves to preserve the integrity of the whole: the gestalt they called the Guild. And the Guild covered the whole coast, extending further than the sailways. The communication network was essential to the life of True Human and Specialist alike—and it was too big an organization for El Tigre to take on.

"We *cannot* bend the rules," said the little man. "You must see the agent."

And the two of them became suddenly still, watching him.

Mordecai! thought El Tigre. *They're waiting for me to kill them!*

He turned and descended the ladder rapidly, jumping the last few meters to the ground, landing lightly on all fours. Then he began to run back to North Stage, moving with that bounding felino gait which covers the ground at deceptive speed.

There was no point in seeing the Guild agent. He was another fierce little man who went by the book and would undoubtedly refuse to send the message on the grounds that felinos had no authority over sailway captains and that such an instruction would make the Guild party to an illegal act.

So El Tigre followed the sailway back to North Stage, where a large crowd of felinos was being whipped into a frenzy by the sly words of Manoso, stage managed by

Dozo. There were no True Humans in sight. The other Specialists, feeling it was not their problem, stood aloof. *Fools,* thought El Tigre.

"I'll speak to them now," he said to Dozo.

"Better not. Manoso's doing fine. This is a time for exaggeration and deceit, El Tigre. A time for politics. One of your talks on brotherhood and rights would bore the hell out of them. They want blood."

Arrojo added, "We're going to catch that bastard Tonio and string him up!"

"How are we going to catch him?"

"We'll get after him, right now!" Arrojo's eyes were alight with anticipation. "We'll follow him to the ends of the Earth, if needs be!"

"There are larger issues." El Tigre visualized all the best felinos galloping to Patagonia, leaving the camp unguarded. His fury had abated now, and he was able to consider the situation more calmly. There was much planning to be done. Instead of chasing wildly after Tonio, they should call a Council meeting and decide on their tactics. The long-promised revolution was at hand. . . .

"And now we hear rumors that the evil Fire-god Agni himself had a hand in the building of this machine!" Manoso was telling the crowd. "Well, friends, I think that Tonio has suggested his own retribution. We will tie him to his own poopdeck and kindle the Wrath of Agni beneath his accursed sailcar, and he and his machine will perish together!"

"But what about the next machine, and the next Tonio?" El Tigre asked Dozo.

Arrojo broke in. "Is the great warrior preaching caution? What's happened to your talk of war, El Tigre?"

"I am talking of war, you damned fool. I'm saying we shouldn't waste time running after one man. I'm saying we should get home and hold a meeting."

"*A meeting?*" Arrojo regarded him incredulously.

"El Tigre!" It was one of the signalmen. People regarded him in astonishment. Members of the Guild were rarely seen in felino camps even though their families might make an exception on Festival day.

"Yes?" El Tigre stepped forward irritably. The reminder of the frustration in the signal cabin added to the fires of his annoyance. "If you have a message for me, you'd better pass it through your agent. Guild rules, you know."

"Listen to me, El Tigre. There's been an accident at Torres involving *Rayo*, and—"

"*Rayo* is stopped there?" Arrojo uttered a yell of triumph.

"Yes, but—" The little signalman was still regarding El Tigre.

"We've got him!" shouted Arrojo. "By Agni, we've got him! To the mules, men!"

"What is it, signalman?" asked El Tigre quietly. His heart was pounding. There was something in the little man's eyes. They had lost their fierceness, and watched him with a new expression.

"One of your daughters, El Tigre. One of your daughters was . . . involved."

Now Arrojo was quiet, and so was the rest of the crowd. They edged closer, sensing tragedy.

"Involved? How? Which daughter?" El Tigre towered over the man, fingers hooked as though to tear the details bodily from him.

"I don't know which—the signal only spoke of the grupo. But. . . ." The little signalman looked away, regarding the mountains almost wistfully, as though he'd rather have been there. "They say she died, El Tigre."

The sound El Tigre made was wordless. He turned

away, snatching reins from Arrojo, jumped into the saddle and flogged his mount into a gallop. After a moment's shocked hesitation, others began to climb onto mules and ride after him.

Dozo watched them go. "So much for the reasoned tactics of our leader," he said quietly to himself.

The death of Haleka.

The Song of Earth makes little mention of the tump. It is not a flamboyant animal. It does not capture the imagination of the listener in the way that the kikihuahua space bats do, with their thousand-kilometer wingspan; or the beacon hydras whose roots have been known to permeate an entire planet and throw it into a new orbit. No, the tump is a dull lump of meat. On the happentrack of our story it is doomed—although, as you will hear, there are happentracks on which the tump thrived and multiplied.

One couplet only describes the tump:

"Across the hills of Old Brasil the landwhales eat their way.
Their herds are ever-dwindling, their future in decay."

Not exactly a song of hope. The tumpier Haleka was not even mentioned—on this happentrack.

Haleka's life's purpose was ended. The tump had halted at the beach for a short rest before its death plunge. Haleka sat astride, prepared to die with his mount. The sun was sinking behind him, and the tump cast a huge shadow across the sand left wet by the outflowing tide. Haleka looked to the south, and saw in the distance another vast form. It might have been a big rock, but it could have been another tump in a similar predicament.

And on another happentrack, it was.

Haleka didn't investigate. He had no curiosity, no interest. In the last few minutes left to him, his mind slipped into the past. The image of a beautiful, tawny-eyed girl faded for a moment, and childhood memories began to soothe him. He remembered his early life in the Women's Village; his mother, and a sister named Andra. The Women had taught him gentleness, patience and philosophy, preparing him for his youth as an apprentice. Those had been quiet years, for the Women's Village was a fortified kraal in the jungle where adult males came only occasionally, where tall fencing kept out all animals except monkeys, where the jungle outside the fence was guarded fiercely by Bachelors—men who had not qualified as apprentices and so would never become tumpiers.

Even the felina grupos left the Women's Village alone.

In later years, when Haleka succeeded to his father's tump, he visited the Women's Village a number of times. It looked the same as he remembered it, but now he had changed himself. He came driven by emotions he hadn't known as a child, and as a result the Women's Village held a new and urgent significance. The Madre—the elderly head of the Village—recognized this when Haleka appeared narrow-eyed and panting outside the fence, having defeated the strongest bachelor in bloodless wrestling. She let him in.

They were times of fierce delight, those visits to the Women's Village, and the bright memory stayed with Haleka always, sometimes coloring his dreams on tumpback. He visited a number of times over a period of two years until, one day, the Madre met him at the gate and said, "Enough."

The bachelors carried him away, struggling.

Back on the tump, he knew this rejection meant one of two things: either he had sired enough children to sustain the Village balance, or the Madre suspected that an emotional relationship had developed between him and one of the Women. This had been known to happen, even though the Madre always ensured that the Men lay with a different Woman on each occasion.

And Haleka did have a guilty memory of one Woman who had held him afterwards, and stroked him in a quite unnecessary way while he murmured things to her instead of leaving.

Years later, they had brought him the boy they called his son, so he was at last able to forget the Woman. Seasons of peace followed while he taught the boy, and when Mauo, as he was named, was apprenticed to a tumpier over Torres way, it was the proudest day of Haleka's life.

Just one thing disturbed him.

Mauo, before he departed, said hesitantly, "There's a girl—she'd be a Woman, now. My half-sister. Your daughter, Haleka. I often think of her."

Of course the Madre hadn't told Haleka about the daughter; why should she? It was no business of his. . . .

And as Haleka sat on his tump waiting for the moments of dying, the phantom face of this unknown girl took on substance, forming in his mind as a clear vision of beauty—a girl with eyes that looked into his soul, with hair like the Wrath of Agni.

"Oh, Karina!" he shouted to the sea. "Why did you leave me?"

Behind him, the swiftest sailcar ever built fled southwards, her sails like transparent membranes against the late sun.

The tump began to move again.

The glory of Haleka.

As we know, all of Time is composed of diverging happentracks. Starquin used this quality to direct events towards the fulfilment of his Purpose. He concentrated on favorable happentracks, but even he could not prevent unwanted happentracks from branching off into the Ifalong—because they were part of an even greater scenario than his Purpose.

Through an odd quirk of the Ifalong, some of these happentracks found their way into the memory vaults of the Rainbow on *our* happentrack, in the here and now, and on this hillside.

Listen:

"Why do I have to hurt someone I like?" Karina said. "You made me run out on that poor little man Siervo, and he died. Now you want me to run out on Haleka. What will happen to him?"

"He will die."

"And if I stay with him?"

"He will live a few years longer. Just a few years, Karina. It's nothing compared to the sweep of the Ifalong."

"But it's a hell of a lot to Haleka!"

"You gave your word, Karina," said the handmaiden.

Karina gazed down towards the ocean, where the slumped silhouette of Haleka could be seen atop his doomed tump. "Well, I'm breaking it. I'm staying with Haleka. To hell with Starquin and his Purpose and the Dedo and the whole rotten lot of you. You're only interested in yourselves and you don't give a damn for anyone else!"

For once, the handmaiden lost her serenity. "Karina,

my child. The Purpose of Starquin is the most important thing on Earth."

"Not to me it isn't. Right now, the most important thing to me, is that I go and look after Haleka, because if I don't I think he'll drown himself." Her eyes were blazing as she uttered the traditional felino disclaimer. "So piss on Starquin!"

"As you will."

"What? You mean you don't care?" The hand-maiden's sudden indifference nonplussed Karina.

"It's of no significance now, because on another happentrack you have obeyed my wishes. Happentracks are infinite, Karina."

"Damn you! And damn that other me!"

"The other Karina will become famous. But you will not, and you will never see me again."

"See if I care," said Karina, turning her back on the tall woman and walking away.

"So Mauo told me he had a sister—my daughter. I never saw her, but I often think about her. I think she might have been something like you, Karina. . . ."

Haleka's voice droned softly on, telling of his child-hood while Karina sat facing him on the broad back of the tump. They were boring, these endless pointless yarns, but they were better than suicide, thought Karina. Haleka had to talk things out.

"Look!" she said suddenly. "There's a car—that must be *Rayo!* What's wrong with her?"

The swiftest sailcar ever built limped southwards, her sails like transparent membranes against the late sun. The mainmast had broken and the car had been crudely jury-rigged, the two pieces of the mast splinted together with a crimson liana, the sail hanging crooked like a broken wing.

"So she wasn't so fast after all," said Karina. "After all that trouble and secrecy, she's slower than any of the others."

"Speed is the enemy of man," said Hakela. "This is one of the first lessons a boy learns in the Women's Village. I recall one day the Madre—"

"What are your plans, Haleka?"

"My work is done. As the Madre once said—"

"I think we should build a boat, you and I. We should sail off east to the Magic Islands, where women live in grass castles and men ride whales, so the legends go. Wouldn't that be fun? We could build a castle and send for my sisters, and we could all live there, forever."

"What would we eat?" asked Haleka tolerantly.

"We'd catch fish, of course, like the Magic Island people do."

"Eat flesh? Me? Never!" said Haleka, whose ancestors came from the floating islands of Polysitia themselves, if he did but know it.

The tump began to move again, heaving itself towards the water, and Karina's heart missed a beat. "Look!" she cried desperately. "There's another tump further down the beach. I think our tump looked at it. Maybe it's a girl tump!"

"Tumps have no sex, Karina. That's the whole problem. That's why they're dying out."

"How do you know they have no sex? Have you ever looked?" Karina warmed to her theme. "Can you honestly tell me anyone's ever rolled a tump over and *looked*?"

"Don't be ridiculous, Karina."

"Well, then!" The tump had reached the water's edge. Karina and Haleka still faced each other. Haleka watched the sea, Karina the land.

Haleka said, "The very fact that a tump can't roll over

ought to tell you it can't mate." The conversation was becoming distasteful to him. Tumpier culture dictated that Men ceased thinking about sex once their reproductive duties were done, and much of the childhood teaching was conditioned to this end. "It wouldn't be able . . . . It couldn't. . . . Even if it had. . . ."

"It couldn't bring its organs to bear," said Karina with relish. Then, with the subject seemingly at an end, the sadness rolled back like a sea fog. "Are you really going to kill yourself, Haleka?"

"That is the way."

"I'm not going to let you—you know that? I'm going to fight you and drag you back, and the whole thing will become ridiculous. You know I'm stronger than you."

"Please let me die with dignity, Karina."

"No way." She took his hands in hers. The tump was in the water now, and a wave touched her feet. She kicked at the water, hating it.

"Karina! Please don't take this away from me!"

The tump was buoyant, rocking beneath them in the light swell. Karina held Haleka firmly around the wrists. His eyes were shut. Tears of shame started from under the lids. Karina blinked, wondering if she was doing the right thing. Haleka wanted to die, but she wouldn't let him because. . . . Because she was just as selfish as the Dedo and the handmaiden and lousy Starquin.

"All right, Haleka," she said quietly. "Goodbye, now. I love you." And she kissed him on the cheek.

She slipped from the tump's back and began to swim alongside, unwilling to head for the shore just yet. Looking around, she saw the other tump was closer now, a low mound showing above the water with a tumpier sitting on top, shoulders drooping. Haleka's tump rocked, nearly unseating him. The bulky animal was not nearly so stable in the water as on land, and Karina moved away a couple of meters, fearing a capsize.

A capsize. . . .

"Haleka!"

"What is it now?" He was trying to compose himself. He loved her, but couldn't she leave him alone?

"Why do tumps take to the water?"

"To drown, of course, when their time comes. Just as I shall do. Our time has come."

"Haleka—suppose this stuff about times coming is all garbage! I know it's traditional, and so on. But I can't really believe the tump wants to die. I can see his eye from here, and he looks pretty lively to me!"

On an impulse she swam up to the tump and laid her hand on its head. The tump sensed her presence but this time it didn't shy away from her; rather, it moved her way, recognizing something in her. Something flowed down her arm, flowed back. Karina smiled.

"So *that's* it," she murmured.

Years later, Karina thought to visit the tump pens.

By now she was a mature felina with three grupos behind her, and a lot of good memories. El Tigre had died several years previously during a brawl on the outskirts of Rangua but he'd taken three True Humans with him, and further assured himself of a place in felino legend. Karina was still beautiful, with the fleshy, wild beauty of the older felina, and the gray streaks in her red-gold hair lent her a slight vulnerability which added to her appeal.

It was not surprising that the man in charge of the tump pens stared in admiration as she walked slowly along the beach. Twenty meters from him she stopped and looked out to sea. There was a breakwater out there; a rocky wall which had taken several years to build, enclosing half a dozen rectangular pens. The backs of the tumps could be seen breaking the surface, two to a pen.

In the pens nearest the beach were the young tumps.

They were being conditioned by the rise and fall of the tide to the feel of dry land under them. Each year another two or three young tumps were ready for the fields. It was simply a matter of training. Left alone, they would have spent their lives in the ocean, like the whales they were descended from, grazing the continental shelf. Trained to live on land they thrived just as happily—until, after a thousand years or so, they matured. Then, like an amphibian, they returned to the water to mate.

But this essential part of tump lore had been lost until recent years.

Tentatively, the man approached the beautiful woman. "Can I help you?"

"No. . . . I was just looking. Tumps fascinate me."

"They're interesting animals. I've studied them all my life. There was a time when we thought they were dying out—that would have been a bad thing for you felinos, eh?"

"Oh, I don't know. . . ." The Examples weren't so rigid, these days. Two nights ago she'd led her youngest grupo into the jungle and they'd feasted on capybara, and felt not the slightest guilt.

He laughed suddenly. "We tumpiers like to feel indispensible, you know. Don't mind me."

Her eyes flashed, as though this show of humility had annoyed her, and she said sharply, "The tump is the most important animal on the coast. Many felinos would have starved if the secret of the tump's life-cycle hadn't been discovered."

Still smiling, he said, "You said it for me. But tumpiers would have starved too, with nothing to trade in. We both owe a debt to Haleka." Now he glanced at her, glanced away. "He was my father, you know."

"Oh." She scrutinized his face.

"Yes, really."

"You must be very proud to have a father who is a legend." He was a couple of years younger than she—yes, he could be Mauo. "The old Pegman sings of him often—Haleka, the tumpier who solved the riddle of the ages, and saved the felinos. How does it go . . . ?" And she sang, in a low, melodious voice, the song which begins,

"From the tumpfields to the ocean,
Sing Haleka, sing Haleka.
How he earned Mankind's devotion,
Sing Haleka. . . ."

"Of course," she added with a mischievous grin, "he may have had a little help."

"Nonsense! He told me about it often—how his tump went loco, and he prepared to die with it according to custom, how the tump began to swim, and suddenly it all became clear to him. And later he designed the tump pens and supervised the building of them—he was a famous man by then, all down the coast."

"He told you all that? Nothing more?"

"Isn't that enough?"

She came very close and his head swam with her loveliness, her unbearable sexuality. She put her hands on his shoulders and the fullness of her breasts touched his chest. By the time her strange eyes had looked into his for a moment he was in no condition to deny anything.

"Nothing more?" she asked sweetly.

"Well, there was. . . ." And suddenly his eyes widened, and the spell was broken. "You're Karina! You must be! He was always talking about you—even when he was dying."

"It is I," she said composedly.

And then her composure left her because, quite unexpectedly, he took over. He was already standing close, so all he had to do was slip his arms around her, crush her body against his, and kiss her with an intensity that no other lover had even approached.

"That's from Haleka," he said by way of an excuse, grinning.

"Haleka would *never* have. . . ."

"Well, maybe he wasn't so bright after all."

"I'm glad you admitted it."

"I do, lovely Karina. But ask yourself this—who does the old Pegman sing about?"

And he was right, of course. On that happentrack, nobody sang of Karina. As so often happens, the truth of the matter had been forgotten in a very short time but the legend grew fast and strong in the fertile tumpfields and the Women's Villages; and since it was a tumpier legend it had a tumpier hero. Nobody wanted to hear about a mere felina who happened to be around at the time. Haleka's protestations were seen as the becoming modesty of a great man and when, millennia later, the vast body of human lore had been distilled into the Song of Earth, the little legend of Haleka had its place on this happentrack which Starquin rejected.

"Some men shoot the antelope while others use the knife.
"Haleka loved the animals and gave his creatures life."

But there was no mention of Karina.
And the Incarceration of Starquin lasted forever.

The bend at Torres.

"I can't understand what's got into you," said Teressa. "He was only an old tumpier. Liven up,

Karina. This is the Festival, and we're at Torres. Nobody knows us!" And she struck an outrageously seduc-
tive pose as a young True Human walked past, arm in
arm with his girl. He colored and looked away, and
Teressa's laughter followed him up the hill. "Wouldn't
he just like to have," she said.

The Festival at Torres was similar to that at Rangua;
a large gathering of vampiro tents and other temporary
structures on the north slope of a hill, attended by a
colorful throng of humans of all species. At the base of
the hill was the bend in the sailway tracks, and the
felinos with their teams of shrugleggers. Then came the
stalls and the pitchers of ale and the mating tents, the
minstrels and their songs. The Pegman was there, his
ramshackle sailcar drawn onto a siding. He cavorted
about the camp, swinging his mallet and singing peg-
driving songs.

The first sailcar arrived in mid-afternoon.

The sails were sighted and a great shout went up.
Then followed a scene which would be repeated down a
thousand kilometers of coast over the next few days—
the felinos began to jockey for position.

This was different from the careful, polite and almost
mathematical calculation of the felinos at Rangua. Few
of the Torres felinos had made prior arrangements with
the captains; it was every man for himself. Added to
which the cars would be arriving over a period of time,
so the felinos who secured the first tows could conceivably get back down the hill in time for another.

They jostled and pushed, and the shrugleggers, as
though understanding the implications, shouldered one
another roughly aside. Grupos began to gather on the
outskirts, awaiting a sign from their men.

"What fun!" said Teressa. "I wish we did this kind of
thing at Rangua!"

In fact, over the years the grupos had been only rarely

189

involved because it was tacitly agreed that the resultant free-for-all would delay the sailcars unduly. So it was usually man against man. After a while, the big felinos began to aim powerful blows at one another.

Captain Herrero came sailing in.

Two teams were in advantageous positions and their felinos traded punches while the shrugleggers spread out to prevent interference. Herrero watched from the deck as *Urubu* rolled to a stop. "You!" he shouted, pointing to the tallest of the combatants. Unfortunately the shout coincided with a decisive kick and his selection fell writhing to the ground.

"Me!" shouted the other, and fastened his team to the towbar. The shrugleggers leaned into the harness and *Urubu* began to glide up the hill. Lower down, fighting broke out afresh as another sail was sighted.

The El Tigre grupo hung about the guiderails, watching with open-mouthed excitement.

All except Karina. "Don't you find all this a bit degrading?" she asked Runa. "Fighting for tokens thrown to us by True Humans?"

"She's in a bad temper," Teressa explained, "Just because she had to leave her precious tumpier friend."

"Yes, she's beginning to sound like father," added Runa.

"Well, at least El Tigre wouldn't stoop to fighting with his own people for the chance to serve a True Human," said Karina hotly.

"No, because nobody would fight with him, not if they valued their life."

"Shut up, you three," said Saba. "There are more cars coming."

For a while the felinos were too busy to fight as the cars arrived one after another, some switching tracks to slip ahead of opponents. Ripe tortugas began to make their appearance as Torres' only merchant bought a small quantity. They were quickly cracked open and handed round. Then the sailcars were gone.

"Let's go and see what's happening up the hill," said Karina, and ran towards the vampiros. As she peeped inside the first, hoping to catch someone in the act of mating, shock hit her like a physical blow.

The handmaiden sat in there.

"Go back to the trackside, Karina."

"Why?"

"It is necessary for the Purpose."

"Oh. . . ." This time, it was no big thing. "All right," she said. She ran back and met her sisters on the way. "There's still another car to come," she called to them.

"*Rayo*," observed Teressa, adding maliciously, "and Karina's boyfriend."

"How many times do I have to tell you I can't stand the sight of Raoul?"

"Why do you ride with him on Captain Tonio's old sailcar, then? And who was following him in the jungle not so long ago, and got caught?"

Karina flung herself at Teressa who met her with a short jab to the ribs. The usual battle was developing when Saba gave a shout.

"*Rayo's* coming!"

Karina and Teressa paused to watch, still locked together, neither one wanting to surrender her imagined advantage.

"She's moving fast," Karina said.

"Of course, you would think *Rayo* is the best car."

"No, I mean really fast. Just look at her." Now the rails were roaring and Runa, sitting on the guiderail, could feel the vibration through her buttocks.

She looked up from her scrutiny of a young bachelor to see *Rayo* coming towards them faster than she'd ever seen anything travel before.

"Mordecai!" she shouted, jumping to the ground. "Let's get out of here!"

There was something different about this car, and this trip.

Astrud sat at the forward end of the hold, just behind Tonio. The wind funnelled like a hurricane through *Rayo's* nose and Astrud would have gone on deck except that it was bedlam up there, the crew fighting with the sheets while the ground sped past at an insane speed. It wasn't *right* for anything to travel so fast. It was against nature. And it was surely against the Examples, although Astrud couldn't quite work out why.

Anyway, she was quite certain they would be punished.

She'd even worked out how it would happen. The whole cargo of tortugas would suddenly explode, scattering *Rayo* and its inhabitants across the pampas.

"Tonio. . . . Do we have to go so fast?"

But her words were whisked away by the wind, drowned in the terrible noise. Not that Tonio would have paid any attention, even if he'd heard. . . . That was another thing. He'd been behaving so strangely. He seemed to lose control of himself at the slightest setback. And just before they'd finally got away from the yards, he'd vomited.

She caught hold of the ladder and, with difficulty, climbed to the deck. It was like climbing a tree in a gale. And just as she reached the top of the ladder, *Rayo* passed the hill they called Camelback, and a gust of wind almost lifted the mast out of its tabernacle. She actually heard fibers parting. As she staggered, Raoul caught her. His eyes were bright with excitement.

"Steady, mother!"

"And just what would we do if the mast broke?" she asked shrilly, fear making her snappish. "Where would we be then? What's the point of all this speed?"

"If the mast broke we'd jury-rig it." He pointed to a locker full of crimson lianas. "It's a chance we have to take, if we want to catch the others."

"And the way those felinos looked at us, at Rangua. Shouldn't we have stopped? The things they shouted after us! I've never heard of a car not stopping before!"

"*Rayo* is no ordinary car."

Even on the swaying deck, with the noise beating at her mind, Astrud sensed something odd in Raoul's tone. He might not be her real son, but she'd known him a long time. "What are you saying?"

"Nothing, mother."

"Raoul!" She clung to him. The car was flying across the plain like a thing possessed. This was the work of Agni! It had to be! There was evil in this speed! "How is *Rayo* different?"

Her stepson was silent. . . .

In the fulness of intuition, she said, "There's something in this car which is against the Examples."

He didn't reply. He moved away, face averted, and began to help the crew replace a fraying line.

Astrud leaned against the deck rail, weeping with terror, while the hellish car bore her headlong into perdition. Her head whirled with the terrible speed of the ground beneath, and when the voice of Tonio snapped commands from the pipe nearby, she felt it was not her husband but the Fire-god Agni himself who sat in the nose, the wind forcing his lips back into a fierce, hungry grin.

She was hardly aware of Raoul running past her some time later, grabbing the voicepipe and yelling into it.

The Fire-god yelled back, unintelligibly.

Raoul was dragging at some kind of lever, and after a moment she was dimly aware of the rest of the crew bunched there, adding their strength to his. It was of no consequence, because a few seconds later Agni struck, as she'd known he would.

Smoke rose from below, acrid and evil.

Something was screaming inhumanly, stabbing into her ears.

And finally the Wrath of Agni, crimson and yellow and painful to look at, blossomed around the nose of *Rayo*.

This was what burned into Astrud's brain. The Wrath was crawling towards her, reaching for her with scarlet tentacles so fearful that she hardly noticed the screaming had stopped, hardly heard the great crash of parting timbers, hardly knew that *Rayo* had left the track and was leaping blindly towards destruction.

"Let's get out of here!" shouted Runa.

Karina and Teressa disentangled themselves and began to run. All around, people were scattering as *Rayo* bore down on them, swift and terrible, her vast sails filling the sky like thunderclouds.

"Mordecai!" someone exclaimed. "The Wrath of Agni is upon her!"

"She's going too fast! She's—"

Down by the bend Karina ran on, bounding over the coarse scrub, reaching the pebbles of the beach. She was aware of Teressa at her shoulder, Runa panting behind her, others near, all running.

Saba!

She halted so suddenly that Runa ran into her and she staggered, scanning the fleeing people for a sign of Saba.

She heard an enormous, splintering crash.

Rayo hit the curve and the outside guiderail snapped

like a dry stick. The car leaped from the running rail, trailing smoke and flames, and flew thirty metres through the air before landing with an impact that toppled the mainmast.

Embedded in Karina's mind was the vision of a small figure hurled through space and striking the ground under the very wheels of *Rayo*.

The great ship ploughed on, her decks a tangle of sailcloth and ropes, the flames sweeping aft and flaring over the waxed fabric. The mizzenmast still stood, catching the wind and tilting the ship. The nose, already a skeleton of smoking timbers, crashed through the first of the vampiro tents and the huge bats reared up, screeching, teeth bared as they were swept aside.

Karina ran forward. "Saba!"

The crowd further up the hill realized, too late, that they were not safe. They began to run. *Rayo* slid on, slowing now and toppling so that the mizzenmast cut a swathe through stalls and huts, flinging aside pots and fabrics, jugs of ale, fruit and other merchandise. In her wake, shrugleggers and humans struggled to their feet, but some lay still. Then the vampiros, crazed with fear and pain, staggered in among them and began to strike viciously with tooth and claw, great wings flapping loosely like tarpaulins in a gale.

Karina ran among them, ignoring their thrusts, searching for her sister. The injured lay around screaming, arms held up to ward off vampiros. The shrugleggers were easy meat, tangled in their harness.

Rayo shed parts of her structure as she ploughed on. The mainmast jammed in the doorway of the community hut and twisted the entire building around before snapping off. Flames from the sail spread into the thatch, and people tore their way out through a wall, jumping clear and running. The mizzenmast caught against a tree, sending a cloud of screeching macaws into the sky as tongues of flame licked into the branches. The deckrails lay scattered on the ground like broken ladders, smouldering. The blazing brake shoes snapped off against a rock outcropping, and lay in a growing pool of fire.

Karina saw Saba.

The whole camp was in motion now, as the spreading fire sent everybody into a frenzy of superstitious terror. *Rayo,* now a blazing cylinder unrecognizable as a sail-car, struck rocks and slewed around, beginning to roll down the hillside towards the sea, gathering speed and crushing vampiros as she went. One animal, brushed by fire, rose clumsily into the sky on burning wings before tilting and sideslipping into the sea to flap for a while on the surface, raising wisps of steam before disappearing. Finally *Rayo* came to rest on the beach, the fabric of her hull totally consumed. She lay there smoking like the blackened skeleton of some huge marine mammal. The tortugas began to explode with a popping, growing to a roar.

Karina held Saba's hand. There was no life there. The felina lay twisted, her tunic torn and bloody and a sliver of hardwood projecting from the ribcage just below one slight breast.

Karina stood.

A vampiro approached, eyes glittering, totally reverted to the wild state. It bent over the still form of Saba.

With an inhuman yell Karina leaped at the creature's throat, hooking her fingers into the folds of skin. As it began a ponderous flapping, seeking to carry her off, her toes slashed into its abdomen and entrails cascaded to the grass. It fell back with a strangled whimper and Karina, her feet planted on the ground, pivoted with all her strength and threw the huge creature onto its back. She hardly felt the neck snap, didn't realize as she stepped away from the body that she had decapitated it, and the head was still hanging from her hooked fingers. . . .

Standing over the body of Saba she gazed at the scene of devastation. The stalls were on fire and the community hut had collapsed. Several of the smaller huts were smoldering. Like gigantic scavenging birds the vampiros stalked among the casualties, pecking here, clawing there, seeking easy meat first and feasting off the dead, leaving the injured for later. Everyone else had fled.

All except for a small group near the siding on which the Pegman's sailcar stood. Two huge men were there, restraining three people who seemed to be trying to get away.

Karina could not see them for tears.

"Is this what you wanted, Starquin?" she shouted at the darkening sky. "Are you satisfied, damn you? Siervo and Haleka, and now *Saba!* Is this your great Purpose? Well, I tell you this, you bastard. I'm through! To hell with my Word—I take it back! From now on I'm going to do everything in my power to wreck things for you. Can you hear me?

"I'm going to start by finding Captain Tonio and his wife and his goddamned son, and if they're still alive I'm going to kill them. Then I'm going to hunt down that burned creep the Dedo keeps sending, and I'm going to kindle the Wrath under her goddamned skirts and finish the job Agni started.

"Then the Dedo. . . . I'll really enjoy that. I'll do it slowly. I'll take her apart, piece by piece—your flesh, your bones, and I hope I'll hear you screaming up there. . . ."

There was more but it was becoming disjointed, merged into the sobbing, and in the end she dropped to her knees and laid her cheek on Saba's breast.

She didn't hear the quiet hoisting of sails, and she didn't see the Pegman's car glide from its siding and roll away up the coast.

"Oh, my God. . . . Oh, Karina." Raoul let his breath out in a shuddering sigh and rolled over, face to the deck, trying to rid his mind of the image of the demented cat-girl, drenched in blood with the head of a vampiro hanging from her fingers, standing over the body of her sister and screaming her murderous intentions at the evening sky.

While nearby, Tonio and Astrud lay watching with scared eyes as the huge, silent Us Ursa handled the ropes.

The importance of balance.

The handmaiden said, "She's resisting—I think I've lost her. Her sister died, you see. I think she blames us."

"Quite rightly, of course."

The Dedo stood against the Rock which was unlike any other rock. It was translucent blue-gray and it seemed to consist of a multitude of interconnecting facets, each one flat and about the size of a human hand, set somewhere just below the surface so that the handmaiden could never be sure they were there at all. And the facets glowed with a light of such eerie violet tint that it was almost beyond the spectrum. They glowed and flickered, passing flashes of dull color from one to the next in a bewildering pattern which seemed to exist in the handmaiden's mind rather than in the Rock itself.

The handmaiden, her emotions dulled by years of

contact with the Dedo, ate a small fish which had been baked before the fire. The Dedo had caught the fish. In the valley, you had to be careful about that kind of thing.

The valley was *in balance*.

When the handmaiden first came, the Dedo had explained.

"The caiman takes what he needs and no more. Certainly he *kills* more than he needs, but that is unavoidable when the prey is large. The surplus food goes to feed the scavengers, who also have their place in the valley. The ungulates graze. The rodents gnaw. The jungle lives in balance. You're probably wondering where I fit in. Well—I grow my own vegetables and I sometimes play the role of a scavenger. Occasionally I am a predator and I kill a deer, or maybe do a little fishing if the stocks are high or if I can see a surplus in the Ifalong." She indicated a row of smoked fish hanging from a beam.

"I choose my role," the Dedo said, "because I'm by far the strongest creature in the valley, and that includes Bantus. I arrange the whole of this place to suit my own needs. I balance predator against prey, browsers against foliage, grazers against range. I do it in such a way that every creature retains its place, at the same time allowing the weak to die and the strong to breed. This way, the valley will support me until I die. It is in balance.

"I've adjusted the balance to include yourself."

Now the handmaiden wondered how this was going to work out, because the Dedo had hinted that she was expecting several visitors in the nearby Ifalong. The handmaiden mentioned this.

"The balance of the valley will work towards the fulfilment of the Purpose," said the Dedo. "Before very long, your work towards that fulfilment will be complete, and John will be conceived."

A moment of human frailty caused the handmaiden to shudder.

**HERE ENDS THAT PART OF THE
SONG OF EARTH KNOWN TO
MEN AS
"TORTUGA FESTIVAL"**

**IN TIME,
OUR TALE WILL CONTINUE
WITH THE GROUP OF STORIES
AND LEGENDS KNOWN AS
"IN THE VALLEY OF LAKES"**

Where El Tigre loses and wins his battle,
Karina loves,
And John is born to the furtherance of
Starquin's mighty Purpose.

Exile

"Should you espy a monstrous beast who shoulders a tree to the ground in passing, tell yourself the trunk was rotten, but get out of the valley of Bantus nevertheless—for sometimes safety is more important than sanity."

—Tales of Old Brasil, anon.

Astrud's shoulder hurt so badly that she could hardly move her arm, her legs were bleeding from a network of scratches, and blisters were erupting on the palms of both hands—the Punishment of Agni.

She wondered how she'd come out of it alive. She'd seen the ground rising to meet her, then she'd known little more until she'd found herself lying on the deck of this squalid little sailcar, with two giant men handling the ropes.

"Palace Guards," Tonio whispered to her. "They must have been sent here to make sure we had a clear track. The Canton Lord looks after us, you see, Astrud." There was a dreadful bruise on the side of his face, and much of the skin was missing so that his cheek looked like raw tumpmeat, wet but not quite bleeding.

"Raoul . . . ?"

"He's fine."

Raoul turned and looked at her then, and his eyes were full of pain. "She said she was going to kill us. She had this terrible . . . head in her hands, I don't know what it was a head of, but it looked as though she'd pulled it off some animal. Ugh. She will kill us, you know. I'm sure of it. She looked crazy."

"The Canton Lord will protect us."

"What, from every felino in the Canton?" Raoul voiced Tonio's own private fear. "How in hell can he? They could get us any time. They could attack the *Cadalla*—they could even come to the house. You ought to have seen her face, father."

"I knew no good would come of this year's race," said Astrud. "*Rayo* was touched by Agni, and in the end he claimed her. That's what happens when you forsake the Examples. Tonight, I'm going to pray for forgiveness. And I'll make sure you do too, Tonio. And you, Raoul. You were involved in this, too."

Raoul said, "I'm not sure we'll have much time for praying, mother."

"What do you mean? What does he mean, Tonio?"

Tonio said carefully, "When news of the accident gets back to Rangua, we may find the felinos in a trouble-some mood. It might be better not to spend the night at home."

"There were so many hurt. . . ." The vision of carnage was reborn in Astrud's mind; the flames, the screaming, the crazed vampiros. . . .

Raoul said, "I think one of the El Tigre grupo died. That's what Karina was crying about."

"Mordecai!" In his perturbation Tonio swore like a Specialist. He turned, staring through the open tail of the old *Estrella del Oeste* at the rosy glow in the south-ern sky. Torres still burned.

The Us Ursa were slackening sail as the hill of

204

Rangua South Stage loomed ahead. The rails gleamed palely against the darkness, and no sails were to be seen.

"What happened to the rest of the cars?" Raoul said. "I've been expecting a head-on collision."

"I think. . . ." Tonio hesitated. "Perhaps the felinos refused to tow them, after the news of the accident reached them."

Astrud said, "If you ask me, they'd be more upset about the way we sailed straight past them up the hill at Rangua." Although her head still throbbed, the wind had helped and she was beginning to think clearly again. "I simply can't understand you, Tonio. How could you hope to get away with a trick like that? You know how touchy the felinos are. Now you've probably tied up a dozen sailcars the wrong side of Rangua. I don't blame the felinos one bit. You as good as told them they were redundant. It's against the whole culture of the coast!"

Tonio looked away, discomfited by her accurate summing-up. "There are other pressures," he muttered. "You wouldn't understand."

"Your only hope is to apologize to the felinos."

At this totally inappropriate suggestion Raoul, with Karina still vividly in his mind, uttered an almost hysterical shout of laughter. "I think it's gone a little beyond that, mother."

The *Estrella del Oeste* glided to a stop at the foot of the bank. The Us Ursa climbed to the ground and the True Humans followed. The grass was wet with dew and South Stage still deserted.

For the first time in over an hour, one of the Us Ursa spoke.

"You will report to the Palace in the morning."

Then the two big Specialists melted away into the night.

Over the past few moments Astrud had been reappraising the situation. Her head was aching abominably, the strangeness of her surroundings was oppressing her greatly, and some inkling of the dreadful implications of recent events was coming home to her. They were not safe. The Specialists, those odd animal-people, could present a genuine menace. Rangua was going to be uncomfortable for a while.

"I'm glad the Canton Lord is going to discuss this with you, Tonio." That great palace on the hill represented a rock of permanence, normality and security. "It would be quite unfair to expect you to handle this alone."

With something that sounded like a groan of terror, Tonio plunged off into the night to round up three mules. They would have to ride home from here. He hoped they wouldn't meet anyone on the way.

The Canton Lord didn't speak for some time, and Tonio sat watching the screen while the sweat dribbled from his body and his stomach contorted itself into knots.

"Say your piece, Captain Tonio," said the Lord at last.

"I . . . we're in trouble. The felinos are after us. You'll have to hide us somewhere, just for a while."

"I'll have to, will I?" There was amused sarcasm in the voice. "You wreck my car and kill a number of people through your own incompetence, and you want *me* to help you? I don't think so, Captain Tonio."

"But they'll kill us!"

"Think of the sailways. The daily commerce, the interlocking cultures. A thousand miles of coastline. What's one captain more or less?"

"I did it for you, Lord Benefactor! It was all for you, at your request! You promised me—"

"Oh," purred the voice. "Just what did I promise?"

"Well, I assumed you'd make sure I. . . . After all, you did organize the whole thing; *Rayo*, Maquinista. . . . If the felinos knew the Canton Lord was responsible for—"

"Are you trying to blackmail me, Captain Tonio?"

"Absolutely not. But, Lord Benefactor. . . . Surely, we're in this together. . . ."

"Partners, you mean? You and I?"

"No! I wouldn't presume . . . !" Tonio was weeping with despair.

"Of course not. What you must understand, Captain Tonio, is that there are bigger issues here than your personal well-being. I had hoped that *Rayo* would be an example to the whole coast of what could be achieved— and coastal unity would have outweighed the felinos' objections. But you failed to demonstrate the craft's capabilities. Now I cannot expect any support from the other Cantons if the felinos become . . . dissatisfied with their lot. And I understand they are dissatisfied. They have refused to assist the remainder of the tortuga fleet, which is now immobilized north of the town. The next step—so I should imagine—is that El Tigre will lead his people in some undisciplined raid on Rangua Town and, possibly, this very Palace."

"No, I don't think so," said Tonio eagerly. "I really don't think we have to worry about that. No, no. El Tigre? That fool? Never!"

The Canton Lord sighed, as though the effort of unintelligent conversation had finally exhausted him. Slowly and distinctly, he said, "You will leave, now."

And an Us Ursa entered, carrying black clothing. He dumped this on a chair and approached Tonio. There was no expression on his broad face, but his fingers were curled slightly.

"All right," said Tonio.

"Put on these cloaks," said the figure behind the screen. "They will hide your faces—and people in cloaks are generally left alone. My guards will escort you to the Palhoa sailcar. After that, you are on your own. My advice is to take to the mountains. It will be unwise for you ever to come back to Rangua—particularly since I intend to cast you in the role of scapegoat for this disastrous enterprise. It may go some small way towards maintaining law and order in the Canton, and then again it may not."

"I will never come back," said Tonio woodenly.

"You didn't tell me that felina had found out about the tortugas, Tonio."

There was nothing he could say.

"Goodbye, Captain Tonio."

Revolution.

That same morning a band of felinos on muleback rode north through the drizzling rain. Wet and tired, they had been riding since dawn, and they had not exchanged one word during that time.

A cold, animal fury burned within them.

They'd helped bury the dead, all except the four crewmen of *Rayo*. Two of those men died in the accident, but the other two had taken to the hills under cover of gathering darkness.

The felinos had sent the grupos after them.

They were caught at midnight, hidden in the branches of a tree on the edge of the tumpfields. A grupo had winded them and had dragged them out of there, screaming. They had every reason to fear for their future. Within an hour of their arrival back at Torres they had been sentenced to death by an ad hoc court and, together with their two dead comrades, had been nailed to crosses on the beach, facing out to sea, in the glow of the still-smouldering *Rayo*. The grupos spent the rest of the night in fruitless search for Tonio and his family and at dawn the search had been called off. The general supposition was that the fugitives had somehow managed to board one of the other cars which was on the hill at the time, and had been whisked south.

It was no problem, the Torres felino chief assured El Tigre. The signalmen would be busy by first light, and descriptions would be flashed all the way to Patagonia. There was no escape.

Meanwhile, the True Human inhabitants of Torres huddled indoors, with doors and shutters barred. . . .

Now El Tigre rode into Rangua South Stage. The camp had been re-erected overnight, and a number of people from North Stage were there too, because it was generally felt that South Stage would be where the action was.

They expected El Tigre to initiate that action—and this time they would be listening.

"Pegman's here," Karina said to Runa. They rode behind the men, like errant children being brought home. "There's his sailcar. He must have come back right after the accident. Strange he didn't stay."

"Have you ever known the Pegman to do what we expect?"

Teressa said, "Probably he's gone into hiding. After all, he is a True Human. He got out of Torres while the going was good. Did you see how those crewmen kicked, on those crosses? And the yelling—True Humans died noisily, that's for sure."

El Tigre and his followers rode grimly up the hill in the direction of the community hut, where a crowd was now gathering. The girls lingered beside *Estrella del Oeste,* pondering the whereabouts of the Pegman. Suddenly their whole world had changed; their sister was dead, the Canton was in an uproar—and the Pegman represented a link with the past; with the childhood they'd left behind so suddenly. Karina fingered the ancient woodwork, slippery with rain.

"Nothing's ever going to be the same," she said.

And a voice suddenly spoke, hollow and ghostly.

"Who's that? Who's that?"

Karina said, "It's the Pegman. He's in there."

"Have they gone? Huh? Is that you, Karina?" The Pegman's eyes appeared at a gap in the warped timbers.

"Have who gone?"

"The Palace Guards. They were here, didn't you know? They commandeered the *Estrella*—stole it, if the truth be told—and sailed it back from Torres. I was scared, I tell you. When I saw them coming I hid in the hold. I knew they wouldn't be poking about amongst the kegs of grease." There was a scuffling and he emerged from the cargo hatch, swung himself to the ground and glanced around nervously. "What's happening?"

"Father's holding a meeting," said Runa.

"We're going to wipe every True Human off the face of the Earth," added Teressa.

"I'm a True Human."

"You're out of luck, Pegman."

The Pegman's eyes sought Karina, but he found little comfort there either. Her face was set, the lips clamped together. Then, after a moment, she said,

"We didn't find those bastards, Enri. We've been looking for them all night. They got clean away."

"You mean Captain Tonio and his wife and son?"

"That's who I mean."

210

He was silent, remembering the unintelligible discussions on the deck. And those final words, couched in tones of quiet menace, *You will report to the Palace in the morning*. Captain Tonio's family, in trouble. Enri didn't know the whole truth of the matter; but one thing he did know, it was easy to misjudge speed in a sail-car.

Rayo had been so fast. . . . Unnaturally so. He'd seen a car break away from the shruglegger team once, and run backwards down the bank at Jai'a. And, like *Rayo,* it had hit the curve at terrifying speed, and the guiderail had collapsed. . . . One felino had been killed. Enri had pitied the captain. . . .

The El Tigre grupo stood before him, a fighting team. . . . Enri decided to keep his mouth shut. Casually, and just to change the subject, he asked, "Where's Saba?"

And their eyes told him.

"Saba?" he said, as something seemed to hit him in the stomach. "Saba?"

"Her neck was broken," said Karina. "And other things." She was watching him strangely and, after a moment, she stepped close. "Tell me, Enri. Tell me right now!"

"They were on *Estrella*," he muttered, unable to look into the furnaces of her eyes. "They're probably at the house right now. The guards told them to report to the Palace in the morning. They may have left."

"Come on!" said Karina, beginning to run. "Let's tell father, quickly!"

The Pegman looked after them. "I couldn't help it," he said to himself. He walked to a nearby team of shrugleggers. Cupping his hands trumpet-fashion he bawled at the leader. "Couldn't help it, couldn't help it! Couldn't help it!"

The creature regarded him in dumb puzzlement.

"But father, we've got to get after them! Isn't that what this whole business is about?"

El Tigre regarded Karina somberly. They stood in the community hut on a makeshift stage. The place was jammed; the audience spilled out through the doors. The South Stage leaders were grouped around El Tigre: Diferir, Manoso, Dozo, all the influential felinos united in a common cause.

El Tigre said, "There are more important things, Karina. Tonio is small fry."

"But Saba. . . . Your own daughter . . . !" Karina was shaking his arm trying to get him to look at her; but El Tigre had learned the folly of looking into Karina's eyes. "How can you fool around with some stupid meeting when the murderers are getting further away all the time! We have to get after them, *now,* and nail them up like we did the crew!"

El Tigre said, "Listen, Karina. The important thing is, the True Humans have started using metal to build ships fast enough to spell the end of us. Look at this crowd. It's the biggest we've ever had—half of North Stage is here, too. And this time we're united. We're going to put our plans to these people, and they're going to agree with them. It's the revolution, Karina." Yet there was no excitement in his voice. The spark had died at Torres, with Saba. . . . "Now, what are they going to say if I send them all running after a couple of True Humans? They'll ask what kind of revolution this is. They'll say instead of dealing with the big issues, El Tigre is pursuing a personal vendetta. Can you understand that, Karina?"

"No, I can't! I can't believe it, either! We're just back from burying Saba, and we know who the murderers are, and all you want to do is talk!"

"I'm sorry." El Tigre's attention was wandering. Torch was calling the meeting to order and he needed to marshal his thoughts. "That's the way it is."

"Well, if you're not going to do anything about it, I am! I'm going to Rangua with the grupo, right now, and we're going to hunt down those bastards, and you're not going to stop us!"

The girls headed straight up the hill at a run.

Arriving at Tonio's house, they found every sign of a recent hurried departure. Although the rain was still falling steadily they were able to follow the trail into the forest, where three mules had obviously been tethered overnight.

"They headed west," said Runa, examining the grass.

The felinas loped through the forest. "The Palace," said Teressa finally, halting and motioning the others to stop, too. Ahead of them lay the vast open area; the grounds, the private sailway running through, and the huge ancient building. And the guards, too powerful for even the grupo to tackle. . . .

"So what do we do now?" asked Runa.

"There are the mules—see?" Karina pointed. "So they're still in there somewhere. We just wait for them to come out, let them get clear of the guards, then we take them." Her fingers itched.

But it didn't work out like that. Eventually Tonio, Astrud and Raoul emerged, accompanied by two guards. For a while the True Humans stood under the portico, sheltering from the rain. They put on black cloaks, drawing them tight around the neck and pulling the hoods over their heads. Presently a sailcar arrived, halting nearby. The five people climbed aboard, the crew let off the brakes and hauled in the sails, and the car accelerated quickly away, heading north.

"Quick!" shouted Teressa. "After them!"

"No!" Runa grabbed her arm as she was about to run
across open ground. "There are guards everywhere.
Let's go back the way we came. If we hurry, we can
catch them at the station in Rangua!"

When they reached the station some time later, however, the Lord's private car was already at the platform
and there was no sign of the True Human family. The
two guards were there, furling the sails in leisurely fashion, but otherwise the station was deserted.

"They've gone into a house somewhere," said Karina
in despair. "How are we going to find them now? It's no
good asking the guards."

"Maybe when the revolution comes, it'll flush them
out," suggested Teressa. "According to father, we'll
sweep everything before us. We'll roust everyone out
and line them up, and kill them." Teressa warmed to her
theme. "Then we'll take their places. We'll be top cats.
We'll capture the Palace, kill the Lord, and live there
with El Tigre as the new Lord. The guards will obey us
and we'll rule the Canton, and if anyone has the gall to
step out of line, by Agni we'll set the guards on him!"

Runa laughed. "I love you, Teressa."

"We'll try the inn," said Karina decisively.

That moment, when the El Tigre grupo entered the
Rangua inn in search of Captain Tonio and his family,
for some reason caught the imagination of the later
bards. It was a moment of some drama, although the
couplet in the Song of Earth exaggerates a little. But
then, few epics would be worth a damn without poetic
licence. . . .

*"She led the fearsome hunting girls into the house of
sin,
And terror gripped the drunken soul of every man
within."*

In point of fact there was little drunkenness, since it was only mid-morning. And annoyance, rather than terror, was the emotion uppermost in the souls of the men. Specialists were not welcome in the house of sin that morning, with revolution in the air, and the Town Elders holding a meeting upstairs to discuss defensive measures.

Karina stood in the center of the floor eyeing the drinkers who sat around the walls. Teressa and Runa stood in the doorway to discourage anyone from leaving.

"We don't want any trouble here, now," said the innkeeper, pausing in the act of filling a pitcher with ale.

"Throw them out!" somebody called.

Karina spat briefly in that direction, then said, "Anyone seen Captain Tonio?"

There was a sullen silence.

"Maybe you didn't hear me too well." Karina took the pitcher from the innkeeper and threw its contents into the face of the nearest customer. "We're looking for Captain Tonio and his family. They were last seen wearing black cloaks, headed this way."

The customer, spluttering and dashing ale from his eyes, said, "*I* don't know. Why pick on me?" He was elderly, and shaking with impotent rage. "He hasn't been in here, that's all I can tell you."

Suddenly a voice said, "I think I know where he might be."

"Pegman!" Now Karina saw the figure in the corner.

The Pegman rose, draining his mug. "Let's go outside," he said. "It wasn't doing me any good in there, anyway."

He followed the grupo into the street, blinking at the light. The sailway ran nearby and he sat on a running rail.

"Well?" asked Teressa impatiently.

But the Pegman was not to be hurried. He uttered a couple of strange cries while he collected his thoughts. Finally he said, "You remember a little while ago, Karina, we talked about . . . the Dedo."

"That bitch! I'm going to get her!"

"She lives in the rain forest above Palhoa. Now, Captain Tonio once worked on that old sailcar track that ran from Palhoa up to Buique. It's all wrecked, now. It's a region nobody ever goes to—even the mountain people stay away—because of the Dedo, I think. Anyway, things are a bit strange around there and Tonio knows that. I think that was the real reason why the sailway track was abandoned—you could almost smell the strangeness. Tonio's mentioned it to me more than once. It's a perfect place to hide out—no people, plenty of food. . . . I think that's where Tonio's headed for."

"You don't think he's in town here?"

"Not if he's got any sense. This town will be a battlefield before long. The signalmen reported a big gathering down at South Stage—but I expect you know about that. No. I think Tonio caught the morning car to Palhoa."

"But the cars aren't running, Enri."

"The Palhoa car is a square-rigger, remember? It doesn't need felino help. It'll be back later on today. All we have to do is ask the crew if three passengers in black cloaks travelled to Palhoa today. And if they did, we take the car tomorrow."

"You're coming?"

"Of course," said Enriques de Jai'a, hoping that he would be able to prevent bloodshed, not expecting success, and wondering why all this seemed predestined as though the Ifalong had suddenly become inevitable.

"Was it worth all those years of disappointment, El Tigre?" Dozo asked his chief.

The meeting had been a rousing success. The hillside still resounded with the roars of acclamation. The felinos were pouring out of the community hut prepared to do battle now, this minute. Mules were being brought, and the few precious horses. Even the shrugleggers had drawn near, mouths hanging open in dull astonishment.

"A moment's cheering?" El Tigre regarded the crowd, which was now being marshalled into three armies. "No."

"Still not satisfied, El Tigre?" Manoso gave his sly grin. "Maybe when I'll capture the delta for you, you'll smile then."

"No." The chief felino stood for a moment in thought. "When we control the whole Canton and I'm satisfied that people—*all* people—are better off than they were; and when the Canton is running so well that we can start giving things back: the tumpfields to the tumpiers, the town to the True Humans, the delta to the cai-men; and when I can see that everyone has his fair share, and no one race is setting itself up as chief; then maybe you'll see me smile. But even then," he added with a faint grin, "only if I'm happy."

"I'm surprised to hear you considering giving the True Humans a share in anything," said Diferir. "I mean, *you*, El Tigre."

"My personal feelings have no place in the revolution."

Dozo said, "It never occured to you that this racial segregation is the real cause of the problem?"

"No—that's natural. It's the very existence of races which causes trouble. Which takes me right back to a question I've asked myself many times. Was the great Mordecai—our creator—a saint or a devil?"

They followed the tail-end of the crowd outside, where the rain still fell steadily. Like the Pegman, El

Tigre felt he was caught up in an inevitable flow of events. The revolution was not his doing; it had been brought about by a series of happenings culminating in the accident at Torres. He was a tool, and so was everyone else. Just for a moment, he allowed himself to wonder who was wielding that tool. . . .

They were watching him, waiting for a sign.

"Move out!" he shouted.

The revolution had started.

The felinos were divided into three fighting units, commanded by Dozo, Manoso and El Tigre himself.

Dozo headed west. His task was to take his army into the foothills to deal with the tumpiers and any True Humans who might be around. It was the easiest job of the three and little active opposition was expected although —and this was why El Tigre had chosen Dozo for the task—a considerable amount of diplomacy had to be used. The tumpiers had to be won over rather than conquered, to ensure the continuance of the food supply. They were proud people with their own culture and traditions and El Tigre did not want to antagonize them any more than necessary. In order to demonstrate good intentions, Dozo's army consisted of good-natured bachelors. He had been given strick instructions that the Women's Village was not to be entered.

Manoso headed north with a mixed army of bachelors and felina grupos to conquer the delta region and to seize the yards, workshops, and tortuga pens. The Canton's whole economy was based on this region, and stiff opposition was expected. There were a number of True Humans in the jungle, Maquinista himself was known to have unusual and effective weapons, and the cai-men were an unknown quantity. Logically, as Specialists, they should side with the revolutionary forces;

but past experience told Manoso that, once stirred up, the crocodile-men would probably fight both sides indiscriminately, just for the hell of it. El Tigre had faith, however, that Manoso's devious mind would be equal to any challenge.

El Tigre headed northwest with a strong force of grupos plus their closest males and other chosen felinos such as Torch. His target was Rangua Town, and here the fiercest fighting was expected. Rumor had it that the Town Elders had already declared martial law, that all Specialists were being interned and that defenses were being organized.

These rumors were substantiated about a kilometer further on, when the advancing army met Karina, Teressa and Runa hurrying downhill.

"They're putting barricades across the streets," Karina told them. "And they've sent word to the Palace asking for a contingent of guards."

"Guards?" echoed Diferir nervously.

"They won't fight in Rangua," said El Tigre confidently. "The Lord will keep them back at the Palace. He'll want to protect his own neck."

"All the same, guards. . . ."

"The Palace . . . ?" somebody else said. "Are we intending to attack the Palace?"

"Mordecai!" roared El Tigre. "My only hope is that True Humans have even less guts than you. Torch! Round up the men for a frontal diversion. Iolande! take your grupo and fifteen others and circle west. Attack across the sailway, near the station. Tamaril! East, and keep below the ridge. Twenty grupos. Attack through the residential areas. Now. . . ." He regarded them broodingly. "We don't know what to expect. But one thing we do know—if we fail, we won't get another chance in our lifetimes. Now, we're not used to killing—

the Examples forbid it. But just for a few hours we're going to have to forget the Examples. Kill if you have to, but only as a last resort. Make a few examples, scare them into surrender, and take prisoners. Then stop. No looting, no vandalism. We have to live with these people afterwards."

"And if we find Tonio?" said Torch.

"Bring him to me. I want him alive. I want to be sure he dies correctly, in the utmost pain."

"What about the rest of us?" asked Amora, the well-built mother of a strong grupo.

"Wait with me," said El Tigre. "I want plenty of reserves. Now, Torch, Iolande, Tamaril! Move!"

The attack on Rangua Town began.

Into the mountains.

Astrud looked back on her old life, knowing she would never see it again, and the collection of shacks which was Rangua shimmered into tears. Raoul seemed to accept things better; he looked forward, up the track towards the jungle-clad hills, and there was a gleam of excitement in his eyes.

Tonio sat beside her, somehow shrunken, the lines of sorrow and defeat radiating from his eyes so that he smiled too readily, too watery when people glanced at him. He wore the cloak tucked closely around his neck, the hood barely above his eyes; and he'd shaved off his beard and mustache as a further disguise. Not only had he lost his sailcar and his pride, but he'd been forced to lose his identity too.

Now they bumped inland on an ancient square-rigged sailcar full of strangers escaping from the rumored felino attack, with the timbers gaping so the wind whistled through—which was probably as well, because

220

it alleviated the stink of the goats which were wandering up and down the aisle. Astrud huddled down into her cloak as a mountain-girl caught her eye. Even on this branch-line to nowhere, they could still be recognized; and by now all Rangua must know the story of *Rayo*.

The mountain-girl smiled tentatively. "I think Rangua is a good place to be leaving, just now. But what takes you to Palhoa?" She was pretty. There was something about her features—her graceful neck, long eyelashes and full lips—which made a connection in Astrud's mind.

The mountain-girl was a Specialist. She had vicuna genes. In her sheltered existence Astrud had rarely encountered her race.

She instinctively pulled the hood tightly around her face as she realized for the first time that she was surrounded by llamoids—eyes heavy-lidded, heads carried high. She hoped Raoul would have the sense to keep his mouth shut. For herself, she was not used to being among a crowd of Specialists and she found the situation oppressive as well as fearful. Once you recognized them, Specialists looked more like animals than human beings. Tonio probably didn't notice; he stared straight ahead, lost in thought. The mountain-girl was waiting for a reply.

Astrud panicked. "My husband is surveying the old sailway above Palhoa."

Then the girl's companion spoke, and her attention was diverted.

Out of the corner of his mouth, Tonio asked, "Why in hell did you have to say that? She may remember, if anyone asks her."

Her fear turned to annoyance. "Well, why are we going to Palhoa, anyway?"

"It was the Canton Lord's idea, and it has its conveniences. I know the old track up there well."

Raoul asked, "What kind of traction did they use?"

"Shrugleggers, mules. . . . Not like this line. Here, the wind always blows up the valley so the car carries big square sails for the inland run, then rolls downhill back to the coast. Above Palhoa, it's too steep for sails."

"Do you think everything will be all right, Tonio?" asked Astrud for the tenth time.

He gave her his watery smile. "Of course it will."

In the valley of lakes above Palhoa, there was a mystery. There were tapirs and hoatzins, capybaras and jaguars, marmosets and seriemas, common animals, rare animals, and fish too—and there was the Dedo. All living in perfect balance, century after century, with nothing gained, nothing lost. Some lived short lives, some long. Some evolved, some held their own, some died out.

One animal was like no other, and it lived a very long time. Even the omniscient Rainbow had no record of its origin, nor of its death—so, for all we know, it may still be there. The Song of Earth mentions this animal obliquely in an early couplet:

"Above the silver ocean and below the mountain's peak,
There dwells a sacred animal of which men rarely speak."

The part this animal played in the story of Karina is, however, well known. At this time, the animal was known as Bantus. . . .

Bantus was hungry. Feeling the rumblings in his stomach he padded to the mouth of the cave and regarded the jungle. The rain fell, washing away the scents and sounds. He sniffed, snorted and lumbered downhill, following the well-worn trail to the creek. A lone capybara, sensing the hunger of Bantus, took fright and left the trail, trotting piglike into a deeper thicket. Bright macaws watched from branches as the beast passed; they were for once silent, their plumage streaming with rain. Then a tapir, perhaps blinded by the downpour, blundered onto the trail.

And Bantus ignored the beast, almost brushing the tapir aside as he plodded along. The tapir stood stock-still on the trail for a long time afterwards, trembling with terror.

It couldn't know that today was not Bantus' day for tapirs.

Today was fish day. But Bantus did not know who had placed that unusual instinct in his mind. As he descended the hill he passed an overgrown stone dwelling and didn't give it a glance, even though a face of human appearance watched him from the window.

Bantus reached the creek and the little fish were there, but he couldn't see them. The surface of the water was in dancing motion with the rain. Snorting with hunger and annoyance, he made a ponderous slash at a half-seen flash of silver, and his paw came up empty.

The nearby lake was about twenty meters across and quite deep; one of an interlinked system of five small lakes. Above, the stream descended narrow and cold from the mountains. Below, a waterfall fell a hundred meters down an escarpment, sealing off the valley from that direction. How the fish got there, Bantus didn't have the intelligence to ask himself.

Now, irritated, he prowled the banks of the linking streams and soon came across easy prey. A huge fish hovered in the current, facing upstream and totally unaware of his presence. Bantus tensed. He would leap into the center of the stream and straddle the fish—that was the most certain way. The bases of his claws itched.

He sprang.

And something in the very fabric of his cells said: *Today is not the day for Torpad.*

Torpad?

No, he didn't want the big fish today. Someday maybe, quite soon. But today the fish was too big for Bantus' hunger. It would be wasteful to take him.

And Torpad, having no curiosity in his dim senses, fled into the next lake and instantly forgot his narrow escape. Soon he was feeding on small fish—never taking more than he needed—while the smell of mammal washed out of the waters.

Bantus grunted in disgust and plodded away. It was too wet for fish, yet it was no day for meat.

Not in the valley. . . .

But he remembered that food was available outside the valley. He need not be hungry today; not if he climbed the rocky hill towards the brightness. Outside the valley, food was unlimited. He quickened his pace, and soon the wind was cool against his coat as he climbed into the barren ground, leaving the jungle behind.

In Palhoa they bought food, utensils and a llama. They paid the villager well—money was no problem for Tonio—and led the animal away. They soon found that llamas do not necessarily agree with human concepts of ownership, and this particular llama was very much his own animal. He consented to take a small share of their baggage, but any attempt to load him further resulted in a display of sullen temper and spitting, until Astrud said nervously,

"We'll carry the rest. It's not too far, is it?"

"About six kilometers." Tonio shared the remainder of the baggage between them while the llama watched with ill-concealed triumph.

They took a trail into the bush and within minutes were in a different world as the rain forest closed about them. Tonio led, ploughing through the vegetation, Astrud followed, then came Raoul, leading the llama.

That was how the villagers remembered them: squat coastal True Humans walking into the jungle, loaded down with provisions, the boy jerking a reluctant llama behind. They looked completely out of place. There was much speculation. Some said they were spies of the Canton Lord; others, having heard a little of the happenings in Rangua, guessed they were refugees. Later, they learned the truth.

"It doesn't matter," one of the village elders said. "We'll never see them again. *La Bruja* will get them. . . ."

In some places the abandoned sailway had completely disintegrated into the jungle floor, but the route could still be followed and in places the rail supports still stood. Some rails were even in place, a webwork of vines holding the rotting logs together.

"Why did they abandon it?" asked Raoul as they rested, sharing a moss-covered running rail while the llama ruminated nearby.

"They said something in the village about a *bruja*," said Astrud.

"Nonsense!" Tonio said loudly. "Typical Specialist superstition."

His face was red with exertion and he looked unhealthy, *but at least he's lost some of that beaten look,* thought Astrud.

In fact he seemed to have gained in stature since they'd left civilization. He strode ahead again, balancing on fallen rails and eyeing the forest with new interest as they climbed higher. From time to time he would exclaim as he recognized things: marked rocks at the trackside, or the overgrown clearing which denoted an abandoned stage. Astrud drew something from his new confidence, ceased to shy at every yell of the howler monkeys, and even took in her stride the unearthly rattling roar of a jaguar.

"It's nature," Tonio said. "We have to get along with it, if we're going to survive. In some ways, the kikihuahuas were right. They say you could put a kikihuahua down anywhere and he'd fit in, and he'd have the animals and plants working for him in no time." Incongruously he slapped at a mosquito, examined the little smear of blood on his palm, and swore.

Fitting into his mood, she quoted:

"They float about the Greataway, their ships are monster bats.
Live hemitrexes cook their food, their clothes are made by rats."

It was a childish rhyme which her mother had told her, years ago; but somehow it had stuck in her mind.

Before the last words had died away into the wetness of the jungle, Tonio stopped. "What's that?"

"What?"

He stood tense and staring, watching a part of the forest where the trees thinned out and a rocky ridge could be seen. They had climbed out of the clouds and the ridge baked in the afternoon sun, brilliant beyond the darkness of the jungle. "I saw something . . . big."

"They say jaguars don't attack in daylight."

"This was not a jaguar." He was whispering, watching the ridge, while he fumbled blindly with the fastenings of his pack.

"What was it, then?" She was whispering too, and the fear had returned. She watched as he stole quick glances at his pack, drawing out a leather sheath while he continued to keep the jungle under observation.

"It was gray and . . . enormous. I only caught a glimpse, you know? Its head—it seemed to be all teeth! Agni, what a brute!"

She watched in horrified realization as he began to screw pieces together. The thing was metal. Touched by Agni. He'd carried it all this way.

"Tonio!"

"Shut up!"

"Maquinista gave you that," said Raoul quietly, flatly.

Tonio didn't reply to that. His instrument was complete. He hefted it in his hand, fitted a bolt, then sighted at the trees. He was trembling—and suddenly Astrud knew it was excitement, not fear. He was actually enjoying this moment of danger. "This was bigger than any bear—more like a huge caiman with long thick legs and gray hair. It ran down the ridge, fast, on its hind legs. I've never seen an animal run so fast." Suddenly he brandished the crossbow. "Come on, you bastard! I'm ready for you!"

Raoul said unhappily, his eyes on the bow, "You could have been mistaken. It could have been quite small, really. Or two animals running together. Giant anteaters."

He uttered a bark of derision. "In the mountains? I don't think so. Well, we can't wait for him. We'll see him again, I'm sure of that. And when we do. . . ." He waved the crossbow like a banner.

"Have . . . have you noticed how quiet the forest is? Even the monkeys." Raoul followed him, jerking at the llama's rope. The animal's reluctance had become more marked.

Astrud stood staring after them and, in a moment, followed.

The track steepened as they pushed on—then, before Astrud realized it, they had reached their destination. The ground levelled out. There was an old signal tower which had almost become part of the jungle; just four more creeper-entwined trunks among many, and she had to follow Tonio's finger carefully before she could make out the rectangular shape of the cabin among the branches.

"They'll never find us here," said Tonio.

"Are you sure it's safe?" Raoul asked. "It looked very old."

Tonio was already climbing the ladder, testing each rung. "I'll have to replace a few, but they'll be all right for the time being. Come on up, Raoul. Tie the llama to that post." His face looked down through a mass of foliage. Raoul ran nimbly up.

"Come on, mother!"

So she climbed, in fear of each rotting step, and stood in the cabin which was to be her home. The roof had fallen in and the floor was slippery with stinking, decayed fruit. It couldn't have been more than four meters across, and much of that space was taken up with the controls for the lamp: wooden levers and a ladder leading upwards. She knew nothing of signalling. The cabin was incomprehensible, dank and frightening.

"Not bad," said Tonio, kicking away filth and unrolling his blanket on the floor.

They ate a supper of dried fruit and it seemed to Astrud that the shadows were full of moving things. Afterwards, it took a long time for her to get to sleep although the other two were snoring lightly within a short while of lying down. She lay awake listening to the menacing sounds of the jungle night and watching the sleepy movements of a colony of spider monkeys silhouetted against the stars. When eventually she slept, she was soon awakened by a commotion on the forest floor.

Tonio, opening an eye, said, "Only a jaguar hunting. We're safe up here."

It didn't reassure her at all. She dreamed of jungle cats, and in her sleeping mind they gained a new dimension of menace.

And Tonio ran with them, waving a brand from which flared the Wrath of Agni.

The battle for Rangua.

Iolande's grupo scored the first successes.

The True Humans' makeshift militia had been strengthened by farmers and others from the foothills and delta regions, and by the time the first attacks came most of the perimeter was covered by lookout emplacements at strategic locations, backed by large reserves within the town itself.

Iolande's grupo overran one of these emplacements. They'd approached upwind, smelled True Humans from some distance away then, with the utmost caution, crept nearer until they could hear snatches of conversation. The enemy were located in a small thicket, lying down, scanning the foothills. The sun, breaking out for a moment, glinted on something which Iolande guessed to be a hemitrex for use in signalling back. She motioned her grupo to lie still. The others were further away to her left, grupos creeping down the run-off gullies like clawed fingers reaching for the town.

Iolande glanced upwards. Although hidden from the True Humans, they were in full view of the signal tower. She could see the tiny head of a signalman, and wondered whose side he would be on. Then, parting the grasses before her, she surveyed the thicket again.

There were four of them in there; three men and a woman. They were farmers; their scent told her that. They would be accustomed to defending their crops and livestock against marauding animals. They would have weapons, and they would know how to use them. Iolande had her ironwood sword, but this weapon was more traditional than practical. When it came to fighting, she would use fingers and toes. She felt an enormous excitement, and a great pride in her grupo— the best she'd ever mothered. She glanced around at them as they crouched behind her, eyes slitted, nostrils flared, urinating quietly as they wound themselves up for the charge. Iolande chuckled, a small purr of delight. She'd taught them well. Away to the left, she heard a brief scuffle. Another grupo had attacked.

"Now," she said.

Screeching, she bounded forward like a charging tiger, hitting the first man squarely in the chest as he rose from the ground. He went over backwards and she went with him, her fingers hooked into his shoulders, her knees bent and her toes slashing at his belly. She felt warmth as her toenails bit into flesh and the man groaned, falling back, his body slack, staring incredulously at his own intestines spilled out over the wet ground. His eyes met hers, and there was a cowlike bewilderment in them. He said quietly, "Why . . . ?" and then he died with a small sigh.

Iolande turned in time to knock aside a quick thrust from a short dagger and, as the other woman fell forward, she slashed at her throat and saw blood spurt. "Mordecai!" she swore. "Can't you protect my back?" One of her grupo grinned sheepishly; she'd missed her spring and the True Human woman had slipped away from her.

The other two men were already dead; one had his neck broken and the other lay face-down in a lake of blood.

"We did it!" said Iolande. Her eyes were shining, her face pale with excitement. "This time it was for real, and we did it!"

"But. . . ." The felina who'd mistimed her leap looked unhappy. "Didn't El Tigre say we shouldn't kill unless we had to?"

"Piss on El Tigre! This is what we were created for, don't you see? Generations of play-fighting, and now this. Next, we go into town and take them apart!"

"Iolande!" It was a gasp of horror. Iolande, without thinking, had slaked her thirst with a cupped handful of blood.

She looked at her hands in mild surprise, then said, "True Humans created us, and now they have to take the consequences. If you don't like it, Lastima, you're not the felina I took you for."

"But *this*. . . ." Lastima indicated the carnage.

"Ha!" Iolande picked up the dagger the True Humans woman had used. She turned it over in her hand. It was not obsidian, as she'd first supposed. "Look at this," she said quietly. "See? This blade has been wrought by the Wrath of Agni. Well, now. Isn't that something? And see—the spear, this tip? And another knife here. . . . Lastima! You have no stomach for this fight—so here's what you can do. Take these weapons to El Tigre, say where we found them—and *then* listen to his views on killing. If I know El Tigre as well as I think I do, he's going to change his mind pretty damned quickly!"

So Lastima left. The remainder of the women advanced to the sailway track and began to move north to link up with the other grupos.

The felinas made swift gains elsewhere, too. Tamaril, another of El Tigre's erstwhile mates, had a larger army than Iolande. Although her discipline was not so effective and she lost contact with seven grupos early on, she pressed home her raid into the eastern outskirts of Rangua, cleaning out a number of houses and advancing until stopped by solid barricades and massed defenders. A hundred felinas paused, spitting fury, as they faced over two hundred True Humans on the other side of piled furniture and vehicles, in a narrow street. Knives, swords and spears glittered in the hands of the defenders.

"Charge!" yelled a felina who had no right to give orders, and she paid the penalty as she ran forward alone. She reached the top of the barricade in one leap, then died as a spear was thrust into her belly from below.

"Wait!" shouted Tamaril. With some difficulty she achieved a withdrawal and regrouped her forces behind a projecting wall. "This isn't our kind of fight," she said. "Right now, the True Humans have all the advantages. But if we hold on here, and wait until dark. . . ."

The felinas grinned as they visualized the night fighting.

"True Humans don't see well in the dark," somebody said, shivering with anticipation.

A single voice was raised in opposition, like Lastima who was at that moment making her way sadly back towards the main force under El Tigre. The felina said, "I. . . . I think I killed a woman in one of those houses back there. I kind of lost control. El Tigre wouldn't like it, if he found out. The Examples. . . ."

"Shut up," said Tamaril.

"But if we attack in the dark. . . . There's no knowing what. . . ."

232

Tamaril said, "Most of us have killed back there, you fool. That's what war is all about. My main concern is, what's happened to the rest of our grupos? I lost contact when we reached the first houses." She glanced around the wall. The defenders stood grimly behind their barricades, waiting for the felinas to come to them. Behind them, stilted above the low buildings, was the signalbox. "El Tigre should have made plans for that box," she said.

In fact, El Tigre had. At that moment Teressa was climbing the ladder, followed by Karina and Runa. Around the base of the tower stood a circle of felinas facing outwards, while groups of True Humans hovered in doorways of the houses opposite, muttering but unable to take any positive action. The thrust had come too quickly, straight up the hill, hidden by the long grass on the far side of the sailway track.

Teressa kicked open the cabin door.

This time, however, there was no opposition from the little signalmen. They sat on tiny seats which jutted from the walls, their hands folded and their heads bowed in attitudes of defeat.

"Send a signal to Torres for relaying right down the coast," said Teressa. "Tell them the felinos have risen against True Human rule. Tell them the days of slavery are over, and that half of Rangua is in felino hands. Tell them to rise up themselves. Tell them El Tigre has spoken."

One little man looked up, the ghost of a smile on his hatchet face. "Tell the sun to come out."

"Well, by the Genes of Mordecai, you're supposed to be the experts!"

"We borrow from the sun, but we can't command it." The signalman quoted an old Guild saying. Outside, the rain drizzled down. Above the box, little puddles of water had gathered in the blind, upturned eyes of the hemi-trexes.

"We're wasting our time with these fools, Tess," said Runa.

Karina, staring out over the town in the hope of catching sight of fierce fighting, said, "Look!"

The Palhoa car, sails furled, was rolling gently down the grade towards the station.

"Send the signal just as soon as you have enough sun, signalmen!" commanded Teressa. "We have other things to do. But we'll send some felinas up here to make sure you do as you're told."

The El Tigre grupo hurried towards the station. They passed several grupos on the way; members of Iolande's army holding their positions having eliminated the True Human outposts, but unwilling to cross the street to attack the heavily-fortified houses.

They met Iolande at the station. "We're waiting until dark," she said. "We'll wipe them out, then."

"Where are the prisoners?" asked Karina. She'd always mistrusted the tall woman and, for a moment, doubted whether Iolande had encountered any opposition at all.

Iolande merely smiled, however, not deigning to reply. She lifted a hand and, with a sliver of wood, began ostentatiously to clean her fingernails of reddish-brown residue.

The sailcar rumbled into the platform and braked to a halt. Karina swung herself to the deck and descended to the open nose.

"You know Captain Tonio?" she asked the captain.

"Of course."

"Did you take him up to Palhoa this morning?"

"Well. . . ." The man hesitated, made nervous by the oppressive combination of sexuality and violence which this cat-girl brought to his cabin. "There were a lot of people leaving Rangua—there were rumors of trouble, you see. The car was full. I didn't pay too much attention. . . ."

"I think you're lying," said Karina frankly.

"No! I can assure you. . . ." There was dried *blood* on the girl—and what was happening outside? There were felinas on the platform, and along the track!

"Yes," said Karina, following his gaze. "Things have been moving around here since you left. You're in occupied territory, captain. In fact you're my prisoner, and so are your crew. You're our only prisoners, because I suspect the others are all dead. Somehow, our grupos don't seem to understand the concept of prisoners. But then, what do you expect from ignorant animals?"

The captain said, surprisingly, "I don't think you're an ignorant animal. I think you're a beautiful woman."

"Well, thanks." Karina was taken completely off-guard. "All the same, I—"

"My name's Guantelete," said the man. "If I tell you what you want to know, will you guarantee the safety of my crew?"

Somehow the initiative seemed to be slipping away from Karina. She said, recovering, "I'm not guaranteeing anything!"

"Then I'm not telling anything."

"Oh. Well, all right, then. I'll make sure nobody harms you."

Guantelete regarded her sadly. Why did it have to be like this? The girl was a vision of loveliness and he was a sentimental middle-aged man who had been relegated to the Palhoa backwater because of his failing ability to cope with the rigors of the coastal run. He would have liked to be friends but now, apparently, there was war between them. And worse, he had to betray Tonio because it was the lesser of two evils.

"Tonio was on the morning car," he said.

"And his wife and son?"

"Yes."

"All right. You'd better come with me. I'll have to find somewhere to lock you up."

"There's something else. My wife, she lives in the town. I wonder, could you. . . ."

"I'll make sure she's all right."

"Bring her to me. You see, you're going to need me and my crew to take you up to Palhoa on the morning breeze. Then, I think we'll stay there for a while until things blow over down here."

Karina bristled. "Blow over? Nothing's going to blow over. This is the revolution! Nothing will ever be the same again!"

"Of course it won't," said Captain Guantelete pacifically, and gave her instructions where his wife could be found. "I'm sure you'll have captured the whole town by morning," he said.

"You're not very loyal to your people."

"Just practical."

As Karina led Captain Guantelete and his crew along the platform, she noticed an odd thing. The Canton Lord's private car was still there, and the guards were shaking out the sails ready to depart. But nobody was making any attempt to stop them. Iolande was talking to her grupo, and although her gaze rested on the huge figures a couple of times, she made no move. It was as though the revolution flowed around the guards; as though their awesome power rendered them automatically neutral.

Yet she knew—and her father had said many times—that the main objective of the revolution would be to overthrow the Canton Lord.

How could they do that, if they were afraid to capture just two of his guards?

Shortly afterwards El Tigre brought the main force up the hill and they set up camp for the night in the southwest corner of the town, around the base of the signal tower. They hung skins from the sailway guiderails to form tents for the bachelors, the children and the mothers, and any others who did not care to join in the fighting. Nobody was forced to fight. El Tigre had enough willing warriors with the grupos.

As darkness fell, the reports started coming in.

Dozo had accomplished his mission. By mid-afternoon he'd held a meeting of tumpiers and put the situation to them. Following this, he's entered the Womens' Village in the company of the Madre and addressed the Women. It seemed to him that both audiences were somewhat unenthusiastic—he'd been used to felino meetings, with their roars of acclamation—and this was something of an anti-climax.

"They don't seem to care," he said to his henchman.

This was probably fair comment. The tumpiers were philosophical people and used to regarding life in the long-term. Rulers would come and rulers would go, but the span of tumpier existence was dependent on the tumps themselves.

Tamaril sent word back that she was holding her position inside the eastern borders of the town, that she'd joined up with the errant grupos, and that she would attack around midnight over the rooftops, coming down behind the barricades. All was well and the grupos in good spirits. There had been little loss of felina life. . . .

Iolande's front had now joined the main body so that the felinos were in command of the entire western side of the town, from the station to the signalbox, including the sailway and a few buildings. The town was thus cut off from the Palace further west.

The iron weapons captured by Iolande were examined and discussed. Like the earlier news that the tortugas were, in fact, animals, this was seen as merely another example of True Human perfidy. It did not present any immediate danger. At close range, an iron dagger was little more effective than ironwood or obsidian. The weapons did not cause anything like the furor which occurred when the remains of *Rayo* were found to contain metal bearings. . . .

"When we rule the Canton," El Tigre had roared, "The Examples will be law! The kindling of the Wrath of Agni will be punishable by death!"

So the discussions continued, and as night deepened the grupos crept among the houses, infiltrating the barricades and scaling the walls. Every so often a muffled gurgle would be heard, as some True Human guard fell and bled his life away; and sometimes a screech startled the night when a felina's enthusiasm overcame her caution; but El Tigre thought little of this.

He was more concerned about the situation in the delta. He'd heard no news from Manoso since the morning.

Torpad.

Shocked, they regarded the carcass of the llama.

"That's a jaguar did that," said Tonio. "I'm going to kill the brute, you'll see." The excitement was in him again, and he looked alert and refreshed after the night's sleep. "Today I'll go hunting."

Astrud said dully, "The Examples." Her dream was still vividly in her mind; Tonio and the cats, hunting together. "Of course you can't *hunt*. Don't be stupid, Tonio."

238

He glanced at her. "Survival," he said. "You're going to have to change your ideas, Astrud. We don't have time to plant crops up here. It's primitive, violent—don't you feel it?"

Raoul had been examining the remains of the llama. "This wasn't a jaguar's kill, father. Look at the way the thigh bones have been bitten through. A jaguar couldn't do that."

The smell of blood, the smell of death, the smell of decaying vegetation, and the monkeys chattering in the trees overhead. Astrud suddenly clapped her hands to her ears.

"I can't stand it! Take me home, Tonio! Anything is better than this!"

Ignoring her, Tonio bent to examine the carcass. It was an unusual kill. The llama had been forcibly dismembered and the bones chewed. Very little flesh remained; the few shreds were crawling with ants.

"Can I come with you, father?"

"No. You stay behind. Somebody has to look after your mother."

After a breakfast of dried fruit, Tonio climbed to the signal light and detached a hemitrex from its mounting. Then he found a patch of forest floor where the sun slanted through the trees and used the shell to focus the rays onto a little heap of tinder. Soon a fire was burning, the smoke curling up among the branches.

By now, Astrud was past speaking, huddled against the ladder, eyes wide with shock.

"See it doesn't go out," said Tonio to Raoul and, taking up his crossbow, headed off into the forest.

As he walked, he wondered at the sense of well-being which flowed through him. He felt as though he was one with the jungle; a predator just as much in his element as the jaguar. He moved quietly through the trees and soon reached the barren ridge he'd seen the previous day. He climbed into the morning heat and, arriving at the crest, sat down on a rock.

More jungle lay before him, a forested valley very similar to the one he'd left, sandwiched between saw-edged ridges and ending on the seaward side in a sheer escarpment. He could hear a waterfall and, through the trees, he caught a glimpse of a small lake. There would be fish.

Some time later he came to a clearing in the valley floor and the tiny lake lay before him, sparkling in the sun. He knelt and peered into the water. Sure enough, small fish swam there, each about as long as his forearm —easy targets for his crossbow. He slipped in a bolt, took aim and shot.

Thunk! As the ripples cleared, he could see a fish transfixed, thrashing on a bolt which pinned it to the mud. He reached in and drew it out, removed the bolt and laid the fish on the bank.

"What are you doing?"

Startled, he looked up. A girl stood there. She wore a long black dress and her hair was drawn back from her face and fastened above her neck. He found himself staring. There was an unearthly beauty about her, and something touched a memory from the past. There was no trace of expression on her face, and this he remembered, too.

But it couldn't be. This girl was no more than twenty years old. . . .

"I said, what are you doing?" she repeated without impatience, as though she had all the time in the world.

"Well, fishing. We're staying over the ridge—you know, the old sailway track? We're living in the signal cabin—well, it's not very comfortable, but we'll soon have it fixed up. . . . Haven't I seen you somewhere before?"

"You can't fish in this valley."

"But there aren't any pools in our valley—just a small stream. Drinking water, that's all we've got. You live here, do you? Surely you can spare some of your fish—there are plenty. I saw them."

"I can spare them. But the animals who live here can't spare them. Neither can the big fish, Torpad, spare them."

"Listen, I don't know what you're talking about. Fish are fish. They're there to be caught." He wound up the crossbow, took aim and shot.

He missed.

The fish darted away as the bolt hit the water. He shot again, and missed again. Sweating and becoming annoyed, he looked up at the girl. "Go away, will you! You're scaring the fish!"

She didn't move.

He unleashed shot after shot into the pool, and now his bolts were disappearing into the mud so that he could not retrieve them. The fish were still there but they could not be caught. Finally, hot and enraged, he was out of bolts.

"So now you'd better go back to the signal cabin," said the girl placidly.

"But I'll be back!" he blustered, a beaten True Human around thirty-five years physical, too ready to submit, feeling an odd need to weep as he strode away.

Now, as he walked with empty bow, the game abounded. Deer wandered across the trail, fat birds perched on nearby branches and watched him. Soon he came to a stream and a huge fish was there, just idling in the current, begging to be shot. He regarded it for some time, and as he stood there in the suddenly-silent forest a name came into his head.

Torpad.

The fish was gigantic. It would provide food for days, and all he needed was just one bolt. Again he felt a compulsion to weep. Everything was against him. He jumped into the water after the fish, but it evaded him easily. He walked on empty-handed and by the time he arrived back at the cabin it was late afternoon.

"Did you get anything?" Raoul asked.

"No."

Now Astrud spoke for the first time in hours. "Good."

"There was a girl."

"A girl?" Astrud showed dull surprise.

"Over in the next valley, a girl living alone. She was . . . strange. She scared me, in a way." The beaten look was back; the crowsfeet, the sudden feeble grin.

"How old was she?"

"Oh. . . . Twenty, maybe. It wasn't easy to tell."

"Was she pretty?"

"And there was this fish—it was huge. We could have fed off it for days, but I had no more bolts left. She didn't want me to catch fish, or anything else. She wanted the whole valley to herself. I'll show her. Tomorrow I'm going right back there and I'm going to get that fish."

"I don't want you to go back there," said Astrud.

It was at that time that Raoul began seriously to consider the possibility that the stress of recent events had driven his father insane.

That night Astrud relived the strangeness of her day; the hours in and around the tower, the terror of the Wrath of Agni in the glade, the queer threatening noises from the forest, the sudden scuttlings nearby. She'd cleaned out the cabin and fixed part of the roof with branches and overlapping leaves. Raoul had helped her, saying little. In the forest close by Raoul had found a relic of the past: an old sailcar, overgrown but still intact, lying on rotting rails. He'd gone inside, disturbing a sounder of peccaries which scampered off into the jungle, scaring her—she must remember to tell Tonio about it in the morning, take his mind off that girl—and she and Raoul had sat in the tiny forecabin, remembering the past, imagining phantom rails flying by, the tramping of the crew on the deck above, Tonio's quick warm smile when something pleased him. . . .

Tonio was different, now. Astrud had noticed a big change, too.

Whimpering, she awakened and looked around with wide eyes.

By morning Tonio's determination had increased. "Tonight we eat fresh fish," he said, slipping crossbow bolts into his pack. "You'll see."

"I'd rather you didn't go. Oh, Tonio—there are some peccaries near! Raoul came across a whole herd of them in an old sailcar, in the bush over there!"

"I'll shoot one tomorrow." Shouldering the crossbow, he strode off into the forest.

"Oh!" Unwittingly, Astrud had sentenced a peccary to death. . . .

It was raining, but the ridge was already warming up as the sun tried to burn away the clouds. Tonio descended the other side—and now, as he re-entered the rain forest, the place seemed to hold a different atmosphere. The air was fresh instead of fetid. The cries of the parrots were musical rather than harsh. The rain dripped softly through the leafy canopy and the other sounds—the animals and reptiles moving through the bush—were no longer menacing.

He was welcome.

He reached the nexus of pools and began to search the

interconnecting streams. The water was clear despite the rain and Tonio became aware of an unusual sensation. It was a feeling of total certainty: he was going to catch that big fish, Torpad. The feeling was so definite that it was almost as though the event had already occurred.

And on many happentracks it had. A few Tonios had failed, a few had even drowned, and one had received a slashing bite from the fish which would turn septic and ultimately cause his death. But in general the fish had been caught.

Tonio saw Torpad. The great fish hovered in his accustomed position, facing the flow of water, keeping station with minimal fin movement. Tonio loaded his crossbow and knelt on the bank directly above the fish, which gave no indication of fear.

Tonio shot.

Torpad thrashed on the bright pebbles of the stream bed, while a mist of scarlet flowed away. His tail came clear of the surface and water sprayed about. Tonio made ineffectual grabbing motions, *nearly* overbalanced, *nearly* received a bite; then, satisfied the fish was securely pinned by the bolt, sat back to wait for him to tire.

"So you killed Torpad."

The flat tones of the girl came just as Tonio was wading into the stream to claim his prize.

"I said I would, didn't I?"

"And you did."

"Well. . . . He didn't even try to get away." Tonio laid the fish on the bank; it was well over a meter long. "He just stayed there as though he wanted to be caught."

She said seriously, with no trace of anger or recrimination, "Perhaps he did. Perhaps he knew his time had come, and he wanted to get it over with. But those little fish you were after yesterday—perhaps their time *hadn't* come."

"I knew I'd get him."

"You didn't know yesterday. It was only this morning that you knew—when the number of possible happentracks had diminished enough to make the Ifalong easy to foretell."

He stared at her. The words were strange, yet they made a kind of sense. "Are you saying its possible to forecast the future?"

Her face was like a stone. "Nothing so precise. But it is possible to foretell the Ifalong." Now she smiled, but there was no humor in it at all. "Come with me. You must be tired and hungry after your walk. My cottage is near."

"You mean you could foretell *my* future?" he asked, trotting behind her like a pet animal, the fish forgotten beside the stream. She was young and very attractive, this girl, and she couldn't possibly be the same one who had given him the infant Raoul, all those years ago. But the resemblance was uncanny. . . .

The pursuit.

The battle for Rangua was virtually over by daybreak. Under cover of darkness the grupos had infiltrated the True Human lines and attacked from behind with terrifying ferocity. Although outnumbered by five to one the felinas had the advantage of superior night vision and, in the confusion, many True Human casualties had been inflicted by their own people hacking with swords at anything that moved.

Barricade after barricade surrendered and the prisoners were herded into the inn and other buildings on the main street. The felinas were not compassionate jailers. Their fighting instincts were still aroused and they were quick to punish anything which remotely resembled an attempt to escape. In point of fact no True Humans *wanted* to escape. The dark interior of the inn was a blessed sanctuary after the streets with their murderous, half-seen predators.

Shortly before dawn, Iolande reported to El Tigre.

"The northern half of the town is ours. Should we move south, or wait for Tamaril to work her way up to us?" She was panting with excitement and drenched with blood; an unnerving sight in the early half-light.

It was probably at this moment that the first intimations of disaster came to El Tigre. . . .

"Wait," he said.

"We could fan out north, mop up the farms and link up with Manoso in the delta." Iolande was unwilling to stop fighting. Only her affection for El Tigre—and a certain fear of him—had prompted her to report back at all. Now she wanted to return to the battle.

"No. Hold your positions. Have there been . . . ? How many died?"

"No more than necessary," she answered. She gave him a quick hug which left a dark stain on him, then ran swiftly back to her forces.

As the sun rose out of the ocean El Tigre was watching from the top of the signal tower. The town was quiet; all fighting seemed to have ceased. Nearby, a great crowd of silent True Humans spilled out of the door of the inn and nearby houses, guarded by felinas. El Tigre wondered at their silence. It was though they were in the grip of a kind of mass shock. Even the children made little sound.

There was no joy in El Tigre as he descended the ladder, having seen Iolande and Tamaril heading towards the tower. They had obviously linked up, the battle was over, Rangua was theirs. A single cry of desolation rose from somewhere in the town like the crowing of a lonely cockerel. What about Manoso? Why was he silent? And in the foothills, the Palace. How should he approach that problem?

By the time he reached the foot of the ladder Karina, Teressa and Runa were there. His girls. . . . He put his huge arms around them, feeling better, for a moment.

Karina said, "I think we've won, father."

"That may be."

Now Torch, Iolande and Tamaril arrived, looking alert and ferocious despite having been busy all night.

"You must come and address the prisoners, El Tigre," said Torch. "We must make our position clear —this is no temporary occupation. We must get certain guarantees out of them before we allow them to go home. We must assign responsibilities—"

"Yes, yes. First I'd like to inspect the town."

"Of course." Torch understood. It was natural that El Tigre should wish to gloat over the scene of conquest.

"Father," said Karina, "we've captured the captain and crew of the Palhoa car. Can we get them to take us to Palhoa now? We must get after Tonio while the scent's still warm."

El Tigre looked at her, shaking his head slightly like a baffled bull. "No—come with me first. There's plenty of time for Tonio." And he thought: *I need you with me for a while, children.* . . .

So they paced down a nearby street; El Tigre with his head thrust forward, his grupo glancing at him and each other nervously; Torch, Iolande and Tamaril with light step and an air of pride and excitement. The barricade in this street consisted of a row of ox- and mule-carts, with pieces of furniture pushed into the gaps: chairs, cupboards, a baby's crib with the blanket still in it, tables, beds, anything which had come readily to hand. There was something pathetic about the futility of this barricade. It might have stopped a runaway tapir, but felinas . . . ?

El Tigre sprang lightly to the top, standing on an ox-cart.

A score of twisted bodies lay on the ground beyond.

They lay as they had died, hunched around terrible lacerations, in puddles of blood now turned to jelly and glistening in the new sun, surrounded by trampled entrails. They were both sexes and all ages. They hadn't stood a chance.

Iolande jumped to the ground. "See, El Tigre?" She held up a metal knife. "You see the kind of two-faced bastards we're dealing with?"

The others joined her, stepping carefully through the carnage.

El Tigre said nothing.

Karina gulped, and walked away. She looked at the sky, clean and bright and blue, the clouds of yesterday gone. *What's the matter with me?* she wondered.

"Let's take a look in there," said El Tigre suddenly, pointing to a house where the door leaned open. . . .

They found the bodies in the bedroom; an elderly man and his wife. It seemed the old couple had locked themselves in and pushed a heavy dresser against the door; it lay on its side nearby. The man lay beside it with his throat slashed open; the door lay across his legs, torn away from its lintels. The woman had tried to get out of the window; the shutter was ajar. She lay in a huddle with her neck twisted back and her eyes open, staring at El Tigre as though in surprised recognition.

He said, "Why?"

"Well, hell, what do you expect?" Iolande answered briskly. "Have you ever tried to control a dozen grupos with the smell of blood in their nostrils? Have you ever tried to control *one?* All right, so a felina got a little out of hand in here. It's a small price to pay."

They left the house and walked on, but now El Tigre insisted they examine the whole town, house by house. He wanted to see the results of the battle personally, before anything was removed.

He saw enough to sicken him of revolution forever.

The barricades were bad enough, with their heaps of corpses and pools of blood; but at least the people there had died fighting. It was in the houses where the pathos lay; where the elderly and the children had barred the doors only to have them broken down by the powerful felinas; and where, in all too many cases, the felinas— already crazed with blood lust—had gone berserk.

El Tigre was relentless, and saw it all.

Some time in the afternoon Iolande said, "All right, all right!" and she began to cry. She collapsed on a doorstep, her head in her hands.

Tamaril, who had been silent for a long time, said, "Perhaps we shouldn't reproach ourselves for the way we're made. After all, the great Mordecai Whirst was a True Human."

El Tigre said slowly, "No—the blame lies with us. We didn't understand one another well enough, felinos and felinas. We didn't understand what war meant, because we've never known one. The bachelors wouldn't have done all this, if I'd sent them in instead. But then, the bachelors may not have won the war. Our men are clever and strong, but they are lazy and easy-going. I am such a man, although I drive myself to lead because somebody must. Our women hunt in packs and they're cruel and violent when aroused—and I *knew* that—yet I sent them into Rangua. I must take the blame. I didn't realize what I was doing, because we've never fought a real war before, and we didn't know our own strength. But I should have known. I should have seen what I was committing the Canton to, once the revolution became more than just my talk.

"Iolande—stop snivelling and get up. Last night you did what you were born to do—only daylight has changed the picture. Now we must face our prisoners. This should be our moment of triumph. This is my moment of vengeance for what they did to Serena." His bitter smile did nothing to hide his sorrow. "But instead I only feel guilt."

Karina said quietly to Teressa, "You and Runa stay with father. I'll go after Tonio alone."

El Tigre, overhearing, said, "More killing?"

"This is a special case." Confused and desperately unhappy, she hurried away. Time was getting on. She'd be lucky if she reached Palhoa by nightfall.

She went to the house where Captain Guantelete and his wife and crew were being held, obtained their release and assured the uncertain grupo guard that she could handle them.

Later, as the great square sails were spread and the car crept into the foothills on the last of the wind, she sat on deck and watched Rangua recede. The True Humans had left their temporary jails now, and were assembled before the signal tower, where her father was addressing them from half-way up the ladder. She hoped her sisters would look after him; right now, he needed their support and affection.

She felt she needed support too; and she was relieved when an ungainly figure came bounding out of the bush and swung itself aboard. It was the Pegman, who had left town in time to avoid the night's killing.

He sat beside her. "So Rangua belongs to the felinos now."

A bluff hid the town from view and the setting sun

illuminated the wetness of the delta region. For a moment she wondered how Manoso had fared. His silence had alarmed El Tigre, who had a vision of Manoso's entire force being wiped out by the ferocious cai-men. Thinking unhappy thoughts, Karina was carried towards Palhoa and her historic meeting with the Dedo.

Years afterwards, they were still telling the story in Palhoa of how the cat-girl had awakened and stood, head high and nostrils flaring as she sniffed the morning air. Her beauty was unearthly, they said, but no man would have gone near her that day—except for the Pegman, a one-armed True Human freak from somewhere down the coast. The cat-girl awakened from where she'd been lying and the vicuna people edged away, tossing their heads. After sniffing she uttered a wordless sound—some said she *roared*—and she plunged into the jungle, followed by the freak. . . .

The Pegman had prevailed upon Karina to spend the night in Palhoa. "I'm beat," he said. "And you must be tired, too. The jungle around Palhoa is dangerous. I know. I've been there. We're going to need our wits about us." So they'd slept on the deck of the car.

In the morning they were climbing, following the overgrown sailway. The scent was cold, but the Pegman assured Karina this was the route Tonio would have taken.

"He may be headed for Buique or even further. He'll be expecting to be followed, for a while at least. He's almost two days ahead of us, but he doesn't know that. Maybe he'll get careless. . . . There are other things besides jaguars here, so they say. . . ."

Karina had been casting around. "Somebody's been this way—look!"

"Do you really want to go through with this,

Karina?" asked the Pegman later, as they sat gnawing at a fungus.

"Is that why you've come? To try to talk me out of it?" Her voice was high. She was much affected by the happenings in Rangua.

"I wouldn't do that." He sat regarding her somberly. He was behaving with unusual normality, and hadn't uttered a single insane yell since entering the jungle. He, like others, had a sense of converging events, of an inevitability in recent happenings which even his mad clowning could not disturb. "You have to make up your own mind, Karina."

"I've made it up. I made it up when I found Saba dead."

"So you will kill Tonio. Will you kill his wife and son, too?"

"Of course."

"What did they ever do to you?"

"If you want to stay with me," Karina cried suddenly, "You'd better keep your damned mouth shut, Pegman!" Her eyes were bright with tears.

Picking up the scent.

After a while Tonio found he was talking about himself, telling this girl the story of the disaster. When he'd finished, she said,

"If it's any consolation to you, Tonio, consider that on many happentracks the guiderail didn't give way, and the people of Torres lived. Consider also, that on a few happentracks you rose to become a Company man, even in a couple of instances rising to the position of second-in-command to Silva. Consider again," she added quietly, "that none of this matters, because the

252

Fifty Thousand Years' Incarceration has run more than half its course, and within twenty millennia the Triad will free Starquin to roam the Greataway once more."

He glimpsed a vastness. "In the Ifalong," he said.

"We work towards that day."

"And what about me?" His chest was tight. "What happens to me?"

"Many things."

"Yes, but what's the *norm?* What might I expect?"

It was late afternoon already; where had the day gone? The rain had stopped and a fresh breeze stirred the trees outside the cottage. The birds were screeching in anticipation of night and the jaguars stretched and unsheathed their claws, limbering up for the evening hunt. And another creature stirred too; a huge beast, the only one of his kind.

Leitha said, "You will take your place in the scheme of things."

"What do you mean?"

"Tonio, you've been at odds with your surroundings for some time now. You must have known it yourself— you've been fighting things instead of going with the flow. Soon, things will be different."

As he left, he said, "You didn't mind me shooting the fish, then?"

"Mind? No, I don't *mind.* Today you shot the fish. It is a fact, and it was going to be a fact before it happened. It makes no difference to the overall scheme—in fact, it's part of the scheme."

He walked away, musing on the disturbing fatalism of those words. He was almost back at the signal cabin before he realized he'd left the fish behind. Astrud greeted him, and immediately accused him.

"You've been with that girl!"

"I talked to her, yes." He was abstracted, still back at

253

the strange cottage in spirit, still seeing the girl's cold face.

"It's not like you're thinking, Astrud. She's an odd person, but I think she could help us a lot." He leaned out of the window, looking east. It was possible to see where the old sailway had run; the jungle was thinner, the roof of the trees just a little lower. From a certain position he could just see the ocean, probably fifteen kilometers away. "If they ever came after us," he said, "I think she would hide us and look after us."

"Why? Because she likes you?"

"Because it might fit in with the nature of the Ifalong," he said, and she stared at him.

Later Raoul tackled him. "We have to move on, father."

"I think this will suit us fine, Raoul."

"You didn't see the way she looked! She's after us, I know that—and she'll be bringing a few grupos with her!"

"Are you still talking about that *felina*?"

"Yes I am, and I think she's a lot more important than that *bruja* you're always with. It seems to me she's got you twisted around her finger! 'You will take your place in the scheme of things,' mimicked Raoul furiously. "What about us, father? What about mother and me?"

By the Sword of Agni, he thought, *the young bastard's been following me*. Tonio glanced around, saw Astrud was out of earshot, and said, "The jungle is a dangerous place, Raoul. Particularly that valley where the girl lives. You could get yourself killed, going in there." He said this quietly, and there was no doubt as to his meaning. *A different world,* he thought. *Survival of the individual is what counts*.

Raoul had backed off as though Tonio had struck

him, and now he was staring incredulously at him. "Are you threatening me, father?"

"Just pointing out the dangers."

"Right," said Raoul. "I understand. . . ."

They hadn't made such quick progress as Karina had hoped. After a few kilometers' climbing they'd left the sailway on the Pegman's advice, heading south.

"Tonio will have made for Buique," said Enri, but he lied. "This is the quickest way. The sailway took a roundabout route, because of the gradients."

His own fury at the death of Saba had subsided and he was regretting telling the El Tigre grupo where Tonio might be. There had been enough killing. He'd heard some of the screaming from Rangua during the previous night and he knew that, so far, Karina had had no part in it. He wanted it to stay that way.

They spent the night a few kilometers below Buique, having bypassed the area where the Pegman supposed Tonio to be. Congratulating himself, he settled down to sleep. Tomorrow he would continue the wild-goose chase until Karina cooled her intentions. He slept heavily and it seemed only a moment later that it was dawn and Karina was shaking him awake, oblivious of the fact that her breasts jiggled in full view under the loose neck of her tunic.

"Enri! Wake up! Look!" She shook his shoulder violently and he dragged his gaze away from her to look in the direction she indicated.

A wisp of smoke rose above the trees, several kilometers below them.

"We've come too far," said Karina.

"We can't be sure it's them."

"Of course it's them! Who else but a True Human like Tonio would kindle the Wrath of Agni? And now—"

her eyes narrowed to fierce slits as she squinted against the wet brightness of the rising sun "—we've got them! Now we close in. Come on, Enri!"

Resignedly, the Pegman allowed himself to be led downhill, and soon they came across the upper reaches of the old sailway.

"We should never have left the track," said Karina, with a glance at Enri.

"You've met Astrud?" asked the Pegman later.

"No. I've seen her, though."

"She's a nice woman. Simple, really. Very religious—she really believes the Examples. I was in her house once, and I saw texts all over the walls."

"I know. I . . . kind of spied on them a while back, and I saw into the house."

"And you want to kill her."

"*Rayo* had metal bearings! How two-faced can she be!"

"She didn't know. I'll swear to that, Karina."

"Huh."

They scrambled down further, walking in the bed of a little stream which followed the sailway. Then Enri said,

"You know. . . . One time, I thought you rather liked Raoul."

She didn't turn round. "Oh?"

"Well. . . . I hear you rode with him up to Rangua one day—and got into quite some trouble about it, so they say. And you followed him into the delta. . . ."

"And I got caught, and he didn't do a thing to help me! Mordecai, what a creep! He's weak, weak!"

"You're right. He doesn't have the guts to stand up to his father. It's the way True Humans are raised, I suppose."

"Maybe," said Karina.

Later the track levelled out to a platform and there,

barely visible among the dense trees, was a signal tower.

"Look at this, Enri!" Karina stood in a glade. At her feet, the remains of a fire smouldered. "They're here." Her gaze snapped this way and that, finally dwelling thoughtfully on the signal cabin at the top of the tower. "Up there," she said.

But the cabin was empty. There were signs of recent habitation however; some food, skins, and blankets laid on the floor.

"Right," said Karina grimly as they climbed down to the foot of the ladder. "They're not far off, and the trail's still warm. We've got them, Enri. Follow me, and don't think of making any loud noises."

Raising her head, she sniffed the air delicately.

"Are you sure you don't mind?" asked Tonio. "Four fish would probably be enough, but five would be better. They're quite small. My wife, she must learn to eat. . . ."

"The valley will be in balance again before long," Leitha said. "When you arrived there was a certain imbalance, but that will right itself. Meanwhile you can keep the fish."

She looked at him in a way which he might have thought calculating—but dead eyes cannot calculate. His gaze strayed to the water. Today the fishing had been good—and there was another big fish there. He'd seen it. Not so big as Torpad, but big enough.

Yet the blood lust had left him. When he'd successfully shot his first small fish and laid it on the grass there had been no elation; just a relief that his hunger would be appeased.

Suddenly, the Dedo stood, glanced around, then walked off up the trail without a word. He watched her go. It was warm in the sun and he was drowsy. He'd lost all sense of time, but figured he ought to be getting back. The signal cabin had begun to feel like home; although Astrud's mood had become unpredictable, and Raoul was showing signs of youthful rebelliousness. . . .

In fact Astrud was close by at that moment, having tired of fixing up the cabin, and having begun to wonder, not for the first time, just what Tonio spent his days doing.

She emerged from the trees in time to see the Dedo disappearing up the trail. Tonio sat by the stream as though in a trance. He'd taken off most of his clothes and he looked pale and flabby. Rage began to gnaw at her. She stormed down to the riverbank.

"You've been with that girl!"

"Yes."

"Well, it's not right! I've been working back there while you spend your time idling about with some forest girl!"

"I wasn't idling. I caught some fish." He indicated them.

"I won't have you playing around with that girl! Listen, Tonio, I haven't stuck by you all this time for you to run off into the woods with some Specialist."

"Leitha isn't a Specialist."

"And you know all about Specialists, don't you? After all, you killed plenty of them!"

"What's happening here?" Raoul pushed his way out of the bush. "I could hear you a kilometer away."

"Your father's running out on us, that's what!"

There was a strange expression on Tonio's face, and he was blinking rapidly. "I thought I told you not to come this way," he said. "It's dangerous. You could cause an imbalance."

"A what?"

"It's claptrap," said Astrud furiously. "Claptrap he learned from that girl. Since he met her he's been coming out with all kinds of queer things!"

Tonio was blinking at the water. "Nothing to be done. . . ."

"There's one thing to be done. You come with us back to the cabin, right now!"

"Two happentracks. I do, or I don't." A tic was twitching in Tonio's cheek. Soon Astrud might start screaming. It was in the nearby Ifalong.

"Come on, Tonio," she said, suddenly more gentle. "You're not yourself. It's the reaction. The humidity. Come—"

She broke off, staring.

Tonio had picked up one of the fish. It had been dead for a couple of hours and it was stiff. He clutched it in his fist with the head uppermost.

He regarded it thoughtfully.

Astrud was still. Raoul was still. The forest was silent.

Tonio put the head in his mouth and bit it off, with a crunch, just as though he was eating a stick of celery.

Astrud screamed.

Blood trickled down Tonio's chin as he chewed, watching her vacantly. He took another bite, stripping flesh from the backbone. He chewed with his mouth open. His teeth shone crimson with blood while his tongue rolled a wad of flesh and bones.

Raoul uttered a bellow of despair and ran, pushing his way blindly through the undergrowth.

"Listen. . . . What's that?" said Karina.

Away to the left they could hear a crashing as a heavy body plunged through the forest.

"A tapir," said Enri. "There are lots of them around these parts. They get scared by a noise, and they just run off into the bush."

They heard a woman's voice; a low, breathless sobbing.

"Tapir, huh?" said Karina. "Come on. This way.

259

She's headed back to the signal cabin.''

"Just Astrud?" The Pegman stayed where he was. "She's not so important, is she? Tonio's still up ahead. He's the one you really want."

As Karina stood irresolute, staring this way and that into the dense foliage, she caught sight of movement. "Quiet. . . ." she whispered, and began to creep forward, one careful step at a time.

There was the flick of a black cloak, half-seen. Karina crept on, her heart pounding, her fingers hooked into talons. It was Tonio—it had to be. It was too tall for Astrud. A twig snapped under her foot and she swore under her breath; but, a moment later, she saw the quarry again, crossing a clearing where water flowed.

On the ground beside the river lay some dead fish, one of them half-eaten. "See this?" she said to the Pegman as he hurried up. "They're eating meat, now. Hunting, kindling the Wrath of Agni—it shows the kind of things True Humans will do, when they think nobody's watching."

"I'm a True Human," Enri reminded her, not for the first time.

Now Karina began to run, plunging through brush which slashed at her legs, climbing rocks, clawing her way up through the jungle and wondering at her quarry's speed. She climbed on, the Pegman puffing behind her with no pretence at stealth, and emerged into sudden sunshine.

She was standing on a ridge of short grass and rocky outcroppings which marked the northern boundary of the valley. Fifty meters away the cloaked figure stood in the sun.

And between Karina and this figure lay a ravine with sheer walls, a hundred metres deep.

She stared. "How . . . ?" It never occurred to her that

there might have been two cloaked figures and the Dedo, calculating happentracks, slipped away unseen.

The Pegman uttered a wordless exclamation.

The figure was turning round, slowly, to look at them. The cloak fell away from the face, and the sunlight shone on pale skin, jet black hair. It wasn't Tonio.

It was the handmaiden.

The sun lit the eroded fissures of her burned face and the wind caught her hair, lifting it. Karina's eyes narrowed as the light seemed to intensify painfully—and suddenly the handmaiden was beautiful. Karina couldn't see the Marks of Agni any more; only the eyes and the oval outlines of the face; the tall, slim figure and the lifting hair.

And the Pegman was shouting a name, over and over. "Corriente! Corriente!"

The imbalance resolved.

Astrud ran. She blundered through thickets, flung herself across streams, and burst out of the jungle onto the slopes of the ridge. Her mind was afire with horror and disgust. Every rock, every tree was Tonio, his face an animal's face as he munched raw flesh, snorting with gratification. She stumbled up the slope and down the other side, falling several times, picking herself up and plunging on, scratched and bruised, the heat burning the strength out of her.

She had to get back among real people.

She would pick up a few things from the cabin, then follow the track down to Palhoa. She stumbled on, reached the cabin at last, threw herself at the ladder and began to climb.

The ninth rung split.

She fell, seeing Tonio's face in the ground as it rushed up to hit her. Later she climbed again, dragging herself up with arms shaking from the effort, one leg almost useless. She crawled across the cabin floor, caught hold of the control arms and pulled herself to her feet. Holding onto her last glimmer of consciousness she worked the arms, catching the sun's rays in the battery of hemitrexes, directing the beam downhill, noting the way the jungle shadows brightened and following the line until she was sure the people in Palhoa must see the distant blaze of light. . . .

She fell to the floor, and prayed that someone was looking her way. Some kindly mountain-woman, long-necked with head held high, her eye caught by the sudden glare. . . .

Much later she awakened. It was almost dark.

Somebody, something, was in the cabin with her.

"Tonio . . . ?"

"Rest easy for a moment. I've almost done."

It was a woman's voice.

"What . . . what are you doing here? Where's Tonio?"

"You can stand now. Your ankle was badly injured, but I've healed it." Leitha slipped a smooth stone into her pocket and helped Astrud to her feet. "You signalled the village. You shouldn't have done that. It introduces new factors and creates new happentracks. You're not very rational, are you? I have to get you away from here. There is a need for you in the Ifalong."

They walked. The forest was waking up for the night. Astrud's leg felt good and she found time to wonder at the healing powers of this strange girl; then her mind clouded over. This was the woman who had taken Tonio away from her.

"Why did you do it?" she asked.

262

"Don't talk. It isn't safe to be out, tonight. There's an imbalance."

They descended the ridge into the secret valley and it was very dark among the trees, and the animals seemed to be all around them. Astrud started as a tapir, head down, burst from the undergrowth and pounded so close that it brushed her in passing. She waited, shivering, for its pursuer to appear. Leitha drew her on, and soon they were fording a stream.

"What's that?" There was a big shadow on the bed of the stream, and for a terrified instant Astrud thought it was a caiman, about to snap at her.

And Leitha said, "Torpad. . . . He's just a big fish."

Later they reached the stone cottage. It was empty and weirdly illuminated, and again Astrud asked, "Where's Tonio?"

"He's been helping me restore the balance."

"Balance?" Astrud was intimidated by this cold, self-possessed girl. It was quite obvious, now, that Tonio had not been involved with her in any romantic sense. This girl had never had a man, and never would—although she was quite beautiful in an icy way. Astrud had misjudged Tonio. In a moment she would find him, and apologize to him. . . . "Tonio's coming with me. We're leaving."

"Well, that's possible, on certain remote happen-tracks. But very unlikely. The chances are, you will die."

The cold eyes watched her.

"I'm getting out of here!" Astrud ran for the door, suddenly terrified in a mindless way, in the way of a hunted animal.

"You'll only hasten your own end," the Dedo called after her.

So Astrud ran into the night and stood there for a moment, heart pounding, looking this way and that. She didn't know where Tonio was, but she knew she must find him quickly. They had to get out of this valley, away from the threats of this girl. She called his name, listened for a reply, but heard only the sound of night hunting.

"Tonio!" she called again.

There was a bright moon above and she could see well enough to discern a trail leading downhill. She thought it was the one she'd come by, but she couldn't be sure. Had she been in the cottage for long? She broke into a run. She didn't look back.

Leitha was watching her from the doorway; watching and calculating, because that was her Duty. She weighed predator against prey, scavenger against carrion. She considered the grass, and the deer. Her mind dwelt briefly on the ants and the anteater, the tapir and the rainfall. She listened to the wind and the birds, and the sound of Astrud's retreating footsteps.

She contemplated the Ifalong.

Astrud ran.

A jaguar killed a pacarana. . . .

Bantus lumbered through the forest. He ignored the deer which swerved in front of him, and he paid no heed to the tapir which he could hear browsing nearby.

Tonight was fish night.

The certainty was within his being, like a command which he couldn't help but obey. He salivated, anticipating the flavor of fresh blood. There was a *rightness* about the night. He could sense a rhythm and a pattern, and his own place in it.

Something in his mind was saying: *Bantus—tonight is the night for Torpad.*

Karina had to physically restrain the Pegman from attempting to jump the ravine. There was a brief struggle until finally she pinned him to the ground, during which time the handmaiden disappeared.

"She's gone, she's gone. Oh, Corriente!"

"Is that the Corriente you've been talking about all these years?"

"That's her."

"But she's cursed by Agni, Enri," said Karina gently.

"Does that matter? I only have one arm, now."

How can I kill that woman now? Karina wondered. "I think we'll find her easily enough tomorrow."

The Pegman gave a faint smile. "After all these years. . . ." he murmured. "And now, Karina, if you'll kindly get your pretty body off my old one, we can decide what to do next."

"Oh. . . . Of course." She stood, watching him warily. "Maybe we should go back to the signal cabin. Tonio may be there by now." But the urgency was gone. It was late afternoon and warm here on the ridge. She sat beside the Pegman. "Who is this Corriente, anyway? Where did you meet her?"

"Long ago, before you were born, I met Corriente at the Tortuga Festival in Portina, to the south. I was playing a few tunes for the felinos, singing a song or two; while they were laughing at the idea of a True Human entertaining them. A few of them had been drinking and some things were said which were not really meant. I was thinking of moving on. Then Corriente came and sat beside me, and everyone was silent.

"Because she was beautiful, you see—more beautiful than any woman there, even the felinas. She sang with me, and afterwards we enjoyed the Festival together, the feasting and the dancing and the fun. Later, in the moonlight, we made love. In the morning she cried, and I thought it was because . . . well, True Human women sometimes do cry when it's over. So I asked her to be my wife; and she said she couldn't, because she had to marry somebody else.

Karina said, "True Humans make things complicated."

"Maybe, but there are sometimes compensations—although not in my case. It turned out that Corriente was the daughter of the Canton Lord, so I was wasting my time. She went away the next day. There was just one moment when I might have had her. I sat on a mule beside Portina station and watched her and the Lord get aboard the sailcar and I *almost*. . . . She walked past me so close and her eyes met mine, and I *almost* reached down and caught hold of her. . . .

"And I *almost* rode off with her into the hills, and we almost built a little cabin up there, and raised crops and a family, and we almost lived happily ever after." He smiled. "It was so close. All I needed to have done, was to reach out and catch hold of her.

"I've been trying to undo that moment ever since. You've heard of happentracks? Well, I *know* on many happentracks I rode off with Corriente. I could almost feel them there, right next to my life. I've been trying to jump across to one of those happentracks ever since.

"Maybe this time I've done it."

The sun had gone down behind the trees. Karina said, "So you became the Pegman. What happened to Corriente?"

"She died—or so everyone thought. There was an accident to her car on the way to the wedding. They say a branch fell off a tree and jammed the sails. The car was struck by Agni and it left the track and fell into the river. They never found her body. It happened at Pele North Stage."

And he looked at her, nodding slightly, as if to say, *Yes, yes.* . . .

She stared in growing amazement. "What was the name of the car?"

"*Cavaquinho.*"

"Oh. . . ." She was looking at him as though she saw him for the first time. "And so . . . Corriente must be. . . ."

"Princess Swift Current. Same words, but an old tongue."

"*You,* Enri? *You?* That story—it's almost a legend. One of the great sailway songs. You're the humble minstrel from Jai'a!"

"That's me," He grinned in embarrassment.

"Mordecai!" Things began to fit together; old stories, odd remarks from Enri, *carrera* songs. . . .

"And now. . . . Here she is, in this valley. Those times I've heard you talk about the handmaiden, I never thought. . . ."

Uncertainly, Karina stood. Suddenly her vendetta was beginning to look small against the sweep of Time and events. All the same, it was getting dark, and the familiar restlessness stirred in her veins; the blood of carnivores from long ago.

"Well. . . . Let's go and get that bastard Tonio anyway," she said.

Astrud saw Tonio in the moonlight, face-down in the stream, and she thought he was dead. With a small scream of desolation she stepped into the water and knelt beside him. He lay very still, the water flowing past his hair and down his pale, naked body. His heels broke the surface, his arms lay along his sides.

Then she saw his fingers were fluttering.

She thought it was the flow of the water. She seized his left hand and held it to her. The fingers twitched swiftly.

Then the body squirmed.

She took hold of him. He was cold. He struggled, squirming sideways, feet kicking. She tried to drag him onto the bank but he was too heavy. He didn't try to push her away, yet she sensed he was resisting her.

"Tonio!" she cried, dragging at him, sobbing. She thought he was trying to drown himself. The guilt had been too much for him. All those felino people dead. And she hadn't exactly helped.

His mouth opened and she thought he was going to speak, but it closed again. Water dripped from his lips.

His mouth opened again, and closed.

He gaped, and gaped, just like a big fish.

She couldn't hold him up much longer.

She felt the ground move under her, and the moonlight was blotted out. She looked up.

She screamed.

She backed away, staring, screaming her lungs out, not standing, just crawling slowly backwards while her gaze remained transfixed by the glowing eyes of the most terrible creature she'd ever seen.

The Pegman and Karina watched from the undergrowth.

"Oh, my God. . . ." Enri was mumbling. "Oh, my God. . . ." Quietly, as though the sound of his own voice was a comfort he couldn't do without, even though it might reach the ears of the monster.

Karina was silent while the Little Friends raged through her body, urging her to run.

. . . . It was the way the creature had *scooped* Tonio out of the water with one paw, as though he was a medium-sized fish. And the next part had been quite simple, too. Tonio hadn't screamed. He'd made no sound at all, just opening and shutting his mouth. He'd squirmed quietly until the creature had cuffed him and broken his neck. Then he was gone, *eaten*. There was very little blood. The monster wheeled around, and left.

Astrud lay panting and trembling like a terrified deer. "So sorry, Tonio," she whispered. "Sorry, sorry, sorry. . . ."

Karina's breath rattled in her throat, like a snarl. She'd dropped to a crouch and her eyes were wide and luminous. The Little Friends were quieter now, but the human part of her was scared sick. At last the dull footsteps of the monster died away and she crept forward and laid a hand on Astrud's shoulder. The woman started, stared at her and whimpered. Her eyes were empty of all intelligence.

The Pegman was talking. "There are worse things on Earth than True Humans, Karina."

She glanced at him, took a deep breath, and stood.

"Help me with Astrud," she said. "We're going to find that damned Dedo!"

Death of the Dedo.

A bar of light showed under the cottage door and Karina hesitated. They had found the place quite easily, but now. . . . Only fungus and slimy things—and of course the Wrath of Agni—glowed at night. It was unnatural, that light. She shivered, swallowed heavily, and threw open the door.

Two women were there.

The handmaiden—Corriente—stood on the far side of the room, the ravines of her face like dancing shadows. The whole room glowed, not only because of the Wrath of Agni which was consuming a pile of sticks in a rock alcove.

Sitting before this alcove, showing no fear, was the Dedo. She was a lot younger than Karina had expected, and much more beautiful. Her eyes glowed with the fire-light and a little more of Karina's resolve ebbed away.

"So you're the Dedo," she said, and the Little Friends helped keep her voice steady. "You're not so much. Your neck's kind of skinny and I'll bet your belly's soft."

"Yes, I am in human form," said Leitha.

Karina strode across the room and stood above her, braving the heat and menace of the fire. "Is everything going according to your plan?" she asked. "Are we all dancing along your precious happentrack like puppets? Can you tell us who else is going to die along the way?" Her fingers were hooked and ready.

"It's becoming unimportant, now. The nearby Ifalong is decided. Certain humans have served their purpose, and there is still a slight imbalance in the valley. Those are considerations." The Dedo treated the question on its merits.

"By Agni!" Karina's temper snapped. "I'm going to kill you!"

"No," said the Dedo. "Raoul will kill me."

The certainty in the beautiful woman's tone stopped Karina as her fingers were reaching for the slender throat. "You know that? Then why don't you save your-self?"

"Because my life is of little importance when con-sidered against the Purpose, the Duty, and the sweep of the Ifalong."

Unexpectedly, Astrud spoke. "You took Tonio away from me!" Her gaze darted around the cottage as though seeking her husband in some dark niche. "He's here somewhere, I know it!"

Karina shivered. The Pegman backed away. Astrud

was completely mad; they could almost see the emptiness of her mind.

"Where are you, Tonio?" cooed Astrud in tones of terrifying sweetness. Then her gaze returned to the Dedo. "You've hidden him. He's your lover, isn't he?" Now she blinked, and for an instant there was a glimmer of intelligence like a cunning dog. "And Raoul's your child! You're the girl he met in the forest, all those years ago! You're a witch, a *bruja!*" Then, as though the effort had been too great, she turned away with a little whimper and began to stroke the fur of a strange animal which hung on the wall. . . .

"Raoul is not my son," said the Dedo. "He has a far greater significance."

The light in the cottage had no source. The fire glowed at one end and the Rock at the other; but there was something else, a suffused glow which seemed to be in the air. *As though Agni himself is riding the next happentrack,* thought the Pegman.

"Where did the handmaiden come from?" he asked with studied casualness.

"That matters nothing to the flow of events," said the Dedo. "Her work is finished now, anyway."

"It matters to me."

The Dedo's glance rested on him for a moment. "The handmaiden? She came to me many years ago, sick and badly burned, talking of a sailcar accident. She was of no significance and I might have healed her and sent her on her way, or simply eliminated her, but then my study of the Ifalong revealed she could be useful in guiding events. So I used her. I didn't heal her, of course. Her burns were useful in keeping the superstitious coastal humans from approaching her."

Enri walked up to the handmaiden and took her hand. "Do you remember me, Corriente?"

But the woman stood silent, her eyes vacant, her hand cold and unresponsive.

"What have you been doing around here?" Karina asked the Dedo. "Have you driven her mad, too? Do you sacrifice *everything* to this stupid Purpose? Doesn't it occur to you that ordinary humans have their own Purposes which are just as important to them? Let me tell you why Starquin's Purpose seems more important to you than a human's Purpose. It's because Starquin is bigger and stronger, that's why. That's the only reason! That's the trouble with every god humans ever dreamed up! They're always made out to be important, but the real truth is they're bigger and stronger, and they can stomp on you! They're rotten big bullies!"

"That is the essence of a certain Cosmic Truth," said the Dedo.

"Well," shouted Karina, shaking her fists at the ceiling, "Piss on you, Starquin!"

"If you're hoping he will strike you with a thunderbolt, thereby proving his existence and a certain vulnerability, you are going to be disappointed," said the Dedo. Reaching into a niche, she took out a curious instrument and pointed it at an earthenware pot. Thoughtfully, almost experimentally as though she was not used to doing this, she thumbed the button.

The pot jumped and shattered, the fragments glowed, then ran together in a small puddle of intense heat.

"It is time to reduce the possibility of error," Leitha said.

Then she pointed the weapon at Astrud.

That scene, the frozen tableau of players, entered legend, was etched in the circuits of the Rainbow, and finally emerged in the Song of Earth as the famous couplet:

"The one-armed man, the mother and the cat-girl watched with dread,

As the devil-woman numbered them among the living dead."

Probably the three humans, at that moment, could not quite believe what was going to happen. All three had recently witnessed violent death; but that had been perpetrated by a mere animal. Now they were watching a creature in human guise, a creature who they suspected was living on a plane above them, a greatly superior being one step short of a god.

And yet this goddess of beauty pressed the button on her little machine.

Astrud glowed briefly, and fell.

"She was mad," said the Dedo. "It's difficult to predict what mad people might do. However, normal humans react very much according to a pattern."

She watched the door.

It burst open and Raoul entered, wild-eyed and breathless.

"What's going on here?" he shouted. "Where's my father?" Then he saw the body on the floor. "Mother!" He knelt beside her, laid a hand on her cheek, snatched it away and looked up at them. "Who did this?"

Karina said, "This woman did it with that thing she's holding. She killed your father, too."

There was a stricken look on Raoul's face which changed as they watched. He rose slowly to his feet, gaze fixed on the Dedo.

"Well," said the Dedo softly, "now I think you've served your purpose too, Karina." And she pointed her weapon at the cat-girl.

"No! Not Karina!"

With a howl of rage, Raoul flung himself at the Dedo. *As she had known he would. . . .*

She fell against the wall, brought up the weapon and pressed the button. Half a meter from Raoul's head the wall glowed and dribbled lava. As he jerked away, she aimed at Karina again. This time Raoul threw a bottle which struck the Dedo on the shoulder, and Karina jumped aside as the floor began to glow. The Dedo recovered, but Raoul had sprung forward again, grasping her wrist. The weapon discharged a bolt of light into the ceiling, and timbers cracked and fell, smoking. Raoul, snarling like an animal, jerked at her arm and felt the bone snap as a ribbon of light slashed across the wall.

The Dedo screamed. The weapon dropped to the floor.

Raoul released his grip. The Dedo fell and began to scrabble for the gun. Even though she knew the outcome of this struggle, the instinct of self-preservation remained. Raoul stepped on the gun. As the Dedo tried to pry it from under his foot, he placed his toe squarely on the button.

The Dedo bucked once and lay still, smoking.

For a moment Raoul stood watching her, then his eyes met Karina's and he looked away, embarrassed.

"You did that for me?" said Karina wonderingly. "You could have been killed yourself, Raoul. You don't understand just how powerful the Dedo was."

The Pegman uttered a shaky laugh. "So much for the Ifalong," he said.

Karina was still watching Raoul incredulously. "But I'm a felina, Raoul."

"So?" he muttered. "Maybe I just lost my temper. Wouldn't you, if your mother had just been killed?"

He regarded the scene in the cottage; the two bodies on the floor, the Pegman standing white-faced, Karina watching him with a look he couldn't understand, and the handmaiden still standing in the corner, unmoved by events.

He mumbled something, swung around and left.

They'd run out of things to say about Time and happentracks and other strangenesses, and the dead women lay on the other side of the wall. The forest was very still, and stars were fading with the first light of a new day.

"What are you going to do, Enri?" Karina asked.

"Oh. . . . I thought I'd stay in Palhoa for a while. Corriente has to be looked after. . . . When she's feeling better, I'll take her down to Rangua."

Karina looked from him to the motionless handmaiden and her face was suddenly sad. "Princess Swift Current. . . ." she murmured, and she remembered how she'd first met this tall, silent woman, out on the sailway track beyond Rangua, when her leg was broken. *It is important that you live,* the handmaiden had said, and she'd healed her, and saved her life. . . .

She'd done it with a smooth stone.

Karina said, "Enri, I want to try something."

She drew aside the handmaiden's robe and there, in an inside pocket, was the stone.

Karina took it and, concentrating, thought: *Little Friends, help me if you can. I don't understand the use of this stone.*

Her fingertips tingled.

Gently, she rubbed the stone over Corriente's face. A light came into Corriente's eyes. She twisted away and mumbled, "She told me never to do that to myself."

Karina said, "She's dead, Corriente." She continued to stroke the burned face.

The Pegman sighed.

The marks of Agni were disappearing, smoothed by the healing action. The puckered scars melted away, the twisted eyelids were mended, the eyes became almond-shaped and beautiful, the brows and the hairline grew back.

The lips smiled.

Princess Swift Current was back—older, but the

275

Pegman recognized her still, and marvelled. The Little Friends withdrew, having unblocked certain pathways in her mind.

"What. . . . What's been happening?" she asked.

"Do you remember me, Corriente?" the Pegman asked. Of course, she wouldn't. It was so long ago. So many things had happened.

She said, "Enri. I wanted you to take me away with you."

"I didn't know. . . ."

"You knew I loved you."

And now that he had her at last, Enri lost his nerve. She was too beautiful, and he was a one-armed Pegman. He wasn't worthy. He shrugged, admitting his past foolishness, accepting that it was now too late. He turned away.

Corriente took hold of him, swung him round and kissed him. . . .

For a long time Karina fidgeted nearby, examining the stone wall with embarrassed intensity. True Humans were the strangest creatures—they behaved like people in legends. At last the couple stepped apart. Karina sighed with relief. She'd feared they were going to mate, there and then, and it wouldn't have seemed right for her to watch. Anyone else, but not the Pegman. Needing to change the subject, she said tentatively:

"The Dedo died very . . . easily, didn't you think, Enri? With all her powers. . . ." Her imagination had conjured up a picture of the Dedo sitting in the chair by the fire the way she'd first seen her, sitting there right *now,* on the other side of the wall, smiling to herself, having fooled them all.

"She knew Raoul was going to kill her. It was in the Ifalong. So there was no point in fighting it. I kind of think it was all part of her Purpose that she died."

"Look!" said Corriente. Smoke was puffing from under her door.

They backed off. The smoke thickened, then suddenly the cottage burst into flames. Fingers of fire reached through the roof into the trees and the slates popped and crackled. The roof collapsed and a great breath of smoke puffed out of the windows like the exhalation of a dying dragon. The door fell outwards, flaming, and within minutes the cottage was reduced to a smoking shell. So rapid had been the conflagration that the ferns and mosses growing in and around the walls were barely scorched. As the smoke died, the remains of the cottage seemed to blend back into the forest, giving the impression of an old rock face scarred by a couple of caves.

In fact, thought Karina in a moment of superstition, *maybe that's what it is."*

It had all happened so unnaturally fast, as though Starquin had needed to erase something from Time, and had done it by the most convenient means.

Karina was about to discuss her new theory with Enri when she saw that he was again occupied with Corriente, and looked as though he'd rather not be disturbed. She stood quietly for a while, feeling sad; then at last said diffidently:

"What shall I do now, Enri?"

The Pegman disentangled himself. "Are you still here, Karina? What are you waiting for? Go and look after Raoul—this forest is thirsty for blood. I'll see you in Rangua in a few days."

Karina flushed. "I don't go nursemaiding True Human brats!"

"But he saved the life of a felina brat," said Enri.

"Oh."

"Or did he save the life of a good felina girl who

277

would be happy to return the favor? He's lost and unhappy, Karina. Does it matter that he's a True Human?''

"He saved my life. . . ." Karina was reliving that fearful moment. "Do you think I've misjudged him, Enri?"

"Go on. Get after him."

"Thank you, Enri. Thanks for everything." She threw her arms around his neck, pressed her body against his and kissed him long and hard.

Afterwards, the Pegman chuckled ruefully. "That was every bit as good as I expected. Will you forgive me, Corriente?"

Corriente was watching Karina running into the jungle. "She's a very remarkable young woman. . . ."

"Is there something you're not telling me?"

"Raoul isn't a True Human, Enri."

"What!"

"He was brought here from a distant place. He's the first natural hybrid of True Human and Specialist. According to the Dedo, on certain happentracks he's capable of fathering children. This is the Dedo's Purpose—to create a new line of people. Karina's a descendant of Captain Spring, the tiger-woman who brought *bor* back to Earth. She's not a full jaguar-girl at all—hadn't you noticed? And Raoul—his children may be able to mate with True Humans *or* Specialists."

The Pegman caught a glimpse of the Ifalong. "That could solve a lot of problems."

"But it's incidental to the Purpose. In one happentrack of the Ifalong—maybe *this* happentrack—Karina and Raoul will mate and have a son. This son will be the first of a new line of humans with *bor,* neither full Specialists nor True Humans but having the best characteristics of both, and capable of breeding with either."

"Karina and Raoul. . . . I always thought there was

something special about her; but him. . . . I don't know. Do you really think it's going to happen, Corriente?"

She said, "I hope so. Leitha died for it. That's quite a sacrifice for someone who's nearly immortal."

The importance of love.

There was no love in Leitha. Why should there be, when she was a Finger of Starquin? He is a lone creature, a being without sex, without even a form.

Yet Leitha *understood* love, and what it meant to humans. And she used it in bringing Karina and Raoul together. She'd learned about it long ago; learned of its importance, and the part it had played in Mankind's progress. She'd known the days of Greataway travel, when humans flitted among the stars faster than light, in insubstantial matrices they called Invisible Spaceships.

Love played a very big part in Man's Greataway travel, because the ether is delicate and will not readily accept hostile vibrations. The Three Madmen of Munich, who planted the Hate Bombs, only succeeded in entering the Greataway because of a one-in-a-million chance when a Dedo was unluckily absent from her Rock.

But by the time our story takes place, romantic love has become rare. Most Specialists had no need for a permanent bond between male and female, and only the True Humans carried on the old traditions—a little strained in most cases, like Astrud and Tonio. And only a few remote happentracks can tell what really happened to Corriente and Enri, when he scooped her into the saddle that distant day in Portina. Did they, in fact, live happily ever after?

There is one exception—a Specialist who was essential

to the Purpose—an animal-person who, against all the odds, knew a romantic attachment. He is central to all the events of that momentous year, he is the reason why Serena, and later Raoul, were transported to Rangua, yet he is only briefly mentioned in the Song of Earth.

He is El Tigre, the fierce and gentle man, the only suitable mate for the tiger-woman Serena.

He is an underestimated lover.

There are others in the Ifalong more famous.

The fast and exciting lives of the Dream People in the Domes left little time for the lingering slowness of love. Just one Dream Person is celebrated for her knowledge of real love—Elizabeth of the Triad, also known as the Girl-with-no-Name, from Dome Azul, a long way down the coast. In the same Dome a Cuidador named Zozula lived; in the Song of Earth he is known as the Oldster.

These two Dome people, they knew love. They discovered it over twenty thousand years after the time of our story.

Meanwhile the thread of Karina's descendants continued, and they experienced love too, because *bor* knows it is essential to the ultimate survival of a sexual species.

The Triad is celebrated in one of the most famous verses of the Song of Earth, beginning:

"Come, hear about the Trinity of legendary fame.
The Oldster and the Artist and the Girl-with-no-Name."

In the year 143,624 Cyclic the Triad came together, loved, rediscovered the Greataway and went out there and removed the Hate Bombs by the strength of their love alone.

And Starquin was free.

The Artist was one Manuel, a young Wild Human.

He was a direct descendant of John, who was born during the year after Leitha died.

Karina saw Raoul on a rock at the top of a ridge. He sat slumped, silhouetted against the sky in the warm morning sun. He was clearly visible to any predator, but didn't appear to care.

Karina climbed up to him.

He heard her coming, jerked around and saw her, and tensed as though about to run. He watched her with as much nervous uncertainty as he would watch an oncoming jaguar.

"It's all right," Karina called.

He said nothing as she sat beside him. She'd washed herself in a stream and she was confident that she looked good. Her hair had dried and it drifted like a bronze cloud beside her head.

"I'm not going to hurt you," she said.

"I'm not afraid of you!" he said with a flash of spirit. He forced himself to stare at her and suddenly found that he was not, in fact, afraid.

"I'm sorry about your parents, Raoul."

"Don't give me that! I heard you at Torres! You—"

"I wasn't myself at Torres. I didn't realize how much the Dedo was in charge. She ruled us all, you know that? For a while there, everything we did was dictated by her. Including what your father did. . . . She influenced us in lots of little ways—and when that didn't work, she compelled us."

"But now she's dead," said Raoul.

Karina remembered how he'd reacted when he'd thought her life was in danger. She felt a warm glow spread through her body, almost alarming in its suddenness. "You killed her, Raoul," she said softly. "You killed her for me."

"Well, I don't know about that. . . ."

"So now she's dead," said Karina with sudden forced gaiety, trying to suppress her growing emotions. "And now we can do anything we like!" She wriggled, finding her words had a double meaning—and gave in to herself, admitting to herself what it was *she* would like. She left the rock and the disturbing proximity of Raoul, and lay on the grass, looking at the sky. It shouldn't be hurried.

"Tell me about the Dedo," said Raoul. "I thought she was just some girl my father found."

So Karina explained, from her first meeting with the handmaiden to the occasion in the cottage when his mother had died, just a few hours ago. When she'd finished, Raoul said:

"If she was so powerful, don't you think she might have left her plans behind her? Set up the Ifalong to suit herself, I mean?"

"I don't care," said Karina, yawning. The sun was making her drowsy and for a moment she closed her eyes. Here, on this ridge with Raoul, she had a wonderful feeling of isolation and content. The rest of the world seemed a long way off. She stretched, catlike, feeling her breasts pressing against the tunic and hoping that Raoul was watching her. She cracked open an eye, and saw that he wasn't.

"I can't see why she had to kill so many people," said Raoul. "Do you suppose she set up the whole revolution?"

"I don't want to talk about the rotten old Dedo."

"Well. . . . What do you want to talk about?" He sensed an impatience in her tone and hoped she wasn't going to leave.

"Mordecai! Here we are all alone in the forest and you don't know what to talk about?"

"My parents have just died."

282

"Well, I'm very sorry. But they weren't your real parents, were they?"

"No. But I loved them, I guess."

"I know what you mean. My father. . . . He's the nicest man I know. And I love my sisters, too. But that's not the same thing as, well, you know. . . . A man and a woman. Is it, Raoul?" She'd propped herself up on one elbow, looking up into his face, hoping he could see down the front of her tunic. "Remember a while back, I rode with you in the sailcar, and you kicked Torch in the pants?"

He grinned suddenly. "I didn't like him too much."

"But you liked *me.*"

Trapped, he admitted, "You're very pretty." He could see right down to her navel.

"Why did you kick him? Why did you kill the Dedo? It was because of me, wasn't it!"

"Yes," he said quietly, staring at the distant ocean.

"Well, then!"

"Karina, I. . . ."

"Look at me when you speak to me, Raoul!"

And foolishly, he did. He fell into the pools of her amber eyes and was caught by the nets of the Little Friends who waited there. He leaned forward, unable to help himself, and slipped his hand inside her tunic, stroking the nipple gently, then squeezing the breast.

"Karina. . . . We're different species," he said help-lessly.

He was hers, now. She crawled close, put an arm around his neck and pulled him down beside her. She kissed him long and passionately, as though she'd been doing it all her life.

"Karina, you're not being fair," he said, when he had the chance.

"It's not supposed to be fair. It's supposed to be fun.

Come on, Raoul. Show me what you're made of. Show me it wasn't a fluke, what you did in the cottage."

"But killing has nothing to do with this!" he protested in despair, his hand between her legs, his fingers drawing her clothing aside.

"No," she said in satisfaction. "It wasn't a fluke."

"But this is because I *want* you."

"That's good enough for me."

But not for me, he thought in desolation, as his body did just what she wanted it to. *This only makes it worse. Now I'm trapped, and I'll never, never be free.*

"Oh, Raoul. . . ."

Because I love you, Karina. I love you with all of my heart, and you don't even know what that means.

Then, for a few blessed moments, all thought stopped. . . .

Later, Karina rolled away and stood. "Oh, Raoul— that was so good. Every bit as good as they say it is."

"You mean . . . you never . . . ?"

"Yes, that was the first time for me," she said happily. "I didn't tell you, because I didn't want you to think I was, well, *amateurish,* you know. But you liked it, didn't you?" She was full of life, full of vitality and youth, as though she'd just enjoyed a refreshing swim on a hot day.

Raoul sighed, lost, as he'd known he would be.

Return to Rangua.

Seven days later Karina and Raoul came out of the jungle and told Captain Guantelete to take them back to Rangua.

"I'm not sure about that." Palhoa basked in an Indian Summer and the turmoil of Rangua seemed a long way off. "There's been no news out of Rangua for days," Guantelete said. "God knows what's happening down there.

"Take us," said Karina.

Guantelete grinned suddenly. "If that is your wish, Karina." He had his curiosity. Every day he'd climbed a signal tower and observed the Canton capital for a while. He'd seen no sails moving. The little signalmen were gone from Palhoa; disappeared into the foothills. It was rumored that their Guild had called them off the job due to violation of their property in Rangua. The hemitrexes stared blindly downhill. Palhoa was cut off from the rest of the world.

Some time later the sailcar rolled to a halt in Rangua station.

Nobody paid any attention to Karina and Raoul as they alighted and walked down the main street. A few True Humans were about, and felinas loitered at the corners in grupos, chattering and idly stropping their fingernails on the trees.

They found El Tigre sitting alone on a treestump beside the sailway track. "It's good to see you again, Karina," he said. "The Pegman was here a few days ago, with his woman. He told us the story. It was difficult to believe."

"I hope you didn't harm him."

"Nobody's been harmed for many days," said El Tigre. His eyes were haunted. "Raoul, I'm grateful to you for saving my daughter's life."

"I think I'd do anything for her, El Tigre," said Raoul.

Karina gave a smug grin, then surprised her father. "We mated, up there in the jungle. Lots of times. It was *so* good."

El Tigre watched them silently; his wayward daughter

and her True Human lover, and he was sad. It was a pity that such a beautiful thing wouldn't last. And it was all so pointless anyway, because they were different species. . . .

He found himself thinking of Serena.

"Who did win the Tortuga Race, anyway?" Karina's question brought him back to the present.

"Captain Herrero."

"Oh. What a pity."

"They flashed the news through just before the signalmen walked out. I'd rather not have known. It seems there's nothing on Earth will stop a man like that from winning."

Raoul regarded the houses of Rangua: quiet, defeated, in mourning. "If it's any consolation, I expect Captain Herrero thinks the same about you, El Tigre."

Then Teressa and Runa arrived, and the mock-fight finished with the girls a tangled heap on the ground while Raoul and El Tigre looked on tolerantly.

As the felinas were dusting themselves off, Raoul asked, "What's been happening around here, anyway? I expected to find you all living in the Palace." And for a moment the memories returned; the house with its view over the coastal downs, and his father and mother. He could never go back to that house. . . .

"We've been betrayed," said El Tigre. "How can I deal with the Canton Lord when we can't put our own forces in order?"

"Manoso's double-crossed us," Teressa explained. "He took his army to the delta under orders to capture it, but instead he made a deal with the people there. The bastard. He's got the cai-men and Maquinista and all the Specialists on his side, and he's holding the delta, the tortuga pens, and all the cars in there. Now he's bargaining with us for terms."

"He wants to operate the whole place himself," said Runa. "He's set himself up as a little Lord."

"We should go right in there and slaughter every last one of them!" said Teressa.

El Tigre said, *"There will be no more killing."*

"You see?" said Teressa.

"So what do we do?" asked Runa. "Just sit around here, like we've been doing this last few days? The felinas are getting restless, I can tell you that, father. People are beginning to ask what the Revolution was all about. The signalboxes are empty and the cars aren't running, and the cargoes have all gone bad. What was it all for?"

Karina was watching her father. "Was it bad, the fighting?"

"It'll take a miracle to bring felinos and True Humans together, after this."

Karina said, "There's only one thing to do. We must capture the Palace and take over the guards. How can people respect you, father, if you rule them from a treestump?"

"I don't think we can raise a big enough army to take on the Lord," said El Tigre. "Our people seem frightened of the guards."

"Why do you need an army?" asked Karina, "when you've got us?"

They reached the Palace ground undetected and paused under cover of a dense thicket.

"Where are the guards?" whispered Karina.

"I think I saw somebody at the window," said Raoul. He held his father's crossbow, a bolt already loaded.

"So what now?" asked El Tigre. "As soon as we leave the bush, they'll see us." He'd made it clear he had little heart for the fight. For him, the Revolution had died during that first night in Rangua Town.

"Too bad," said Karina. "Come on, Raoul."

And she stepped into the open, and walked boldly across the grass towards the Palace doors. Raoul walked beside her, the crossbow held loosely but ready.

The guards met them inside the entrance. Karina pushed the door open and strode into the vast, dim hall —then quickly dropped into a fighting crouch. Raoul did likewise, swinging the crossbow in an arc.

El Tigre, following up, murmured, "Mordecai. . . ."

There were over thirty guards standing around the walls. They carried no weapons—they didn't need them. Their strength and size was intimidating enough. They stood with their arms folded across their chests, watching the small band silently.

"Come on, you bastards. . . ." said Karina softly. "Come on. . . ."

Teressa began to creep towards the nearest guard, her lips drawn back. "I'm going to kill you," she said. The guard made no move.

"Wait, Teressa!" Raoul said suddenly.

"Huh?" Surprised, she glanced over her shoulder. "No True Human brat tells me what—oh!" The guard had stepped forward, pinning her arms to her sides. He lifted her and she hung kicking, snarling with frustration.

Raoul said, "Take us to the Lord."

"The Lord is gone."

"Gone? Where?"

"We don't know. He's left the Palace and won't be back."

The guard released Teressa and she dropped to her feet. "Scared, huh?" she said triumphantly. "The Lord got scared of us, and he ran out. We've won, father!"

El Tigre remained silent and thoughtful.

"Who's in charge, then?" asked Raoul.

"Nobody. We await your orders."

"*Our* orders?" Runa's gaze ran along the row of guards in delighted surprise. "You mean you're *our* guards now?"

The guard permitted himself a faint smile. "We answer to Karina and Raoul. They're the new Lords."

"Why them?" asked Teressa in aggrieved tones. "They're not in charge here. El Tigre is. Besides, Raoul here is a True Human!" She spat out the words with the utmost distaste.

"Ask yourself, cat-girl," said the guard. "Will the Canton accept a single Lord from a single species? Can't you see the wisdom in setting up this couple as joint Lords—a True Human and a Specialist?"

El Tigre smiled for the first time in days. "That makes a hell of a lot of sense to me. What do you think, Karina?"

She nodded, wordless, feeling Raoul squeeze her hand.

El Tigre continued. "We have other problems besides True Humans. Manoso, for instance. Do you have any ideas about him, short of annihilation, of course? We're through with war."

"Negotiate with him. Treat him the way he wants to be treated—as an independent ruler. After all—he's already done what you were trying to do, El Tigre. He's united True Humans and Specialists in a single purpose. If the purpose is to make money, is that bad? He seeks power through commerce, and you seek power through conquest. Is either way more right than the other?"

El Tigre shook his head silently.

"Go and organize Rangua, El Tigre. Share the work and the rewards equally between Specialists and True Humans. At the same time work towards restoring good

relations between Rangua and the other Cantons—
they're going to be suspicious of the change, for a while.
It's not going to be easy, but you can do it.

"Meanwhile Karina and Raoul will rule from the
Palace. Ostensibly you'll be working under their orders,
but their main purpose will be to serve as figureheads—
a united couple for the Canton to look up to. Proof that
different human species can live together, and more."

Now El Tigre laughed. "Karina a figurehead? I'll believe that when it happens."

Looking much happier, he ran his hand through his
daughter's hair, saw Serena in her eyes again, glanced
curiously at Raoul as though he was half-remembering
something, gathered Teressa and Runa around him and
set off back to Rangua Town, to begin the rebuilding.

Epilogue.

There never had been a Lord of Rangua, of course. The Lord had always been whichever Us Ursa chose to sit behind the opalescent screen. They took it in turns. In their grim, thoughtful way it amused them to think that True Humans were, after all, ruled by Specialists.

And the Us Ursa wanted no trouble. Power, yes; that was their birthright. But trouble meant danger, and danger was against their creed.

So, in the name of peace, they shared their power with Karina and Raoul for a while. Meanwhile El Tigre worked hard in Rangua, a deal was concluded with Manoso, the impounded sailcars were released, and trade was resumed with the southern Cantons with every sign of a boom in prospect.

The Johnathan Years, as the subsequent Age was called, marked the beginning of the end of the religious movement inspired by the Kikihuahua Examples. Under the crafty guidance of Manoso, metal artifacts began to come out of the delta and were accepted into general use. More sailcars of the *Rayo* type were built. Felino objections to these cars were overcome by allowing increased Specialist participation in sailway operations, and in due course the example of Rangua Canton was followed all down the coast.

Another change was triggered by Manoso. He took charge of tortuga production, making no secret of the fact that the creatures were animals, and that True Humans had therefore been eating meat for a long time. And so another Example collapsed, the felinas began to hunt their food again, and the tumps could safely become extinct—which they did, on that happentrack, a thousand years later.

History, as recorded by the Rainbow, does not relate what happened to the Us Ursa. A little-known stanza of the Song of Earth speaks of a small but powerful tribe of huge Specialists who, in later years, inhabited a certain valley of lakes once rumored to be the haunt of a *bruja*. If this tribe was the Us Ursa, they could be there still. It is equally possible that they discovered the workings of the Rock, and, one day after the Triad had removed the Hate Bombs, took off into the Greataway in search of new worlds.

Early in the following summer Karina went to see her father. By that time the Canton had settled down and he was chief of the Town Elders.

"I'm pregnant," she told him.

He had aged, this last few months. He walked a little more slowly, stood a little less tall. He spoke more carefully, weighing each word, the memory of the Massacre of Rangua still burning in his mind. Torch now handled a lot of his work—in addition to squiring Teressa and Runa.

"I don't see how you can be," said El Tigre, but his eyes told him she was.

She laughed shakily. "Neither do I. . . ." She glanced down at herself, gulped, then burst into tears. "Father, I'm so *scared!* What kind of things am I carrying? *What's in there?*"

He laid a huge arm around her. "It's not like my girl to be frightened."

"I never used to be, before," she sobbed. "Whenever I was frightened or hurt, I used to be able to . . . kind of concentrate, and I could make it go away. I used to call the things that helped me my Little Friends. I never told anyone about them."

El Tigre's eyes were far away, remembering. "Serena . . . your mother. Nothing could hurt her—until. . . ." Until a few months before she died.

"Father, my Little Friends have gone, now. I'm scared the things inside me have killed them!"

"Don't be ridiculous, Karina." He spoke firmly, masking his love. It was the only way. "They're just babies, your first. It's natural for you to be nervous."

"I'm going away. I want to do this by myself."

"That's the usual way."

"I . . . I may not come back."

"I'll be very sorry if you don't. And so will Raoul."

"Raoul?"

"Well, you are. . . . I mean, I thought. . . ."

"Only True Humans stick around one another afterwards, father." Her voice was brittle. "Raoul and I have stayed together for the good of the Canton, but now we do it the felino way. I'd have thought you'd understand that, of all people."

And El Tigre made his confession.

"I've never stopped loving your mother, Karina."

Karina bore John by the shores of Lake Da Gueria. It was a difficult birth because he was so big. Karina lay on the pebbles at the water's edge, mewing with pain. She was alone, apart from a guanaco who watched her with supercilious eyes, chewing. John was born, and Karina bit the cord, and the pain subsided to an ache.

There were no others; John was the only baby and Karina inspected him closely for strangenesses, but he seemed normal enough.

Karina rested.

Later that day, feeling better, she bathed John in the warm waters of Lake Da Gueria and wrapped him in a soft blanket, and held him against her. The low sunlight slanted past her, casting long shadows and illuminating the distant sail of a car beating down the coast. She lay back in some contentment, listening to the ripples spending themselves on the lake shore.

John made a sound.

Karina jerked; she'd been dozing. The guanaco had wandered away.

John looked at Karina directly, his eyes focussed in a way that babies' eyes never do. He smiled.

And something in those eyes said, *I'm hungry.*

"Hello, Little Friends," said Karina happily, and held John to her breast. He was a fine, strong boy.

She found herself looking forward to showing him to Raoul.

HERE ENDS THAT PART OF THE
SONG OF EARTH KNOWN TO
MEN AS
"IN THE VALLEY OF LAKES."

IN TIME,
OUR TALE WILL CONTINUE. . . .

CONAN

WITCH WORLD SERIES